It's Over or It's Eden

Also by Rebecca M. Zornow
Dangerous to Heal
Negotiated Fate

it's **OVER** or it's **EDEN**

Rebecca M. Zornow

It's Over or It's Eden

Text copyright © 2021 by Rebecca M. Zornow

This is a work of fiction. Names, characters, places, and incidents are either the product of the author's imagination or are used fictitiously. Any resemblance to actual persons living or dead, business establishments, events, or locales is entirely coincidental.

Requests for permission to make copies of any part of the work should be submitted online at www.RebeccaMZornow.com.

First Edition
978-1-7377118-0-3

For Nicole,
who was with me

1. Homecoming

The war ended and they all went home.

That's what was supposed to happen.

The war ended and everyone but me was dead. My home was gone, so when I walked away from the smoldering, shit-for-all-the-good-it-did military base, I turned north and never stopped walking. I had a vague notion of finally leaving the desert behind and dying in the woods. A majestic wolf pack could take me out. I'd live on in their stomach cavities for a time, then eventually lie hot and steaming beneath the trees, ready to be ground back into nothing.

I didn't actually want to be hunted down by a wolf pack. My secret plan was to freeze and die in my sleep when winter came on, but it was neither majestic nor dignified so

I kept that from myself most days.

I told myself enough monologuing, Arwen Cruz. It was time to get my ass up the hill.

My breath came heavy, but that was okay. There was no one around to hear it, and I was lucky to make it to the top of whatever I was climbing in one go. I could walk for days on end—and had been—but I was utterly unprepared for the size of the hills in the north. The real mountains were still in the distance, like white-topped knickknacks I could fit perfectly in my hand.

I reached the peak with a wheeze and scanned the grassy hill behind me. It looked pathetically small from this angle. My back was slick with sweat. I undid the metal clasps at the back of my neck and rolled my Titan Suit down to my stomach. There was a great gust of relief under my armpits, and I sat down under a tree to rest.

I thought the north was supposed to be cold, but it had to be a good hundred degrees. It wasn't dry heat like I was used to. It was wet and thick, like the exposed, hairy nook in my shoulder. Other than the armpit quality, it was nice. As a child from the southwest, the behemoth-size trees looked as if they could populate the dark stories of the Brothers Grimm. The glimpses of squirrel and deer made me feel less alone.

My gears churned as I thought more about how to catch and eat one of the critters. Most of my meals came from cans and bags, but it seemed better that I should meld with the forest to gather and hunt. I wasn't in it for farming. First,

I didn't know how long I'd live. I wasn't going to spend my meager last days plowing a field. Second, I didn't want to be tied down. If I had to make a run in the middle of the night, I didn't want to be slowed down with thoughts of all I'd lose.

Still, I was trying to save my ammo—I didn't know if I'd ever get more for my Kronos L85. Production, like everything, was down, perhaps nonexistent, and many supplies would soon approach the edge of shelf life. I worried about the longevity of my combat-enhancing body armor dubbed the Titan Suit, but I didn't know what else I could do. It would simply be what it was. I congratulated myself on the Zen-like thinking.

I'd already gotten good at foraging in mostly abandoned orchards and gardens. I knew the food was *right there* for the taking, but it still felt like I was doing something to survive.

The year I was fifteen, everything changed. The farther we ran from home, the hungrier we got. Mom didn't know what wild greens were good to eat, but anybody could guess that eating from some trees with a fence around them was a good move.

If I could figure out how to set a snare, I'd be good.

The sweat dried quickly on my body, but there was no urgency to get moving. It was weird how after so much destruction, the woods could be so peaceful. The long walk was one of the most disturbing yet serene periods of my life. Disturbing for my head; peaceful for my body. I didn't have to sit through a mission brief or try not to get blown up. I just walked.

An angry pinch stabbed my shoulder and I flinched, jumping to my feet, trying to see down my back. Out of the corner of my eye, I saw a winged insect fly away and I tentatively felt the new welt. A bee sting? Or wasp?

"I didn't provoke you," I said sternly. "This means war." I squinted into the trees, but the bug was gone. I hoped the stinger wasn't left in the welt, but I couldn't bend my neck at that angle to see. If the barb was still there, my body would have to do the gross job of slowly pushing the needlelike stinger out.

I pulled my bodysuit back on and sloshed my canteen—nice and full—before taking a drink. The canteen fit squarely onto a belt latch when I was done. My belt held my whole life. Army-issued, it was sturdy and snug around my waist. There were small pouches for water tablets, ammo, and other loose items, as well as slots for a flashlight and a small knife in addition to the canteen. Only the canteen release latch wiggled from overuse. Most of the time I didn't wear my helmet and jerry-rigged it to the gun strap.

The tough yet silky texture of my bodysuit protected me from bee stings and more when I had the thing on. I was never outfitted for a mech suit—even at the end of the war there was always someone more important than me. Besides the helmet, the only powered component of my suit, a small armband was long out, not that there was anyone I cared to communicate with. My suit could charge wirelessly, but I hadn't been in proximity to any working stations recently. They were quiet. Like everything else.

Altogether, it wasn't much, but it was enough to keep me alive, and nearly more than I cared to carry overland. The suit clung to my body in the heat, but the reinforcement and protection was worth hauling around. Every time I thought about dropping the gun and leaving it behind, it felt wrong. I didn't yet know who was out there.

Even from the plateau, I couldn't see any glorious view or where I was headed next through the thick trees and constantly rising and falling landscape, but that was okay. There were enough streams and lakes that I wasn't worried about my canteen running dry. When I hit a road, it was my habit to follow it until a driveway. Once I pilfered a few supplies from a dusty house or long-abandoned charging station, I headed back into the woods.

It took time for me to locate the afternoon sun through the dense canopy, but when I found it, I put it at my left and started off again. The wide sagebrush fields of a few days ago were giving way to rocky terrain. I was already used to the pine trees all around me. I called them all pine trees, but I suspected there were a couple of different species. Some were tall and skinny. Some had thick branches all the way to the ground. I didn't care much what kind of tree they were. They all made it difficult to see ahead.

A twig snapped. I jerked right hard, taking cover behind a trunk, and pointed my Kronos in the direction of the noise. Sticks fell and shifted at random intervals in the forest, but a scatter of rocks accompanied the snap.

I saw blond—A deer?—no, smaller. I straightened in relief. It was just a dog.

Then I tensed again. I didn't know if the dog was friendly or looking to make my dreams of majestic devourment true.

"Hey, buddy, you back it right up and go the other way. I'll do the same."

The dog appeared to take comfort in the sound of a human voice and crept out from the undergrowth. It had shaggy yellow fur, matted with burrs and mud. I swatted enough red wood ticks from the smooth exterior of my bodysuit to know the dog would be full of them. The animal's sides heaved as it watched me. It was hungry, that was clear.

What was it thinking, I wondered? Did it see me as a lonely, kindred spirit? When was the last time it had seen a person? Had it—

Bowwowow!

The dog's bark startled me. I recoiled and nearly fell on my butt. I looked around, but there was nothing. The dog barked at me again. I barred my teeth and growled back. I didn't feel stupid until I realized how small my growl sounded compared to the canine's.

"Go on, get out of here!" I shouted. I threw an arm up in its direction. The sun was setting. It was time for me to scout out a place to sleep, but first I needed the dog gone.

I took a few steps back from the dog, but it followed, its four-legged steps quicker than mine.

"No, git. Git!" I picked up a handful of stones and dirt and threw them in the dog's direction.

The dog didn't growl or whine. It simply stared. I threw some more. The handful was mostly soil so it fell limply back to the earth. Then I understood the dog's expression. I saw the pleading in its round black eyes.

I couldn't believe it. I felt sad for the wretched dog. There were plenty of animals throughout the forest, but I didn't identify with squirrels; I wanted to eat them. A doggy pal was not part of my plan. I wasn't going to allow it to scare away game. Or be forced to find food for both me and the dog. Or wonder every time I drifted off to sleep if the dog would go for my wet, meaty jugular in the night. I felt bad for it, but I wasn't going to have anything to do with it. It was just another thing to feel sad about at the bottom of a very long list of feels, and the whole dog-thing wasn't what I was doing out there.

With my mind made up, I turned and walked away briskly. After a beat, the dog started in my direction, so I had no choice but to return to our tango. Yelling and throwing pine needles wasn't creating much of an impression on the dog's teeny brain, so I switched my gun's safety on and lunged in the dog's direction.

Like I expected, my abrupt attack shocked the dog. The whites of its eyes rolled, and the animal bounded backward in a half-coordinated hop, alarmed by my uncouth behavior.

I lunged again and this time kept running. I didn't want to chase the dog down; I just wanted to scare it away. The mutt was faster than I was, so every few paces it had time to turn and look back at me, as if it couldn't believe a human would do something so undignified, then sprinted ahead in an easy dog gait.

Soon I'd be tired and stuck with a dog hovering at the edge of my campfire. I pushed into the run, all the way to my top speed, the solid length of laboratory-made material warming from the heat output of my body. The Titan Suit snapped to attention as it tightened against my muscles, supporting my bones and pumping fluidity into every movement. It flexed for attack as if it were an organism, not an article of clothing. My speed picked up, and I felt the strength of a small rhino. If I had my helmet on, I could—

The thought broke the glow of concentration. Suddenly all I could focus on was the helmet and gun banging around on my back, wondering how sure I was that I had put the safety on. I stopped waving my arms so I could balance the gear and instead gave a little whoop—not loud enough to attract any attention, but hopefully enough to scare the dog off its intended path toward Best Friends Forever.

With my Titan Suit at full capacity, I gained on the dog as it scrambled, fighting to hold itself together, against what, I couldn't see. A great gust of wind hit my face. I slowed my pace, but I was running full tilt and couldn't stop when I saw the dog's feet slip out from under it and slide on its side, right over the edge of a cliff.

Training took over and I threw my body's weight and momentum at an angle and tried to dig a heel into the ground for traction. The suit protected me easily as I rolled along rocks and sticks, finally coming to a stop. I scrambled backward, ass dragging, until I was certain I wasn't going over the edge. Shaky adrenaline poured through me, even as I realized I was a good four feet from the cliff drop-off.

My mouth went dry. Where was the dog? I didn't hear anything. Did the dog really fall? Not just fall, but perhaps get chased over the edge of a cliff by the last remaining member of the dog's favorite species?

I crept toward the chasm and poked my head over the side. I spotted the dog immediately. If I had fallen in my Titan Suit, I would have broken a leg or some ribs for sure, if not my neck. The dog. Well, the dog was definitely dead.

I watched for a couple of minutes and then backed away from the cliff's edge. I want the dog to die. I just didn't want it to follow me. I didn't want the responsibility an end-of-the-world buddy brought.

"Shit," I told myself over and over until I realized I was saying it out loud with increasing desperation.

I was mad and *embarrassed*? I don't know why I felt embarrassed when there was no one around, but my cheeks flamed and the back of my neck flushed. I started away from the cliff, staggering a few paces into the tree line. Combat over, my Titan Suit began to relax. The reinforced cloth felt saggy. The regular fit only felt loose by comparison to the flexed, bone-strong exoskeleton the Titan Suit became in moments of combat.

It was a few minutes before I could think clearly and remember how thirsty I was when I realized how wrong everything had gone. It wasn't only the scruffy, dead dog— my hand grasped for the water canteen and found empty space.

I spun around in the dirt and pine needles, scanning the dimming forest floor. I raced back in the direction of the cliff, but neither the cliff nor the canteen ever appeared. For someone with no place to go, I had been wandering the woods, considering it progress every time I lived and headed in an approximation of north. Now I was confronted with how incapable I was of navigating the wilderness. I spent an hour retracing my steps, scanning the ground for my canteen, but it never materialized among the rocks, logs, and pine needles. I couldn't even locate the fateful cliff.

Darkness set in. I had to give it up for a bad job. I could find another water container, but not one that would be so easy to carry. Plus, I had taken a certain amount of pride in my fully stocked utility belt.

I picked a direction with the intention of finding a safe corner to curl up in, chiding myself the whole way. My throat was dry, not just from chasing that blasted dog but from roaming the woods looking for my canteen. I had to find water soon, if not that night, then first thing the next morning.

Even as the trees grayed around me in the fading sunset, I saw a shimmer up ahead.

Water. I took a cautious sigh of relief.

I came upon the shore in the near dark. I couldn't see the other side, but I knew the body of water was a lake. I couldn't see it, but I could hear it. The water didn't run but lapped at the sides.

Without the canteen, I still had a dilemma. I had purified water in the canteen by using tablets except when I found bottled water, in which case I always drank that first. Of course, I had expected my tablet stash to run out at some point, but I thought I'd be ready for it. It was literally counting down in my pouch. Once I was nearly out, I thought I'd find a metal pot and boil the water before pouring it into my canteen to carry with me. Or more optimistically, by that point I would have found an ideal spot to winter in and could collect snow to melt. I never counted on losing my canteen altogether.

Maybe drinking straight from a fresh, running stream would have been okay, but the lake was stagnant. I could smell it as I approached. Putrid. Stale. Not words I would use to describe a refreshing drink. It was full dark when a buzz faintly echoed across the lake. A light sprang on. Simple but extraordinarily rare in this new world.

I froze. I quietly and carefully crept back to the tree line, eyes scanning what I could discern of the new horizon. Kronos in front, I slowly shut off the safety with my thumb. The light was tiny, just a single outdoor bulb, but it illuminated enough to make clear that this was indeed a lake, a big one. It wasn't ordinary for reasons beyond its size. Houses, far from shore, rested atop the water. I thought the structures swayed with the current but, from that distance in the dark, I may have imagined it. What I didn't imagine were the docks that ran through floating buildings like a web.

The buzzing light wasn't the only one to flicker on. A few others sputtered to life in the sector, some portion of the electrical circuit still worked though the people who lived there were long gone and likely dead.

I thought I had a good idea of what the floating town was. In the decades before Arrival, when humans were drastically trying to undo global climate change, water towns sprang up. Families lived in low-rent housing and grew aquaponics for the corporation that owned the house, the lake, and the patented lakeweed. The communities were touted as environmentally friendly because the people who lived there didn't have to clear acres of trees for living space. They could farm and live among nature.

It shouldn't have come as a surprise that humans were ecosystem blights on water as well as land.

Air coursed through my lungs as I forced a deep breath. Likely no one was there. Even if someone was squatting in the deserted village, they'd never know if I stole a dusty bottle.

Once the thought solidified, I stood and crept quietly along the tree edge. I had long since learned to act on instinct. Thoughts only served to pull you back—cautioned you against anything different in the effort of keeping you alive through another dark black night of tigers and bears. But I lived in a different world. You couldn't hunker down in that world. It was only through constant movement and action that I'd survived.

Halfway around the curve of the lake toward the light, I hit the edge of the settlement. The docks were still cast in darkness, which made them my best bet for going unnoticed while foraging supplies. I didn't want to wade into the middle of a camp and find squatters, or worse.

My first bootstep reverberated on the plastic dock. I adjusted my next steps and moved carefully. I wished the headlamp on my helmet was still working. I had a backup flashlight on my belt, but I decided I'd do better to keep my gun out than expose myself in the dark.

A faint tendril of rot permeated the air. I opened my mouth to breathe. The whine of a gnat rushed inside my ear, and I brushed it away once, then twice before the persistent bug was off. The moon was bright enough that I could see the outlines of the shacks. The dorms were small and in such close proximity that living there would have been uncomfortable. So what if you lived in the middle of an endless expanse of woods? If you could hear your neighbor fart, you didn't have an iota of freedom. It reminded me of the army.

I eased one door open and the pungent, rancid smell rose like a specter in the night. I shut the door softly. In the past however-long-I'd-been-out-there, I'd learned to rely on my nose and shy away from strong smells.

At the second door, I entered, pausing in the opening to listen for anything within. I took a gentle step in and lit my flashlight, palm covering most of the glow. There were only two rooms: one the living quarters, the other full of bunk beds. There was no bathroom. I wondered at that, but my experience in the wilderness recently clued me in to what they'd been doing. There were papers and empty plastic water jugs—if they weren't drinking the lake water, I wouldn't either. I found a tin of fish on a shelf and tucked it into my belt.

My senses told me more and more that no one was there. When the light buzzed on, there was no collective sigh of relief. The night was entirely devoid of distant voices or footsteps, no whiff of recently cooked food.

But my skin was crawling. I was used to single farmhouses and vacation homes, places that were abandoned in the aftermath. It had been a while since I rifled through any type of dark community. The sheer number of places someone could hide unnerved me. At least it hadn't been a site of slaughter during the invasion

I sorted through two more dorms. I didn't find any bottles small enough to carry water in, but I did find a book of matches I hoped had stayed dry, coils of long wire I imagined perfect for a snare, and a book. I only glanced at the cover. The book could have been on any subject, but it was my policy to take what I could get. I rarely finished books, as I didn't want to carry them with me, but blissing out of existence via pages was a privilege I reserved now that I was working for myself.

When I spotted a small metal pot in the last house, I grabbed it. It would be inconvenient, but I could mix water and purification tablets in it and it was small enough to carry. I'd have to gorge myself on water in the morning and carry the empty pot through the day. Maybe I'd find another canteen at my next stop.

I went into the last structure on the dock, a relatively sizable warehouse for supplies, opposite the first house I started at. I saved it for last because I suspected it to be least likely to have the common household items I was interested in.

Quiet as ever, my bodysuit muffling any creaks or gurgles my flesh made, I slid a door open and listened. Silence rang in my ears and I stepped in, chancing to shine my light over the contents.

My blood ran cold when I saw the light die in one corner. In an instant, I knew what it was. And that I was dead.

I turned off my light immediately and crouched down, gun ready—I'd be damned if I didn't go out fighting, not that it would do any good. My body wanted to lock my lungs down, but I forced myself to take small, silent breaths as I waited for an attack that didn't come. I listened and counted to a hundred.

At a hundred and one, I turned my flashlight on again. There it was again. *Their* metal. Unlike our own steal and precious metals that brilliantly reflected light back, the inky black metal seemed to suck in and demolish light. The absence of illumination was an indicator you were being watched by a Deadlight Garde.

I had gotten an uneasy feeling, in the barest first impression, that something wasn't quite right about my impending doom. A second look made me understand why. I had never seen a piece of their metal separated from a working body. But there it lay.

It was a metal shard the size of my forearm. I couldn't believe it. Was it bent? As in, broken off during an attack? I shivered to imagine what could harm a Deadlight Garde. Not humans, clearly. Another one of them? But though they didn't move in synchrony, the robots were unilaterally of one mind.

I approached cautiously to examine it. The edges were jagged, as if it had indeed been ripped off. Our targeted weapons couldn't puncture their armor, but the evidence that one of the robots had come through here wounded was undeniable. Or was it still in the vicinity? I shut off the flashlight again.

At that point in the alien invasion, everybody had seen a Deadlight, not just military personal. They were clever, absolutely deadly, and bent on killing every human they could.

I didn't survive the war because I was a hero or impressively strong. It was luck. Once a Deadlight had come straight toward me. It ripped apart a big man in a mech suit as if it were tearing soft bread, turned its faceless mask on me, and then did an abrupt turn and walked away. As if it had met its quota for death that day and I wasn't worth another thought.

It wasn't a calming thought that if the Deadlight Garde was still around I'd already be dead, but it was a thought.

As quietly as I could, I crept out the door and down the dock. I expected something to spring out and tear my head off, but nothing happened. It took me a fast minute to figure out how to carry the pot and keep my gun ready without them clinking together. I tied the handle of the pot to my belt with the thin wire. I slid the thick novel under my arm.

I felt better once I was back on the soggy shore and moving into the trees. I forced myself to turn back to assess the situation. The harsh overhead light still buzzed in the distance amid the soft glow of a few others in the houses around it. I heard nothing but water lapping at rocks and sand. Nothing moved.

I turned to leave, and the butt of my Kronos L85 hit the pot. The clank rang out and, to my horror, echoed across the lake. I didn't crouch and hide. I knew I had to book it, and book it I did. My suit woke and gave me a burst of speed. I crashed through the undergrowth and nearly collided with a tree as I put distance between me, the water town, and any potentially wounded Deadlight Gardes.

I raced and raced, my lungs and mouth burning from exhaustion and dehydration. Finally, I slowed and trekked ahead at a good but quieter pace. Then I stopped in my tracks as it hit me—I hadn't collected any goddamn water from the goddamn lake.

It was in the silence of the dark woods that I kind of wished I had the dog with me.

2. Close Encounters

I worked in the church with the other married women, all of us sweating like pigs while prepping supplies for the winter. All was right in the world.

Though Sister Esther reported that the big thermometer read ninety-eight degrees, it had to be even hotter inside the stuffy side room of the church. Even with the unbearable heat, early harvest was one of my favorite times of the year. My fingers, still stained from early blackberry picking, moved nimbly, almost of their own accord, through the beans. It was my thirty-second summer and I'd spent all of them preparing for winter.

The unmarried girls helped their fathers and brothers in the fields, weeding and harvesting ripe zucchini, carrots, and beans. I didn't miss working in the boiling sun, bending to pick foodstuffs with soiled hands, but I did wish we could sit outside in the shade as we separated pods from vines. *A stray breeze would not go unappreciated by me, God.*

"Sister Marah, pass me that bunch there, would you, please?"

I passed the prickly bunch to Rachel and went back to my own vines. Four of us stood around the table. In Lilium Springs, every person had a place and every person a job. I knew mine well. It was to wheedle out of Sister Abigale if she was pregnant or not.

I waited for her to finish her story about the goats knocking Joel down to nibble his hair. I laughed, but the whole while I rehearsed my lines.

"Joel's how old? Five now?" I asked.

"Yes," Sister Abigale replied. "He's big, but not quite big enough to do the feed chores on his own. He's eager to help his brothers though, and seeing his little body out there is so cute." She giggled. "My mini man."

"And is anything else happening soon?" I caught Rachel's eye. She was in on my theory; we had talked about it on our way over.

Sister Abigale shrugged. "He'll probably lose his first tooth soon."

"I mean with you, Sister."

She slammed her beans down in mock protest. "How in Heaven's name did you know, Sister Marah?"

Rachel nudged me and Sister Esther's jaw dropped open.

"So you *are* pregnant?" Rachel asked.

"Praise the Lord, yes I am," Sister Abigale said smugly. "Only a few weeks along though. I haven't even told Brother Ben. How did you figure it out?" She pointed a thick finger at me.

It was my turn to be haughty. "I got a feeling. You seemed tired last week. I wondered if morning sickness was wearing you out." The truth was, I had been watching all the women of an age with me. I wanted a fourth baby—*A girl finally, Lord*—and I was desperate to know if it was still possible. Sister Abigale was four years older than me, so if she could breed five years after her most recent baby, I could too.

Sister Esther leaned in for a hug with Sister Abigale to congratulate her. I was surprised Sister Abigale hadn't told her the news; they were so close. I would have told Rachel right away. I told her everything. Nearly.

I gave Rachel a smile and smoothed a tangle of stray hairs from her sweaty neck. Her skin was warm and damp, lithe as she's always been. She automatically collected the tendrils and started braiding them.

We chatted for a few minutes about the coming baby and what that'd mean for Sister Abigale's family. A slight line formed on Rachel's brow while she thought. She was so quiet when with the others. I usually didn't find out what was going on in her head until we were alone.

As Sister Abigale described every moment of her commonplace pregnancy, I felt the old dog of jealousy lift its head. The whole while Sister Abigale spoke, I thought,

Why her? And then, *Sorry, Lord*. It was easy to direct my thoughts toward Her. I'd repent for my jealous nature that night too, but the faster I could recant my human ways, the better.

But I wanted another baby too. It was eating me alive. After all those years of service, I wanted my girl-child.

When conversation drifted off, Rachel spoke up, "Actually, I wanted to talk to y'all." Her voice lowered and piqued my interest. She hadn't told me of any big news of her own.

"Yesterday, I was on the trail by the forge, the far one by the hollyhocks, and I saw Elder Sister Hetta." Rachel piled the bean pods for drying, but carefully, as if she had to focus on her words. And when talking about Elder Sister Hetta, one did have to focus on one's words. Rachel set a torn pod aside.

"I caught up to her on the trail. Elder Sister Hetta was moving slowly, almost as if she wasn't well or as if hurt. I called out to her and she turned and smiled like she does now, but all she said was 'Hello, dear,' and kept walking." Rachel's expression pinched and she pulled her braid over her shoulder. "It was clear she was in some kind of pain, but she never stopped to rest. I followed—I mean I was going the same direction—until I turned off to the well."

The three of us set our vines down and leaned forward as Rachel gathered pods in a basket. She was done with her story. I made eye contact with Sisters Abigale and Esther, and the three of us burst out laughing.

"That's your story?" I asked. "You greeted Elder Sister Hetta?

Rachel wrinkled her eyebrows at us, as if we were being absurd. She cast about for some words. "No, it was like I got the impression she forgot my name. Like she couldn't place who I was."

That silenced all of us.

Sister Abigale was the first to speak. "And you think since her stroke, she's getting ready to pass on?" It was a carefully voiced assumption.

"Well, I don't know, now do I? But maybe." She tossed her braid back.

I felt a flame bloom in my chest. What she was saying was taboo. She was just edging around it a bit. No one should speculate on when the Lord would take our Elder Sister. Only She knew. Only She knew when it was time for our Elder to move on and the next woman to rise. Gossip about God's predetermined plan was dangerous work.

Just then, the door creaked open. I was frustrated by the interruption. The children delivering more vines should have knocked and waited to be allowed in. I wanted to talk more about why Rachel was bringing up the succession.

At the door was Timothy with a wheelbarrow. I pushed down my anger and smiled for all to see. "Oh, Brother Timothy," I said. "Do you have more vines for us to separate?"

"Sure do." His baritone voice was suddenly loud in the space we had just been whispering in. Not whispering. Idly gossiping. I peeked at Rachel out of the corner of my eye, determined to interrupt her if she kept at it.

"Thank you, dear," I replied. I didn't ask about the children. If I gave him a verbal invitation, he might stay and talk with our group. I wanted my husband to leave so I could deal with Rachel's issue.

Timothy put four armloads of bean vines on the end of the table we had cleared with our work. "Matty's taking a break in the shade," he volunteered on his own. "He didn't keep his hat on and his cheeks are blooming red."

Sister Esther tutted in response.

"You're a little red yourself there." I reached out to touch his face. Under his lower lip was something bright red. That couldn't be a sunburn, it was a stray red thread or—

It was a tiny piece of tomato skin. We hadn't had tomatoes at breakfast that morning. No one had eaten tomatoes yet. They were just ripening and the Elders would distribute them once picked and sorted.

Once the red flesh was in my fingers, it was pretty obvious to everyone what it was, and Timothy knew it.

"Just a taste test." At least he had the grace to look abashed.

"Tim, you know we shouldn't." It was all I said, but it was enough. I wanted him—and the other women—to know I'd talk to him about it later. No one was supposed to eat from the fields before food was counted, blessed, and given by the Elders. It was selfish and presumptuous, and a community couldn't last if its members were such.

The other women had their heads down, intent on their work, and I felt shamed by my man.

Timothy tried to catch my eye on his way out, but I didn't give him the opportunity. I went back to my place at the table. The silence was oppressive. I knew the other three were thinking about my husband breaking taboo.

"Sister Rachel," I started, "I don't think it's wise to speculate about Elder Sister Hetta's health. That's in God's hands." I wanted to get our minds off Timothy's transgression.

"I wasn't—"

"And it's idle gossip." That was a low blow. That's pretty much all we had been doing all morning, me included.

Rachel shot me a dark look, but I knew she wouldn't challenge me in front of the others.

The conversation turned toward the practicalities of drying the beans under the nets outside—we relied on them all winter for fiber and vitamins—but it was stiff. I knew I was the cause of the tension in the air and I felt the back of my neck burn with more than heat, but I was upset too. Rachel shouldn't have spoken that way in front of the others. If she had a concern, she could have told me privately. An open questioning of Elder Sister Hetta's health? She might as well say she wanted God to smite the Elder Sister down to hurry along the succession and make the beautiful, golden-hearted Sister Rachel leader of us all.

I was upset with Timothy for breaking taboo, but mostly that he had gotten caught so publicly. Sneaking something in the fields is one temptation to give in to—I ate two strawberries early that year, Lord help me—but making an open show of it was an affront to the whole community.

I wondered if I was being too hard on them—in fact, I knew I was—but as we transferred the beans to netted trays outside for drying, I found myself feeling restless.

It didn't make sense. I had everything. It was my favorite time of the year. The crops were good; we'd have plenty to eat when snows covered our fields and iced our wells. Timothy was a hard worker, as was I. My kids were healthy. But as I rested my hand on my empty stomach and felt the curve of my body, it flashed again. This war within me.

It was true, I did want. I wanted a baby, a girl baby to raise up to be leader of the family after me. At the same time, I reveled in newfound freedom now that my last boy was weaned. Without a babe at my breast every three hours, or the endless cycle of teaching little boys where not to pee, I was finally coming out of the baby gloom that had descended on me with Gideon. I was ready to have more time to myself. For myself.

I wanted a baby, and it was my responsibility to birth a girl before my season of fertility passed, but at the same time, I wanted other things. Things I could hardly name to myself.

I glanced at Rachel. A small spot of wet dotted the

cotton back of her butter-colored dress and she blew loose strands of hair off her face.

"1 Corinthians 11:15. But if a woman has long hair, it is a glory to her: for her hair is given to her for a covering," Rachel recited.

I wasn't impressed. It was the shortest Sunday School verse on the list. I pushed myself to memorize the short verses in addition to the long verses, but only to recite the lengthy ones. But pride was a sin, so I set that aside.

"Very good, Rachel," Sister Bethany said.

Rachel sat down, smoothing the skirt she recently finished making with her mother.

"Marah, you're next."

I stood from the pew, a little firefly in my tummy. "1 Corinthians 11:5-6. But every wife who prays or prophesies with her head uncovered dishonors her head, since it is the same as if her head were shaven. For if a wife will not cover her head, then she should cut her hair short. But since it is disgraceful for a wife to cut off her hair or shave her head, let her cover her head."

I sat down before Sister Bethany could answer in affirmation. I knew I got every word correct. I gave Sister Bethany a shy smile and she smiled back.

"Good," Sister Bethany said as she turned to the front of the room. I was the last to recite. The other girls my age, plus me, barely filled a single pew. The room was drafty, but nothing like the fierce cold that would come with the snow.

"Note what each of these verses have in common; our hair is a glory. It is a woman's glory." Sister Bethany smoothed her own tan hair in demonstration. "There is power in our uncut locks. Remember the story about Samson?" We nodded, not allowed to speak out of turn. "Samson received his power from God because he didn't cut his hair. We don't cut our hair, so that we receive our power."

I raised my hand. Sister Bethany waxed on until she saw me.

"Yes, Marah?" She peered over her glasses at me.

"Sister Bethany, if Samson's strength came from his hair, why aren't we strong like that? My dad cuts his hair and he's much stronger than my mom."

"That's a good question," Sister Bethany said even though I knew it was a good question. What I wanted to know was *why?*

Sister Bethany continued, "God allowed Samson to grow his hair, and in return he received immense strength. He could slay a lion and defeat an entire army. Extreme physical strength was his special gift from God. Each of us has a special gift from God, something we all have that She enhances. Samson, as a man, could only receive a *physical* gift. While it's true men have stronger physical gifts than women, that's all they're able to receive. Women have *spiritual* gifts. That's why we're the spiritual leaders of the community. Understand?"

I nodded.

Rachel raised her hand and asked, "Could we let men grow their hair too? Wouldn't it be neat if they could all lift a tree?"

Sister Bethany's nose shriveled in revulsion at the thought of men with a female characteristic. She shook her head quickly. I could tell this was not a good question, but Sister Bethany responded kindly.

"Samson was a chosen one by God. It was a special case. Today, God has chosen you young ladies to be special ones. To be leaders."

The bell rang for lunch and we each went home to our little chaotic corner of the world. My family ate fresh vegetables for lunch and bread with jam I had made from the blackberries. I didn't find it within me to bring up the tomatoes to Timothy again besides a nod and a look at what was on our plate. He went sullen and wouldn't talk until I asked him to pass me a cloth napkin. He was a quiet man, which was good at times, frustrating at others. The boys were boys. Little Gideon was alive with stories from play group. I fussed over Matty's sunburn—I couldn't believe he was nearly a height with me—and I drew some sentences out of our brooding James. Among my family, I felt my cup runneth over. I thought more about my desire to have a girl. Maybe that wasn't God's plan for me. *Lord, let me be satisfied with what You have given me.*

A loose rattle caught my attention. I glanced up from

my plate to see the pans on the wall sway. My teacup rattled in its patterned saucer, and I looked around the house in disbelief. The buzz of a thousand flies filled the air.

"What's that?" Matty asked, eyes wide in terror.

Demons. Demons were coming.

I knew it was not a sound of God. It was no horn calling us home at long last. It was a sound made by the Devil.

I looked to Timothy for confirmation. He was already pulling the children from their chairs. There were only three, but I counted the boys as Timothy swooped Gideon up in his arms. The cabin around us shook harder and I felt a wave of thunder pulse through my body. I was already praying as I ushered Matty and James through the door behind Timothy. Lunch sat half-eaten on the table. I hoped we'd be back to finish it.

I expected to see dark billowing clouds and fire in the sky—the terrors of Hell raining down on us—but the skies all around were impossibly blue. Vibration moved through me more urgently now, and I fought to keep my footing. I pushed ahead of the boys to open the cellar door and took Gideon from Timothy's arms. Once inside, the smell of fresh earth filled my nose and everything suddenly went dark as Timothy slammed the door behind Matty. I stumbled on the last step, and Gideon whimpered in my neck. I didn't know if dishes still rattled in the house, but dusty clouds of soil wafted down on us. Matty coughed and I felt the grime of silted dirt coat my hair. Panic struck me as I imagined our cellar caving in. I clutched Gideon to me even as he wiggled to get down.

The five of us muddled about in the dark without order until James tripped over the lantern and cursed.

"James," I hissed. "Repent now, before we all die and you're damned to Hell."

"Kids, we're not going to die," Timothy said. "Marah, maybe that's not helpful right now."

I lowered my voice, threat evident until James muttered in repentance. I set Gideon down as a spark caught and the lantern sprang to light. Timothy held it over his head, bathing us in an amber glow.

"Boys, come here."

They gathered beside me, and the powerful vibrations subsided as we prayed as a family, the boys all crying to varying degrees. I felt a tug as Gideon wiped his nose on my dress. I put my arm around him. My mind drifted meaninglessly until Timothy's stirring beside me brought me back to the dark cellar. I didn't know how I could lose myself in the midst of such an emergency. My heart raced even though I'd been sitting still. I wondered how much time had passed.

A radiant, blinding sunset broke in as Timothy opened the door. I realized all signs of the demons were gone. Timothy stood, listening intently. I strained to hear as well, but it was all silence. One by one we fled up the stairs out of that dark chamber and into the light.

We found ourselves back at the dining table, staring at each other in shock. Gideon was red-faced from bawling, but James was white with fear. I looked at Timothy and saw the hard lines set around his mouth. I wondered what I looked like out in the red-toned daylight.

It never got easier. Not for any of us.

As soon as I could, once the boys were calmed though shaky, I left the house—Rachel's home, her location, tugged me forward. The gloom of night descended and I felt a shiver break through me. The terrible things were gone, far away, but we never knew when they'd be back, how close they would fly over our homes. It was only the Lord's provision that kept us safe.

I saw a dark figure on the path. It was her. Oh, thank God, she was safe. Rachel's braid had come undone and hair fell around her shoulders in a wild tangle.

"Marah," she cried in relief. She never called me Sister. We were more than that.

Reassurance washed through me, and I closed the gap on the path by running to her. I could see she was still disturbed by the afternoon's events. Dirt streaked the side of her dress, and she smelled like onions and earth.

She opened her arms as I approached and I stepped in to hug her. A beautiful swirl of sensation twisted through my stomach, pulling my heart with it. Rachel was hot in my arms, and I felt her arms warm in embrace. I took another half step in so my hips lined with hers. I was so glad she was safe, glad to be close to her. Wind whispered through the tall pines. We were alone.

Without thinking of who I was or what I was doing, I leaned in and kissed her lips. It was a moment I had imagined many nights, but I wasn't prepared. I moaned, ecstatic to be taken in by her soft, wet mouth—then something pushed hard against my shoulder.

"Marah." She let my name hang in the darkness for the second time as she wiped her face.

I was in shock, unable to respond or defend myself. I couldn't believe I had finally acted upon the impulse.

Rachel cast me a dark look and spit on the ground. "What was that all about?" she hissed. I had never heard venom in her voice before. Not toward anyone and definitely not directed at me.

I couldn't respond. My insides went from a flame of sensation to numbness.

"Are you possessed, Marah? Should I call the Elders? Or is defiling my body some weird joke to you?"

The last thing I wanted was to get the Elders involved. "No, Rachel, I thought…"

"What?" There was unfamiliar steel in her eyes. She had never stood up to me before. In that moment, I realized how easily Rachel could ruin my life. Sacred actions outside the marriage bed? It never occurred to me that Rachel would protest against me, much less point a finger in front of everyone.

"Tell me what that was, or I'll tell Elder Sister Hetta." She bunched up her hair to pull it back.

"You can't," I said quickly. "You can't tell her without

admitting what you did. You're the one that pressed against me."

Rachel didn't back down like I expected her to, like she always did. "Last chance, Marah."

I pressed my limp, dirty hands to my temples before letting them drop. "Rachel, I was so worried about you. I was stricken with terror at the thought of something happening to you today. We're more than friends, more than sisters. I'd give one of my own children to you if you didn't have yours." I could see none of this made sense to Rachel.

"Stop. You need…" her voice shook and she started over. "Never touch me again, or I'll tell Elder Sister Hetta and Brother Timothy. I don't know what's going on inside of you after the terrible things that happened today, and I don't want to get you in trouble, but don't you dare touch me like that again. I'll tell. I really will."

She took one last heavy breath and flew down the now pitch-dark path.

She could tell. So easily my life would be ruined, my whole family in danger.

I fumbled in the dark though I had the path memorized. I felt tired and thirsty and incredibly hungry all at once. I tried pushing thoughts of what happened with Rachel out of my head but couldn't. I was seriously puzzled by Rachel's response. There were so many things we did differently than the men, without men. Why couldn't this be one of them?

I thought back to my long friendship with Rachel. Was it over? My eyes brimmed, but I had gotten good at not crying over the years. I swallowed twice and parted my mouth, chin to the sky. The tears dissipated but the knot in my throat lingered long after.

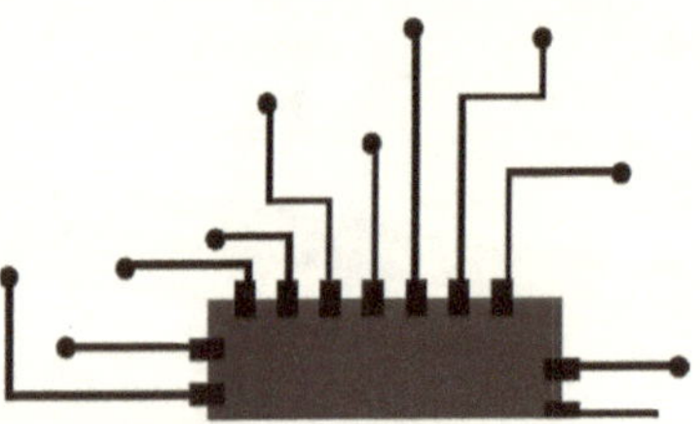

3. Magnificent Mushrooms

I scrutinized the page and compared the mushroom in my hand to the picture. It was a clear identification—white, stringy, and growing on the side of a tree. There were no poisonous look-alikes as with morels. I set the book down on the ground and slid my knife out to cut the lion's mane mushroom from the bark. My fingers dug into the flesh of the mushroom as I grabbed hold. It felt uncomfortable, like cold, dead skin.

The guide said there were some mushrooms that must be cooked or the eater would be subject to a night of gas, but lion's mane could be eaten raw. I was ready to join the club mushroom enthusiast and author Dean Miles called "the last members of our population worth their 'spores.'" Miles was most likely dead, so I let the pun pass.

I held the textured mushroom in my hand. It was big—

half the size of my head—but light and dense at the same time. What I would have given to fry it up in some hot butter. My stomach reminded me what I was doing and I took a bite. I was so hungry anything edible would have been good, but in truth lion's mane wasn't bad. It was weird biting right into the ginormous fungus as if it were a pungent apple. It felt bumpy, almost furry on my lips. Once gummed between my teeth, it was the same as any other mushroom. I stood upright in the forest, gnawing on the woodland fruit when a beetle crawled out of its hideaway in the mushroom and down my wrist—my gloves were hanging at my belt.

"Ewughhh." I shook the mushroom off, trying to dislodge anything else living inside. The plastic water bottle I'd traded for the pot a few stops ago was nearly empty. I filled and purified it at streams and now the thin plastic casing was wrinkled and bound to break soon. There wasn't enough water to wash the mushroom and hydrate myself, so I got on with it and ate until the mushroom was small enough to tuck into one of my belt pouches.

I quickly packed up my belongings and set off again. How many calories could that have been? Fifty? Twenty? I was learning to incorporate foraging into my diet, but not fast enough. I couldn't forage and eat upward of fifty lion's mane mushrooms a day. I shuddered to think of what that would do to my already tenuous digestive system.

Six days back, I crept into a dusty library and used my flashlight to locate a section on foraging. I carried copies of *Magnificent Mushrooms* by Dean Miles and *A General*

Guide to Woodland Edibles by someone who was a lot less colorful than Miles. At the moment, Miles was my only friend in the world. My brother, Julian, had loved mushrooms. But, like everyone else, he had been dead for years.

I was already thin from the low rations and panic of those last drawn-out months in the army. I was muscular, too, from years of training and eating protein packs. When I started the godforsaken walk into the woods, I dropped a few pounds, leaning out even more. That was fine. Less to carry. I barely had the energy to carry the books. I was hungry all the time. As hard as it was to admit to myself, I was starving.

When I splashed my unmentionables with river water, my ribs threatened to come out and beat me unless I found some nice fat to slather them in. My safety blanket was disintegrating by the day. I needed to find a solution, and fast.

My gun prodded along in the beat it'd been keeping since I wandered shell-shocked out of the Arizona base. *BuMP, bump, BuMP, bump.* My arms were full with books—I wondered what it would have been like to forage mushrooms with Julian—and the water bottle. The wire coil at my belt struck erratically at my upper thigh. The regular, predictable bump of the Kronos I could handle. It was the inconsistent wobbling and sporadic clinks of the wire that drove me crazy.

A root caught my foot and I crashed into a clearing,

spilling the books in the grass. I looked up and found myself in a small meadow filled with wheat-colored grass and pint-size saplings. And what was on the other side of the tall grass?

Trees.

Bloody, goddamn trees!

Prickly beasts that wouldn't let you near them or they'd smear sap all over your freshly cleaned bodysuit. Bastards that held precious treasure troves of bird eggs close to their chests. Urging you on for another mile, because they never revealed what might be on the other side.

And 98 percent of the time, what you saw after all that walking was more trees.

Animal noises filled the air, but they were my own. I grunted and snarled as I untied the wire. I dropped my gun more roughly than I ought to and took the lame foraging book in both hands like a baseball bat.

I smashed the hard cover against a sizable trunk. The aged tree's branches started far above my head, so I had clear aim as I hit it again and again. The reverberation in my arms was thrilling because it felt like something. Anything. I wanted to be done walking and feel something and maybe not starve. The spine of the book snapped and pages stuck out like broken white teeth.

Quickly, I was winded and sank down to the ground. I cried and looked at the warped book and cried a bit more. I was going to die.

And it wouldn't be dignified or glorious. I wouldn't go

down under a pack of wolves—I didn't even know if wolves existed anymore. I wouldn't go to sleep one cold winter night in my hand-built shed and freeze, death taking me before I could greet it.

Commonplace hunger was going to take me. And slowly. I couldn't scavenge, forage, or hunt fast enough to survive. That was my truth: without the failure-of-a-society I had left behind, weak and flawed as it was, gone the way of the wolves, I couldn't survive. I'd walk until one morning I couldn't get up again. I'd lie for days in the same spot and softly fade away, mushrooms eventually pushing up through my eye sockets, bending gray eyelids aside. Or maybe I'd crash over the side of one of those rocky escarpments like that dog.

That stupid dog.

I looked around for something to wipe my running nose on, but of course there was nothing. Suddenly my resolve not to use book pages as toilet paper seemed weak. I ripped a page—not from Miles's, never from his—and wiped my boogery nose.

I bunched up the paper and threw it. The crumpled ball landed a short distance past my outstretched legs. I wished the sun would set so I could make camp and settle in to read Miles's manifesto by flashlight before drifting off.

But I couldn't. Not only did I need to find food and water, settling in before sunset would be another personal failure. I already had too many of those on my shoulders.

Tiny white butterflies flitted about among the clouds of

gnats. I stood to my feet, crossed the field quickly, and stepped into the shady pine forest once again. The game I had designed—left around one trunk, right around the other, always going in the approximation of north—formed an unbearable snaggle of threads woven all the way from the empty southwest to the northern forest I found myself in, whatever it was called.

I smelled something sharp, like metal. Instantly I dropped my cryfest and maneuvered my gun to the front. Creeping forward on soft feet, I scanned the trees for any movement. Then I heard it: a low, incessant buzz. I veered in that direction and found a mass of dark flies highlighted by an errant stray of light through the canopy. I imagined one of the flies zooming up my nasal cavity, and my nostrils squished up as much as nostrils are able to do.

On the ground at the base of a tree lay a bloody pile of organic waste. I set the gun safety back on and squatted down to take a better look at the wet mass. The limp and flaccid pile clearly wasn't a whole dead animal. It looked like intestines and blood and organs. The entrails, I realized, as the term came back to me.

If it were wolves or a bear scavenging a carcass, there'd be a half-knitted husk of a body. No, a human had been there. I looked up. They had probably hung the animal—A deer?—from a tree branch as they gutted it. Or maybe they hung the deer before dark, out of the way of predators, and lowered it in the morning to carry home.

I knew then for the first time in a long time that

someone was near. The thrill of that idea lit up hairs along the back of my neck. In anticipation or fear, I didn't know. I had no idea how many near misses there had been along my long route. Maybe there were others, simply always beyond my sight. Or me and this person could be the only ones left. The two of us and a whole lot of *them* on this once-homey rock.

It was clear that no one was coming back to the area. There was nothing here for them except black flies. And me.

I had kept watch for evidence of humans. Partly as a thought experiment—Where were the other survivors and what were they doing?—but also with the hypothetical understanding that if I found them, I could make contact. I could join them.

I walked past the bloody mess, out of earshot of the flies, and squatted by a tree. Throughout my walk, I worried often enough that no one was left. The moment I had real proof someone existed, I was confronted with major questions. Did I want to see other humans? And if I did, how would I find them? They could have gone any direction, but their destination must have been a short walk away, close enough to carry a deer to. No, you couldn't carry a deer. And there weren't drag marks. A vague image of a deer hog-tied to a sturdy branch carried by a man on each end came to mind.

Did I want to meet deer-toting wilderness types? I wanted people like me, not the individualistic, young, healthy men that peeled away from refugee camps to save themselves while everyone else was under attack. The same people my mother complained would run full tilt into the wilderness at the mere mention of group chores.

I asked myself what I was doing. What was Arwen doing in the face of the end of the world? Traveling the woods, trying to survive. A knot of anxiety released under my breastbone. It didn't pay to make assumptions. Anyone still alive was doing exactly what they needed to, like I was.

There was one more problem. If I found them, what would find us?

I hadn't seen evidence of the Deadlight Gardes since that discarded metal at the water village. The Deadlight Gardes generally stayed within two thousand miles of the equator on either side. Something to do with geomagnetism, it was thought. The camp my mom and Julian lived in was in that range. All the makeshift communities we lived in had been. Maybe it wouldn't have mattered, maybe they'd be dead anyway, but I hated the misinformation of the early days. Anyway that didn't stop their ships from making temporary journeys north and south to exterminate humans.

The government told people to band together, and that was a mistake too. The largest cities were the first to go, buildings and people just flattened, nothing left. Only an eight-minute warning before death. Then, over the years, small cities and towns were desolated by Deadlight Gardes on foot until only refugee camps were left. Then, the largest of those were systematically wiped out. There was no safety in numbers. So why was I trying to join up again?

Mind still not made up, I wandered through the woods, slowly, apprehensively but also weak AF.

Then, through the trees, I saw a shelter. I had seen many deserted cabins during my time in the woods, but the knowledge that a heart of my own kind beat close by sent prickles down my back. I crouched and watched, waiting to hear movement inside the tiny cabin. The structure wasn't like the elaborate vacation houses or hunting cabins I had seen. There was no wide porch with a mossy rocking chair or old hot tub filled with leaves to designate it as a former retreat. It hadn't been abandoned in the midst of an alien invasion; it had been built since the Arrival. I was sure. All that stood was a little shed with rough walls and no windows. It felt fairy-tale-like, otherworldly, and ageless because of what was missing. There wasn't even a front step. A witch could step out any minute with promises of candy and pastries. And I would probably accept.

Nothing stirred, and I grew restless as I kept watch. I didn't think anyone could winter there, and it was too small to hold many people. Finally, I decided the homeowner was out doing whatever it was they did and it was worth a peek inside.

I stood and tested my theory. "Hello? Hey, is anyone in there?" My voice rasped unfamiliarly.

I walked to the door and put my ear to it. When I pulled on the handle, I discovered it wasn't locked. The first thing I saw brought relief—bedding but all rolled up and stashed away. The small hearth was long cold. This wasn't someone's home, but a temporary reprieve from being on the move, or maybe a hunting camp. The dead deer and whoever killed it were long gone.

At the same time, I worried I had missed my only chance to see another human being. Relief or guilt, the decision had been made for me.

I looked around, but there wasn't much to see. It was bare bones. My flashlight lit up something overhead. Whoever used the camp had tied up a parcel. To keep the animals out, my instincts told me. Which meant…

Food. There was food in there.

I didn't stop to think before untying and carefully lowering the bundle from a rafter. Glass clinked as the bag resettled. I pulled out several clear jars. One held a flint starter and bit of dry kindling. Another was chock-full of roasted hazelnuts. I twisted the top impatiently, took a handful, and shoved the tiny nuggets in my mouth. Dear God, they were salted. I let my mouth go to work as I examined the other foodstuffs in the sack. There were also dried berries and some kind of brittle jerky.

Then it hit me. I was eating someone's stash. Not just the leftover bags and cans from a generation gone, but someone who expected to come back there and find something to eat. They could be counting on this food. Moreover, the missing snacks might awaken some primeval stirrings. They'd know someone had been there. I hadn't made up my mind yet, but I didn't want anyone looking for me either.

I carefully measured out small portions of the food. I guessed I could take about 20 percent without it being noticed. I packed everything back up the way I found it and hoisted the bag to the rafter once again. Though I was sure the hunter was long gone, I was edgy, imagining someone darkening the doorway to find me messing with their supplies.

Once I finished erasing the evidence of my visit, I stuffed the portion of jerky in my pouch and quickly polished off the handful of nuts and dried berries. They were good but made me terribly thirsty. Like an enchanted cabin in the deep, dark woods, my wish was granted when I spotted a canister peeking behind the door. I tipped it, trying to empty some of the big metal container into my flimsy plastic bottle and succeeded in spilling most of it on the floor. I guzzled half a bottle and then made myself stop while I refilled again.

Then I sat. I thought about how easy that had been. I'd struggled for months to feed myself. Then, in the span of an hour, I had gotten everything I needed. Clearly the person here knew how to take care of themself.

That's exactly who I needed.

In olden days, the adults would have kicked us out, let us run around outside while they discussed important issues, but things being as they were, they cooped us up in the barn and let themselves out. Though we were basically living outside, I hadn't been out from under that roof for five days except to go to the bathroom. It made me angry—I was nearly sixteen years old. Did they think I didn't know how to handle myself outside? I knew how to creep through the woods, quiet as the deer. I knew to avoid open meadows and snake through the trees.

Instead, I was inside. And the grown-ups got to be out there.

"Sneak attack!" Sharp, bony fingers dug into my side.

"Julian, stop it." I pushed him away, dark scowl on my face. "I could have fallen if I didn't hear you coming a mile away."

"Why so grumpy? Did you step in a cow pie again?"

"Doesn't it bother you? Being stuck in here with the kids?" I waved around. Most of the kids were squirming around quietly in the corner their family staked out for them. Lil was with a group of older teens in the middle, talking quietly.

Julian threw his legs over the edge of the loft I was perched up on and shrugged. "We *are* kids."

"Maybe, but not like them." I nodded toward the others, separating myself from them.

The truth was, I felt bad for those kids. My family was the only one there with two parents. All the other kids had just one grown-up, or if they had more than one grown-up with them, the other adult was a grandparent or relative. I knew my mom and dad never would have left us like those other parents. It wasn't right and I felt protective of those kids. But I couldn't help them if I was stuck inside while real decisions were made elsewhere.

Julian tapped me on my shoulder and pointed down. The grown-ups were coming back in through the barn door. I stayed where I was. I didn't want to seem too eager to run down to Mom and Dad. I'd do anything to align myself with the older ones, and Lil and the rest barely glanced the adults' way.

Then I heard a soft sob escape from Mom. A shock ran through me and I looked her over quickly. She wasn't hurt, but she folded her arms up against her chest as if she was squeezing herself together. The front line was half a state away, so I knew we weren't under attack.

But where was Dad? I scanned through the adults until I saw him, over by Lil, pulling her in for a hug. She ducked her head in front of her new peers but followed when he asked her to.

Mom's bleary eyes caught mine, and she gestured for me and Julian to come down.

I picked through the other families and their crap and the five of us, my family, met back at the neatly kept horse stall that did its job as our temporary house. I was proud that everyone in my family only brought a backpack and nothing else. We weren't like the others, slowed down by bags of old photographs and papers, or hastily wrapped heirlooms that people growled across if you got too close. I sorted my pack every night in case we had to run for it in the dark.

When I was within arm's reach, Mom and Dad both touched me, as if to reassure themselves I was there. It ruffled me a bit, but I let them hug me anyway, one of the benefits of still having both parents with you.

Mom cleared her throat and spoke first.

"Sara Wilkens was able to get through on her transistor radio. There's a camp setting up about forty miles east of here." Her voice was off. As if she was trying for upbeat. "It'll take a few days to get there. Some of the other groups have decided to make for it and we can travel together."

"There's supplies there? At the camp?" That was Lil, always looking for the hole in the plan.

Mom nodded. Dad was already packing his black canvas bag. I didn't expect to be leaving right then, but that was fine with me. I was more than ready to leave the musty air of this barn behind.

Lil pressed on, "But won't the aliens go there too?" I hadn't noticed until then that my sister had dark shadows under her eyes, aging her half a decade.

Dad finally spoke up, backpack on. "That's why there's another group heading back the way we came. To join the army." I nodded, that made sense. "Keep the aliens back. Defeat them." His voice hitched and he couldn't say any more.

My heart slowed as I read his tone, what he wasn't saying. No, it couldn't be. He would never leave us. We were family. Family sticks together. That's what he said since the first evacuation—that we'd never split up.

"Dad, should we get our bags ready?" I asked quickly.

He knelt down and grasped for our hands. I saw

realization dawn on Julian's face as it crumpled inward.

"I'm not going with you kids." His body shook with a sob. He wasn't supposed to cry. I didn't want him to be allowed to cry. "I'm going with a few others to help the army."

I pushed away from him to look in his face. "Dad, you can't. You can't go. We need to stay together."

He talked over me, tried to reason. Said the army needed help. Even with renewed support from Russia, they didn't have enough people. That China was battling ships in their own airspace. I didn't care about any of that. He said he had to go; it was the only way he could make things safe for us so we didn't have to keep running. I felt my head go fuzzy, as if my mind was tearing violently away from my body to avoid thinking, avoid feeling. When the clouds cleared, I was *seething*. Dad said he would never leave us. He was different than the other dads, our family was different. *We* were his priority, not other people.

Lil collapsed into Mom, tears rolling silently down her cheeks, but Julian was swathed in Dad's arms, his little shoulders hardly poking out from under Dad's frame.

I balled up my own fists and stood clear of Dad, even when he reached for me. When he tried to hug me, I pushed at him, pushing over and over again and finally slapping him in the face. Tears leaked down our faces; his of sadness, mine of sheer anger.

"I'll come back. I promise."

He promised.

I opened my eyes to find someone watching me.

4. The Long Walk

"I don't understand. If I haven't done anything wrong, why am I being forced to go on a prayer walk?"

"Sister Marah," Sister Bethany said softly. "A prayer walk is a gift. Take this time to reflect and commune with God. This isn't a bad thing."

Yeah, right, I thought. If I went on an unexpected prayer walk—one I didn't request the Elders to grant me for intercessory prayer time away from the business of home life—everyone would think I was backsliding. I knew what everyone would think, because that's what I'd think about them. I'd be a threat to the community's connection with the Lord. They'd think I was sent on the walk to get right with God again. Being sent on a prayer walk wasn't a punishment, but sometimes it was the first step down that road.

The woodwork around us gleamed from polish. It certainly smelled fresh; the young girls scrubbed it down the previous day. Church was home in a way my family's house would never be. This was where everything that mattered happened. Usually when I came, I felt calm, loved, and part of something bigger than myself. But right then I was distinctly uneasy. I didn't like others thinking I had done something wrong, especially when I hadn't.

"But, Sister Bethany, I don't need the opportunity. I'm happy at home."

Sister Bethany watched me as carefully as she could through her cataract-clouded eyes. The next time she spoke, I felt the weight beneath the words.

"Sister Marah, I'd rather not involve Elder Sister Hetta in this." Almost as an afterthought, as if she thought I wouldn't notice the weight of importance, she added, "Not now."

That took me aback. Why would Elder Sister Hetta get involved in something this routine? And *why* not now? Was Rachel right? Was the Elder Sister really facing difficulties?

I sniffed and Sister Bethany waited for my response. This was the Sister who taught me at Sunday School and shepherded me when my mother died. She was second in the succession line and she deserved my respect, not the belligerence that surfaced in me.

"Of course, thank you, Sister Bethany. I will cherish this time."

I turned to leave when Sister Bethany spoke, "I suggest you focus your prayers on your recent transgressions against Sister Rachel."

The blood drained from my face. Rachel told Sister Bethany about our kiss in the dark? How could Rachel have done such a thing? And how could Sister Bethany address me about it now, here in God's temple? It wouldn't surprise me if the veil rent here before us and I was taken down to Hell in a plume of dark smoke.

I wish I had never done the thing. I had already lost my friend. Now, my standing among the women was in jeopardy.

Sister Bethany spoke louder, her voice ringing through the church. "Sister Rachel, please come here."

From the back room nestled to the side of the sanctuary came the sound of a bench nudged back. Then soft footsteps.

"Yes, Sister Bethany?" Rachel asked when she appeared in the doorway.

If I hadn't be so furiously mad at her, I would have been glad to see her. It had been weeks since Rachel and I talked. When I woke the morning after the kiss, I knew she'd avoid me and I decided to do the same. When we were both at church or working on the same group task, we dodged each other's eye, speaking of only the bare necessities related to our work. It would be odd to Sister Bethany if I didn't look at Rachel, which gave me an excuse to do something I sorely missed.

Rachel's light brown hair was wound in a bun on the back of her head. Her shirt opened at the throat and her slender collarbone shone through. She was beautiful in a way that I never found Timothy. With Timothy, it was about duty. Rachel though, she was a vision.

I didn't know what I was thinking. I *still* didn't know what I was thinking. My entire body went wet and warm and I clasped my hands behind me to keep them from shaking. I felt just as flushed as if the whole community had piled into my bedroom to watch while Timothy pumped inside me. It was all too personal. I just wanted out.

"Sister Rachel told me you two had a spat," Sister Bethany continued, eyes watching my face. "Friends like you, in a small community like this, cannot let trivial, Earthly things get in the way of our pursuit of eternal life."

The thing was, if it was a big deal like Rachel implied, why wasn't I already being punished? Did Sister Bethany need a confession? What exactly had Rachel told her? I decided Sister Bethany couldn't know the whole story.

"Of course. I will ask God for more patience. And I offer my sincerest apologies to Sister Rachel for my"—I picked something general out of the air—"rude behavior. A Sister should act better."

Rachel looked out the window rather than at me, but Sister Bethany nodded placidly.

"It's not easy. I've had my own disagreements with Sisters throughout my life. What you learn, though, is none of it is so important."

My heart restarted. I was sure now that Sister Bethany didn't know what had passed between Rachel and me. That was a relief, but why had Rachel given her only vague details? I tried to read her furrowed brow. I could only guess that Rachel was trying to send a strong warning but protect me by ensuring the punishment didn't go too far.

If I had kissed a man out of wedlock, I'd be subject to banishment, and there was precedent in living memory for that punishment. Maybe Rachel personally thought what I did was wrong but didn't have any scripture to stand on. She was offering me an out. All I had to do was take it. And never speak or act on my feelings again.

I nodded again and said, "Thank you for this opportunity, Sister Bethany. I will use my prayer walk well and commune with God so that She may teach me. I only want to be a servant to Her and a productive member of our community."

There was nothing else to be said so I left, without going home, without taking a drink from the water pump. As it should be for a prayer walk. God would take care of me. She would reveal Her message to me. And then I could go home. The unwritten, underlying reason for prayer walks was more sinister than time to pray. Prayer was part of it, yes, but the hidden reason was to give God the opportunity to act. Some women never returned. God removed the stain they left on our community by dealing with them in the wilderness.

But, my mind screamed, this wasn't a real prayer walk.

God hadn't called me to take time alone with Her. This was a sham, almost a lie. I knew Rachel was uncomfortable by what I did, but honestly, this felt more like a lie to me than the beautiful moment I had with her.

I took the east trail, frustrated. I was supposed to do the baking that day. My sudden absence meant there would be no bread in my house that week. Each meal would serve as a reminder of my embarrassment. What would Timothy think?

That drew me up short. What *would* Timothy think? Would he be surprised his wife had been sent by an Elder out of the village? Would he be upset that the spiritual leader of his household was on the verge of downfall, tempted by cackling, dark spirits in every corner?

And what would he think if he knew the whole truth? My link to Timothy was supposed to satisfy all things. It was supposed to make me whole. I didn't let my thoughts linger there.

I came to a fork and decided I would turn left. I spotted wild mint and picked a leaf to chew. I couldn't bring food along on a prayer walk, but I knew God wouldn't mind this. In the woods, She provided.

My shoulders unknotted slowly as I trudged well away from the village. It was hard to stay mad or imagine my doom while the sun shone so brightly. The last crust of summer was a busy time, but I didn't often leave the perimeter of the village at any time of year.

I felt jealous of Timothy's ability to hunt with the other

men. They could go out past the safety of God's perimeter together. When their tangible task was done, they came back. Women only went out and away alone, for the purpose of prayer and guidance. Men were concerned with the physical realm, we dealt in the spiritual.

And anything could happen in the spiritual.

I tried to pray, but I had prayed that morning and there wasn't much to talk with God about. Plus, it wasn't a legitimate prayer walk. This was a misunderstanding on Sister Bethany's part. She and Rachel were both trying to control me. How could I pray when I was trying so hard to figure out what Rachel meant by all of this?

A cluster of nodding onion sprouted along the path. I sighed. If I was going to be forced to traverse the wilderness like an Israelite, I wanted to enjoy the break. My mouth twisted at the categorization of forty years of painful wandering as a break.

I pushed thoughts of Rachel away and slipped off my shoes, like a little girl. That was one of the benefits of a prayer walk. No one but God could see you, as it was in the Garden of Eden. The community wasn't at your back watching how your man behaved or how much milk your goats contributed or the length of your shirt sleeves. The soft dirt of the trail welcomed me. I put a hand in either shoe to carry them easily. I set a contemplative yet bright expression on my face, in case anyone saw me through the trees. No woman wanted to be spotted crying on her prayer walk. That would signal an internal battle between her and the Lord. Exactly not what I wanted reported back.

I thought idly of the boys at breakfast that morning. Lately, at every meal Gideon tried to covertly stick a finger in the butter jar and speed it up to his mouth. That was another advantage of having a girl—they seemed to eat less. And, as the person in the household that carried the huge job of food management, it could be tough. The Elders gave us our allotted food of harvested vegetables and fruits, as well as preserved goods to keep through the winter. Wild or domestic meats were shared as well. It was a challenge making it all last among hungry appetites, but it was the reason our community had lasted so long when others did not.

I walked on the trail, alternating my shoes on and off while I dithered over when to turn around. As I wasn't seeking guidance from God, I expected none to come. So, the awakening that typically signaled the end of the prayer walk would never come; I'd keep walking, waiting for something never promised. It stood to reason that I had to turn around randomly, though it felt shameful.

If I arrived back too quickly, it would seem like my answer from God wasn't earned, that I had fed myself a false answer and sought the comfort of home. But if I stayed out too long, I'd have to sleep in the woods, and not only would I be uncomfortable all night and late to my chores the next day, it would look like God really had to take me to task. Or, worst of all, I'd needlessly put my life in danger by getting lost or crossing paths with a grizzly bulking up for winter. I shuddered at the thought of never coming home—partly from fear of death but mostly that everyone would think I was a massive sinner God needed to remove before I corrupted everyone and brought the demons down upon us.

I turned onto another path, this one less defined among the brush. It was decided: I'd get a drink and turn back. Already, I had probably walked for close to two hours. A four-hour round trip was plenty. If I made good time, I could walk back more slowly, but be sure to be home in time to cook dinner for my family. They'd do okay without me—Timothy would know to lay out some of the produce—but I didn't want the boys going overboard on the preserves. Yes, I would definitely be back in time for dinner.

I followed the trail up to one of the hunting camps. I typically went to them only in the spring to clean. I wasn't allowed to eat the food there—it was taboo once it entered the male-centric structure—but I could drink from the water. Water was a universal gift from God. It had no natural replacement and was always open to those who sought it.

The trail narrowed and I slid my shoes back on. The patchy dirt was layered with rocks and pine needles. I kept my stockings in my pocket so they didn't brown on the bottom. My feet felt grainy from the soil they'd picked up along the way. I spotted the siding of a hunting lodge through the branches. The dryness of my throat bloomed now I knew water was close.

I paused, midstep.

The door was open.

I panicked, wondering who was there. No one should see me on my prayer walk, especially since I was currently seeking the easy way to water.

My mind ran through the list of Brothers, but I didn't hear of anyone out hunting today. In fact, Timothy and Brothers Ben and Barry Garland came back a day ago with a deer. Timothy didn't say which camp they had used. It must have been this one and someone had left the door open. I wondered about that younger Garland brother, so irresponsible—

I turned into the hut and there, facing me, was another human. A human I had never seen before. My thoughts jumbled together as I faced, for the very first time, someone not from Lilium Springs. My breath caught in my throat and I jerked back.

The person was sleeping, leaning upright against the back wall. Enough light poured through the doorway to illuminate the woman. The hairs on the back of my neck rose and, as my thoughts caught up to what my instincts told me, I realized she was dangerous. If she wasn't sleeping slack-jawed, I would have run. She looked like a powerful angel of God. Or, I felt my insides thin, an angel of the Dark One? Did it matter which side she was from if vengeance drifted off her like a scent?

Black material wrapped her body from foot to neck. In

some places, the material was hard, like a shovel, in others, it stretched but with the strength of a wheelbarrow tire. Even as I made the comparisons, I knew they weren't right. What she wore was of another world. A helmet sat by her side and a weapon lay across her lap, but it was a far cry from the shotguns and pistols we had in the community.

I told myself to run, but how could one run from the extraordinary?

My eyes darted to her face, which I drank in while she slept. Two lines of dark lashes crested each cheek. She had tawny brown skin, polished as a river stone. Black hair fell in a tangle barely to her shoulder. The edge was unnaturally straight, and I wondered why the ends had broken off there. Then it struck me—her hair had been cut.

My response was visceral. I drew back from her at the thought of this extreme break in taboo. She definitely couldn't be an angel. Unless she was fallen.

It struck me that she didn't look well. Whereas maybe her skin would normally be rich, it was dull with a gray undertone. And her cheekbones were unnaturally arched. She was starving. She wasn't an angel of death or otherwise. She was human like me, but she was shorn and cast out from her people. She had to have been wandering for a long time for her hair to have grown to that length. What crime had she committed? And had she served her penitence?

As my primary excitement faded, I wondered what to do. I could turn around, go home, and never speak of it. I could go back and tell Elder Sister Hetta. Or I could wake the woman up and talk to her.

I found that my feet had carried me into the cabin some ways, but I had to get out of there, at least go back to the woods and watch while I considered my options. I turned to go but stopped. I felt something powerful draw me in. More than the pity I had for this woman, more than the worries. I felt God move me.

I had already felt Her speak to me on a number of occasions; in church during prophecy sessions, during my hard labor with Matty, and when Papa married Goodmother Kristy after Mama died. But those were all so…expected. *This, Lord, what am I supposed to do with this?*

But hadn't I been sent on a prayer walk? Rachel could have talked to Sister Bethany anytime in the past month. Instead, Rachel did so in time for Sister Bethany to send me out that morning. Everything happened so that I would end up here at this very moment. This woman was my answer from God.

Outside, the sun shifted into late afternoon. I should head back. With my mind set now, I would take her with me. I reached out to wake her up, then thought better of it. I retreated outside the door.

"Yoo-hoo, hello?" I made my voice a little louder. "Hello there. Are you awake?"

The woman groaned and stirred. She moved laboriously and adjusted the gun on her lap. Then, she looked up and we made eye contact. A spark lit in my gut. As I saw her eyes go wide, I felt my own widen.

I put a hand out, palm forward. "It's okay, it's okay," I reassured both of us.

She lurched to her feet, unsteady and obviously not well, and I backed away from the cabin, wary. I was ready to run if I had to, but I was just taking precautions. She looked so weak I didn't expect trouble.

The woman appeared in the doorway, gun in her hands—I froze. She looked me over as she assessed me. The woman did something to the gun and then pushed it behind her, on her back.

"Hi," she said slowly, as if she were tasting the letters. She cleared her throat. "I'm Arwen. Who are you?"

I hesitated. I had never met another person except for new babies. I floundered as I cast about for a response.

"What's your name?"

"Marah Bennett," I whispered.

Arwen looked more and more alert now that she was up. "Marah, I was passing through. I thought this house was abandoned like all the others. I wouldn't have gone in if I had known someone lived here."

"Oh," I said confusedly. "I don't live here. Some of the men stay here when they hunt."

The conversation halted. I didn't know what to say to this woman. And clearly she was out of sorts with her being cast out from society for her sins and all. I wondered if she was even allowed to ask for help.

"You look hungry. No offense," I added quickly, "you just don't look well."

She—Arwen—made a strange laugh. "No, I suppose I'm not doing well. I don't think anyone is."

"Well, let me see if there are supplies in the lodge and get you fed." I covered my awkwardness by bustling past her through the door. I had prepared travel rations numerous times but had obviously never eaten of them. I lowered the sack, opened all the jars, and lay them out for the woman to eat. For myself, I dipped my hand in the large canister and slurped the water from my cupped palm. I felt guilty feeding the woman the hunting food, but I didn't think it was specifically a taboo. She wasn't part of our community. And one of my roles was to care for people who needed care. I didn't know if she would make it much farther, to our community or otherwise, without repercussions from her hunger.

The large woman ate methodically, not letting one hazelnut drop. Like I guessed, she was starving. I let her eat as much as she wanted, but she stopped as quickly as she started, a little left in each jar.

"I don't want to eat all of your food," she said.

I almost smiled as I recognized the passive request. She seemed less like an angel by the moment. As strange as she looked, she was human.

"Please eat. You need it."

It was uncomfortable for me to be in the hunting lodge, but also in close proximity hovering over a stranger. I told her I'd wait outside.

In the shade of a red cedar, I sent up a prayer asking for

guidance.

As if beckoned by God, the woman stepped out. We both sank onto the limp summer grass, more room between us than strictly necessary.

"Do you live near here?"

"I do," I said cautiously. "I live with many other families in Lilium Springs. We're a strong community." I hoped the subtext would be clear—others knew (well, kind of) where I was and that we could defend ourselves.

Arwen—it struck me again what an odd name it was, definitely not Biblical—nodded as if she heard what she expected.

"Listen, Marah, this isn't easy for me to say and I don't want to overstep…but I need help."

It sounded like it pained her to ask for it. My heart broke a little for this Jezebel.

"Of course. I've never been in a situation like yours, but I'd hope that if I was, someone would help me. But, Arwen"—my speech stumbled over the name—"our community will have rules too. The decision is with the Elders, and they will need to know more about your sin before they decide if you can stay."

She looked at me with honest shock.

"What are you talking about? I didn't do any sin."

"We've all sinned," I gravely intoned, hoping I was living up to the severity of the situation.

She laughed. "Okay, let's back up. I'll go first. I grew up in Arizona. When the aliens came, my family was evacuated to Colorado. When I signed up, I was moved around a lot but stayed in the Southwest. So, though I don't even know where we are, it's gotta be the farthest north I've been in my life. There's nothing left of my base"—she stumbled over the words and I knew she had lost something—"so I've been wandering." She paused and thought, weighing something out in her head. "I've been on the move for about three months."

"What's a *base*?"

Arwen stared at me hard, thoughts tumbling in her head. I felt uneasy. I didn't like this meeting new people business. If only Sister Bethany hadn't sent me on an unneeded prayer walk. If only Rachel hadn't ratted me out. If only I hadn't kissed her.

Arwen finally responded, "As in military base. I was a soldier."

I nodded. "And what's the aliens?"

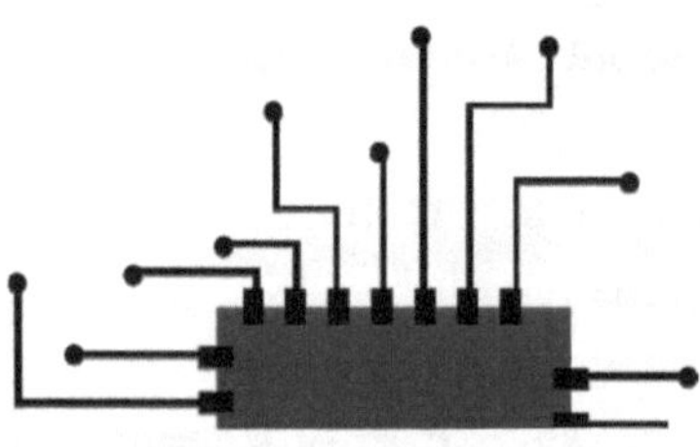

5. What r aliens?

I smiled. And then my cheeks drifted down.

Holy fuck. She wasn't joking.

My eyes darted across her frame. I felt like I was just now seeing it. Her cream button-down shirt was factory-made, but her skirt was homemade in a subdued, prairie-brown material. Long hair ended in uneven tips with summer highlights all the way down. No tattoos, no makeup, no implants, no earrings. It was suddenly conceivable that Marah didn't know about the aliens.

"Marah," I said, just to be sure, "Are you saying you don't know about the aliens?" It felt stupid once it was out of my mouth, as if I asked her if she knew she had eyebrows on her face.

She nodded but squinted at me slightly.

"Yes, as in 'Yes, that's correct, I don't know about the aliens' or, 'Yes, I'm pulling your damn leg, ha-ha?'"

It was the "damn" that did it, not the reference to aliens. She gasped as if she had never heard someone curse. "Lord forgive you."

I ignored her. I hadn't even used the f-word.

"Marah, I was in the military because the Earth is under attack. Alien ships came when I was a teenager—when you were a teenager—and they have been systematically killing humans. We don't know why they're here, but they don't eat us and it doesn't seem like they're stealing resources. Our best guess is that they want the entire planet—without us."

"Oh, I know what you're talking about," Marah said.

I nodded in relief.

"You mean the demons. They don't come here. This is sacred ground."

"Demons?" This was getting weirder by the minute. I hoped she'd burst out laughing. Maybe she'd lost her mental faculties wandering the forest. Or maybe I was the one who had lost it.

She looked thoughtful. "I've never had to explain this before, but what you call the aliens are demons. Heaven and Hell are constantly warring. Their ships have come terribly close, but our leader keeps them at bay." Marah pulled her long hair over her shoulder and combed gently with her fingers. "We lend strength to Heaven by obeying God's commandment and living pure lives. The people in our community are spiritual warriors." She blushed. "I've actually never met someone from outside Lilium Springs before."

No shit.

"But I do know about outsiders, and how many of them give in to sins of the flesh. I knew outsiders lived in towns and cities different than ours." She cast an eye over me. "I've never been far from my community. Now I can see your people live much differently than mine."

"Lived. I've been traveling for months and you're the first person I've seen."

Marah's eyes went wide. We both sat quietly for a minute. I didn't know what was weirder: me discovering someone who didn't know about the Deadlight Gardes, or her discovering that there's this great, huge world out there and that everyone's pretty much dead in the same moment.

"What's it like out there?"

I didn't know how to answer that. Like what was her frame of mind? She was obviously part of a cloistered community. They didn't seem like the survivors I expected to find. There was this weird religious slant, and Marah was wholly unaware of the state of the world. But the dried berries in my belly spoke for themselves. This community, as odd as it was, was alive.

"Well," I said as I fought to organize my thoughts. "All the cities are deserted. The buildings are bigger than your hunting cabin, like, thirty times the size. I came from the south." I could see my words meant nothing. I opened my pouch and pulled out a small sheath of pages I'd ripped from books throughout my walk.

She took the packet eagerly and read the first, a poem.

And what of death do you know
Before its jaws encroach,
Ready to snare your last spoken breath?
In the distance, death is fainter than onion leaf.
Up close, its breath pungent sweet,
Delicious like the moment you first arrived.

Marah wrinkled her nose at it and turned quickly to the next paper. Belatedly, I realized I'd handed over the equivalent of my diary. There was an illustrated page from Dean Miles's *Magnificent Mushrooms*, a quirky page from a pre-Contact graphic novel about alien wars, a small map of the Rocky Mountains, a glossy picture of a Southwestern landscape—the closest thing I had to a picture of home.

Marah examined each page carefully in turn.

"This is…a lot for me to take in. And—"

My stomach growled even though I had just eaten.

"And you're starving."

I knew it wasn't a question.

Marah sighed. "There was no one out there? Really no one?"

I shrugged. "I wasn't looking too hard and I didn't make myself known. I assume others are out there, but how many I don't know."

She nodded as if she had made a decision. "Then you'd better come with me."

"What?"

"You said it yourself: there's nothing out there. A long while back there was a blight on our crops when someone angered God. I remember how hungry I was that winter." She paused, searching my face. "My mom looked like you do now. You won't be on your feet much longer. If you come, we can take care of you." She paused. "You can join us."

It was hard to keep my face even and my panic down. "I would be grateful for some supplies, I really would, Marah, but I better keep moving." I forced a smile. "The life you have in Lilium Springs…it's unlike anything I've experienced. It doesn't sound like the right place for someone like me."

Marah said, "From the sounds of it, it's probably the only place. If everyone out there is gone or fading, you'll do the same. This land we're on, it's protected by God." She nodded stoutly, certain in her belief.

I wondered about that, how they'd lived without interference for so long.

"How many people live in your community?"

Marah smiled, as if relieved to finally think of something good. "One hundred and sixty-three. Oh, I guess it will soon be a hundred and sixty-four because Sister Abigale is pregnant."

I cringed at the title, but my mind churned. There was some secret to their success. Did the lack of advanced tech disguise their presence? Was it something about their mountain location? Even if it was blind luck, odds were that luck would hold out long enough for me to recuperate and gather some supplies. I glanced at the shed. I could learn what I needed to, what would help me survive this new world absent of stocked vending machines, then slip away quietly.

It felt oddly like the moment I decided to join the military. Way back then, I left Mom and Julian behind because I wanted to protect them. I thought I was making the right decision, teaming up with people who were going to make a difference. Instead, the military was a group of assholes fucking up the war against the aliens.

I already had a sense—okay, maybe a prejudice—that Marah's community would be another group of assholes. A bunch of men keeping women like Marah under their thumb. I had to be careful here. I didn't want to wind up as a twelfth wife or chained to a stove. I looked over Marah. There was no mistaking it—she was healthy. She glowed with purpose and good health.

"And what about you? Do you have kids?"

"My husband, Brother Timothy, and I have three kids—Matthew, James, and Gideon."

"And Brother Timothy, does he have any other wives?"

The look of pure disgust on her face said volumes. "Of course not. That's a sin."

Okay, a solid win on behalf of the secret, weird religious group.

Her face softened. "Arwen," she drawled saying the *A* in my name long, "you should know we don't do things like"—she waved vaguely—"the world." She drawled "the world" in the same way. Ah, it wasn't a drawl, it was a sneer.

"We are a very religious group. That means we all play a role in the community during the week and then we worship together on Sundays. I have nothing to compare it to, but it seems like a good life to me."

She was right. It did. And much better than no life at all.

I leaned forward to ask, "I don't mean this offensively. I'm just trying to make sure I understand before deciding. Can you tell me, if I go, is anyone going to try to hurt me?"

Marah looked confused. Or was her face purposefully set?

"No, of course not. We don't fight among ourselves. We teach the kids not to hit. It'd be unthinkable for an adult to hit you."

I took a breath. "One hundred and sixty-five it is, then."

An hour and a half later, Marah and I were arguing like old friends. Old friends where one is a stubborn, sheltered woman who'd never heard the word *no*, and the other a livid, enraged animal.

"I'm not putting my Kronos L85 in there."

Marah rolled her eyes. I could tell her new friend was getting on her nerves too.

"Yes, you are. We've never had an outsider enter our community before. If you look like—well, I'll put it this way: when I first saw you sleeping in the hut, it crossed my mind that you were an angel. A dark one. I mean look at you. You're terrifying."

I still wore my Titan Suit, but the clothes Marah thrust into my hand hung limply. I smiled darkly. "Thank you."

"Arwen!"

"They're going to know I'm lying. Who would be walking around these days in clothes like this with no weapon?" I shook the silky blue blouse she handed me for emphasis.

Marah looked genuinely offended. "I'm not asking you to lie," she hissed. "I'm trying to make this easier for them *and* you. You walk in there like that, you're gonna scare the kids. They'll think the end times have come."

I rolled my eyes at that. "The end times" were here and prospering.

On our way to the rocky outcrop, we took turns asking questions. I learned more about the food they grew and her family, but she had trouble talking about the community's actions within the larger framework of history. She asked me cautiously about how I'd been getting along in the woods on my own. When I tried to describe the war, she clammed up. Then we stopped at the supply shed where Marah took a full outfit of clothes out.

I asked, "Won't someone recognize these clothes and know I took them?"

"We have so many clothes. Foraging teams go out a few times a year and extra clothes wind up in here. None of the men are going to notice you're wearing a shirt they saw three years ago." That was when she first started to get annoyed. It got worse when we circled around to the pile of godforsaken rocks she was trying to convince me to bury all my worldly processions under.

I chalked it up to the huge favor she was trying to do for me, but I couldn't imagine wrapping my Kronos L85 in a tarp, leaving it under this jutted-out rock, and walking defenselessly into the biggest group of people I'd seen in half a year, all strangers to me.

"Arwen," she leveled with me, "you don't have to be afraid. I don't know everything you've experienced out there, but the people in my community are *good*, God-fearing people. We don't do things like hit outsiders."

It was the language that got me. If Marah was a spy, sent out to entice me into coming into the community so they could eat me, she probably would have said, *We're not like those other communities that eat people.* She truly didn't understand my worries. We talked about hitting earlier, so that was the worst example she could think of. She wasn't a practiced liar.

I paused one moment longer, half pouting. "Okay, I'll change. But I have to impress upon you, don't tell anyone where this is. And don't come look at it yourself. It's extremely dangerous."

"Sure thing," she said, all polish now that she had won.

I stripped everything off, even my underpants and put the clothes from Marah on. Civvies felt loose and strange after wearing bodysuits for years on end. Without the ballistic reflective casing and blast-retardant knit, I felt like a clear, easy target. The suit wouldn't fold or roll up but the crevice was deep. I lay out the Titan Suit like a body. We pushed a big rock in front and fit it in. I started to pile rocks on top, to fill the gap, but Marah stopped me.

"No, that looks like someone's hiding something. Rocks wouldn't naturally gather like that." She pointed at the green moss and said how it'd be strange if we covered most of the moss with rocks. I understood then that maybe it was better to hide in plain sight. I wondered what I would learn after a winter in Lilium Springs. Hopefully enough to survive on my own.

I took a handful of dirt and wiped it down the side of the blue shirt. Marah's eyes went big with anger.

"What are you doing?"

"I've been walking in the woods for three months. Don't you think it'd be a little strange if I showed up with a neatly pressed outfit?"

"But you didn't have to do that. Look what you did to that silk. You think anyone's going to make a shirt like that again in our lifetimes? That's a finite resource."

And we were arguing again.

Her wispy hair was pure white but drastically thin on top. Age spots crawled up the skin of her face and her lower lip barely moved when she talked. Clearly, Hetta was the survivor of a recent stroke. Her eyes were emotionless but intent, drinking in everything about me. I felt like a prized pig brought to slaughter.

Pews of all kinds filled the room—the sanctuary, Marah called it. They were all different colors and sizes, obviously salvaged. A giant cross and golden velvet curtain hung the length of the wall behind the pulpit flanked by four wood chairs. On another wall was a larger-than-life gilded lily. I felt a pain in my heart at the sight of Lil's namesake flower. The grandiose effect of it all was thrown off by the ordinary plastic cup and bendy straw set on top of the pulpit.

After the four Elders assembled, all women, Marah briefly summarized how she found me on what she called a prayer walk—and left out the bit about dressing me and hiding my gun and suit. Then she stepped off to the side with a clear face, her job done. I glanced behind me, surprised to see some of the pews filled with curious onlookers.

I had fully expected to be brought in front of a panel of balding, leering, sweaty men, eager, if not for another womb, then for another set of hands to wash dishes. So, I had been surprised when all the Elders were women. Questions broke out in my mind like a rash. Was it because women lived longer, and their council of leaders was simply made up of the oldest inhabitants of the community? Were they elected?

Elder Sister Hetta addressed me directly for the first time. "How far have you traveled, soldier?" Though one corner of her mouth was limp, her voiced carried well enough through the sanctuary.

I cleared my throat. "From the Army Base in Yuma, Arizona, ma'am. And what state might I be in?"

She didn't answer my question but looked me up and down shrewdly. I wondered what I would do if she asked what happened to my gear.

She didn't. Instead, she said, "So, it's you we have to thank for this ten-year war?"

A titter escaped from one of the old women seated to Hetta's right and my cheeks glowed. I opened my mouth to respond, but Hetta kept talking.

"And what about on your journey? What were the sizes and locations of communities you stayed with?"

"Ma'am, there—"

One of the other old biddies broke in. "Elder Sister Hetta," she corrected.

I started again, keeping my annoyance to myself, "Elder Sister Hetta, there were no other communities. Marah is the first person I've seen since I left the base." I hoped she didn't ask more about what made me leave the base.

I heard a baby babble somewhere behind me. I glanced around again to see the pews had filled more while we talked. Most of the spectators sat in small family groups;

there was more than a few kids. They all had the same well-kept look as Marah and wore a combination of salvaged clothes and well-made knit and handsewn pieces. They were better fed and healthier looking than my platoon had been in the past year, and we were eating on the government's coin.

I realized I had expected a sea of white people, but there was one very old man of clear Asian descent and some mixed families of Black and white. I didn't see any other Latinx, but we were very far north. The kids were all either white or biracial. I grasped the community bred only within itself. It was clear there had been no other outsiders and their skin colors were slowly melding together, skewing largely white. I wondered how the group got their beginnings and what they would do when the size of their gene pool became a problem. I filed this away to think about later.

"The situation is increasing rapidly," Hetta directed her statements to the old women around her rather than her congregation, "but that's what happens when a people bring their own extinction down upon them and then cannot defend themselves."

I couldn't help myself. My words came fast and hard. "This is an invasion. Earth has lost a *war* against advanced beings not of our planet. My father and sister gave their lives in defense of you people."

Elder Sister Hetta cast her cold eyes upon me once more. I had trouble reading the expression on her face, but there was no empathy there. The room went silent. As if I had embarrassed myself.

Finally, Hetta looked up at the ceiling. When she looked back down at me, she addressed the whole room. "I'm not surprised that the world has fallen against the demons." There were nods. "Lord, thank You for Your judgment. May we always be worthy of Your protection." The old woman closed her eyes briefly. "Soldier, your report brings me no joy, but your people have been dancing with the Devil for generations. God in all Her wisdom cannot save those that cast Her blessings away."

Her?

In the face of the seriousness of the situation, Hetta maneuvered the bendy straw into her mouth and drew heavily. I realized I was standing there, mouth hanging open, so I quickly seized her incapacitation to speak without being interrupted.

"Elder Sister Hetta and council, the aliens, beings not from our planet"—it occurred to me that maybe we did think more similarly than I had first thought—"came of their own accord. And the people who died in that war were innocent."

"And what of you?" It was the woman who corrected me earlier, sitting in one of the chairs, velvet curtain spread behind her. "Are you innocent?"

I resisted the urge to shrug and changed the subject. "And I'd like to know how this community has stayed standing for so long. Even life in our smallest towns was disrupted years ago. How is it you people have existed here without being affected by the invaders?"

One of the other old women spoke in a wizened voice. "That's all we need to hear, Elder Sister. Likely she's come to scout our territories for her own people." She turned her speech toward me. "Since our founding, others have always coveted our land. Coveted everything we've built." She cleared her throat and directed her words to Hetta once more. "We don't want her leading others back here. I propose banishment. We'll need to ensure she can't find her way back."

Okay, so much for a progressive, female-led take on things. A murmur stirred through the room and I looked around wildly. No, this was not how I was going to go. Why the fuck did I leave my Titan Suit behind?

Marah stepped quickly to the center, near my side. "Sister Bethany," she made a direct plea to the woman who wanted to banish me. "You yourself directed me to take a prayer walk today. If I had not gone where God led, Arwen would have walked past our community. I believe God led me to Sister Arwen for a reason."

Even looking banishment and eventual starvation in the face, I couldn't help but cringe at being called "Sister Arwen."

"I could *literally* be the last person on the planet." I didn't expect to have to convince them I was worth keeping around and felt burned by the realization. I shook my head and poured out my frustration. "Las Vegas was totally flattened, you must know that. It was a thousand times worse than a hydrogen bomb—the weapons *we* threw at *them*. I saw the footage, the aliens arrived and minutes later everything was just suddenly wiped out. No mushroom cloud, no waves of debris. All the buildings smashed and gone." My voice was rising now, but I could tell I had their attention. "On my way here, I couldn't even walk down the streets in Salt Lake City. The city stands, but the people, they were just wiped out. There are severed bodies in the streets. In those cases, people were decimated city by city, one by one. Some cities are filled with husks of people, already old and dying, others are fresh.

"Why the difference between the two cities? And for what? They're not eating us. They're not setting up their own population centers. The Deadlight Gardes—the aliens—are taking their time systematically wiping us out. But why?"

I heard someone stand behind me and leave. Marah stared at me with terror-struck eyes. As mad as I was, I felt better that these people, who had been living a quiet existence while the rest of us suffered and died, should face the pain I had.

"They've been here too," Hetta said.

"What?" Confusion soaked my thoughts. "How can any of you still be alive?"

"They've flown over us three times now, all in the past two years. But we follow the Lord and She keeps us safe."

Someone said "Amen" behind me. I shook my head in disbelief.

"We've been isolated for so long. If God has seen fit to bring a stranger into our midst, it is our responsibility to discern why. Soldier," Hetta barked. "I offer you a place among us."

"I don't—"

"Quiet," Bethany said. "The Elder Sister is speaking."

Hetta continued, "This is no light decision. If you go, you cannot ever return to Lilium Springs, on pain of death. If you stay, you will live by our ways and our laws."

My head spun. I didn't want to sign up with this group. I wanted to hurl their offer back at them and run away. But more than that I wanted to know how they survived so long. I wanted to survive the winter. I wanted to be left standing at the end of all this. It was decided. I'd stay for the winter, recover my health, learn everything I could, and leave quietly in the spring with the knowledge and skills to keep myself alive in the wilderness.

"Understood, Elder Sister." I had years of practice pressing down emotions in the military. This was nothing.

There was suddenly a clear shift in tone. The proceedings were over. I was relieved for the trial to be over, as it occurred to me that that was what it was. I stood, unsure what to do. I cast my gaze again over the families that talked among themselves. I was sure they were curious to see the outsider. I felt frail and unprotected in my dirty blue shirt and jeans.

Hetta beckoned Marah forward as the other Old Ones slid off the stage and into the crowd. I wanted to hear what

Hetta was saying to Marah and edged closer.

A hand touched me on the elbow. I whipped around, but it was a kid, flushing remarkably under his pale skin. My heart pounded and I took a shaky breath. It was just a boy, I reminded myself again. His outfit was the same mishmash of homemade and salvaged clothing that everyone else had on. His dark hair lay in a ruffle on his head. I could tell from his expression that it wasn't kindness that brought him over but curiosity.

"Hey, squirt."

His eyes squinted in response as he tried to figure out if that was an insult. He glanced behind him to see who heard.

"Sister Soldier," he said solemnly, "I wondered if on your travels you found stores."

An older boy—not much taller but definitely denser—stepped in close and pulled at the kid's sleeve, trying to get him away from me. They were clearly siblings, though the older one had summer highlights in his brown hair and the younger, the one who got my attention, looked wan.

"Yes, lots of them. Are you looking for something specific?"

He nodded but before he would tell me, he looked around to make sure no one was close enough to hear us. I had a hard time imagining what this kid could possibly want.

"James," a deep, rich voice said.

I looked up, suddenly surrounded by a man and Marah

and what appeared to be their family, even as the crowd dispersed. She moved possessively toward the kid, taking his hand and putting herself between us.

Marah smiled at me, shy for the first time. "It's decided. You're staying with us."

6. A Simple Commandment

I spotted her figure through the back window. There was Arwen, marching through the sheep pen, Matty running after her. He shot a confused look at his father, but Timothy merely shrugged. James was nowhere to be found at chore time—that was usual—and Gideon stood at his father's side. His normally cheerful face was set in a chubby but stern frown as he analyzed the newcomer and her odd behavior. He'd never seen anything like her. I hadn't either.

Though I'd been in the sheep pen a number of times, the farm animals weren't part of my regular chores. The wool was still short from when we sheared them that past spring, but it was thick enough to give a nice spring when you patted it. Maybe Arwen had never seen sheep before, I mused.

A sizzle reminded me of the task at hand and I turned away from the spectacle. I flipped the eggs to cook—but not break—the yolk for over-medium eggs the way Timothy liked them. I would have asked Arwen how she liked her eggs, but after she went to the pit latrine that morning she never came back to the kitchen. I wondered how long it was taking her when I heard the shouts outside. They weren't serious but bemused to find Arwen tramping about the barnyard, breakfast not yet cooked. It was a reminder of how much Arwen had to learn. I wasn't opposed to teaching, I was raising three kids and teaching was an essential part of what I did, but it was strange to think of an adult that didn't fit into community life.

I set the blue platter on the table. I liked how the sky-like color stood out against the dark stain my father put on our table when he built it. It took merely a moment or two to set out the rest of the spread, and in between tasks I darted glances out the window. Timothy and Matty finished feeding the sheep, and I finally spotted James watering my herb garden, his dark hair bent in concentration. After breakfast, Timothy and Matty would head off to the fields.

As they headed back to the house, James brought up the rear. Arwen said something to Timothy. I was surprised. What could they have to talk about? I felt a strange stir within me. If she needed something, she needed only to ask me.

It all felt strange as I fell asleep the night before.

Timothy and I were in our own bed. Arwen slept in Matty's bed, which moved Matty to James and Gideon's bigger bed, and, James as the middle child, not quite young enough to be coddled and not quite old enough to be respected, was sequestered to a spot on the floor that I made as comfortable as possible.

It wasn't a surprise that Elder Sister Hetta directed me to host the newcomer until we could get her settled. Initially I felt relief. I was curious about this strange woman but also protective. There again, I also rejoiced at the thought of another pair of hands to help me with the house chores. As a family of five with no young girls, it was taxing on me to take care of all the most important tasks myself. I often envied how easy it must be for Timothy with three little versions of him to help. It didn't occur to me that Arwen might be near useless for my purposes.

I exhaled. I typically wasn't looking for more work in a day, but I needed to think of it as an investment in Arwen's future. And I'd be lying if I said I wasn't intrigued. *And, Lord, I do not lie.*

The four came in and washed their hands. There was a stiff moment when I started the family prayer before the meal. Arwen hadn't expected it, but she bowed her head after a moment. It was a shock as I realized she probably hadn't known to enter into prayer that morning. A baby. She was going to be exactly like another baby but not quite what I had in mind. I hid a smile. The Lord does have a sense of humor.

"This is delicious," Arwen said.

"Oh, it's just simple eggs."

"Delicious eggs. I haven't had eggs in at least two years. And bread and butter. This is delicious." She took an overlarge bite as if to prove it.

"I help feed the chickens," Gideon declared.

"You do not, chicken-butt," Matty broke in.

"Yes, I have *too* fed them in the chicken shed."

Matty rolled his eyes. "You did that, um, once."

Gideon's lips puckered, dismayed at the truth in his oldest brother's words. "I'll feed them again, you'll see."

"Boys," I said, squashing the argument with one head shake. I smiled brightly at Arwen. I didn't want her to think my boys were misbehaved. Though sometimes they were.

"Arwen, we should talk about the sleeping arrangements."

James looked up but didn't say anything. His narrow face was always so intense.

Arwen picked up the thread easily. "I get it, I don't want to crowd you. Is there a storage area I can sleep in? Or maybe I can sleep in the barn loft. I'm used to that." She smiled slowly at some memory.

"Timothy, can you talk to Brother Marc about starting another cabin?"

Timothy nodded. Gideon chomped noisily on my left, and I wiped his mouth with a cloth napkin.

Arwen stopped eating in favor of turning red. "Oh, I don't want to put you out. That seems like a lot of work for me." She looked around, as if someone else was going to back her up.

I dipped my bread in yolk. "No, we always build houses for married couples."

Gideon inched a finger toward the butter jar and I moved it out of his reach. When I looked back at Arwen, she looked like a horse ready to bolt. She set her fork on her plate—and I knew it wasn't because she was full.

"I'm not getting married."

Timothy and I looked at each other. It was one of those looks we'd developed over the decade of our marriage. Something incredulous was happening and it was almost as if we wanted to acknowledge the moment.

"Seriously, I'm not getting married. If you can't understand that, I'll leave today."

"But Arwen"—I shook my head—"why—"

"Are you a widow?" Matty interrupted. I was going to tell him off, but I wanted to hear the answer too.

"No," she dragged the word out as if it were two. "There are other reasons someone might not want to get married."

Everyone was uncomfortable except Gideon, who was eating. James stared at his empty plate and Matty looked back and forth between us, waiting to see what would happen next.

"Timothy, Matty, why don't you go ahead and get going. And, Timothy, no need to say anything about a house to the other men yet."

Timothy rose, all too happy to make an escape. He and Matty left their dirty plates where they were and put hats on before heading out.

"James, take Gideon to visit Sister Henrietta—she'll be glad for the company." Sister Henrietta was our closest neighbor. Her kids were grown and led their own households, but there were no grandkids yet. It was Rachel's idea to develop a system for our kids to stop by. She was so...*nice*. I was good, but I wasn't nice the way Rachel was.

Everyone was soon gone except for me and Arwen. The crumb-filled dishes lay on the table. Those could wait.

"Well, if you want to wait to get married that's fine, but the sooner we can make the arrangement, the sooner the Brothers can start building your house.

Her words came out rigid. "Marah, I'm not getting married." She grimaced in disbelief. "If that's a-a commandment or something for the people who live here, I'll leave." I believed she would, even if it meant getting herself killed on the way out.

"No, no," I said quickly. "It's not a commandment." I couldn't help but smile. "I assumed you'd want to get married. The only time we build houses is when a couple gets engaged. And you're alone. I assumed you'd be looking for family."

Arwen nodded, her eyes tight. "I'm not. But I'm new to Lilium Springs, so explain it to me, like I'm a kid. How does all this work?"

I sat for a moment composing my thoughts. I thought I knew where to start, but I kept thinking of more and more things to tell her.

"For me, I was engaged to Timothy when I turned eighteen. We courted for about four months while our families built the cabin. It could have been done a lot quicker, mind you, but it was nice to take it slow. We made or salvaged everything in the house. My mom was a big help of course. Then we got married and moved in." I wrapped up, unsure if I had given Arwen the information she needed.

"And the only people who live alone are widows?"

"No, Brother Bert lived alone. He never married."

Arwen was still frustrated. "And why would you assume I wanted to get married? That's a very personal preference. And, since I've only known you for a day, I'm sure I never mentioned the subject to you."

"I don't know." I stared at the blue platter. Arwen was too intense to look at. "I mean, yes, you can live alone. Of course. I didn't think you'd want to live celibate, not have any kids. You've been wandering so long, I assumed God brought you here to build roots. Start a family. Lead your own household." I shrugged. "I'm not trying to make assumptions about you. It didn't occur to me that you'd do anything different than what, you know, people *do* with their lives."

To ease the tension, I piled the plates and brought them to the basin by the window. After a moment, Arwen stood next to me and took a dish rag I handed to her. We washed in silence until she spoke.

"I don't mean this offensively, but do you not want to go and do other things? When you talked about the prayer walk, it sounded like it was rare for you to go out in the forest. Why should you mind the kids and wash the dishes while Timothy gets to go out and have fun? Why should he be in charge of you?"

I gave a huge belly laugh. A fork slipped out of my hands, and I waved my hands over the basin to get extra water off.

"I'm sorry, I'm just so surprised," I eked out.

Arwen's alarmed expression made me laugh harder.

"God built man and woman differently. I create a family. Men are better suited to work in the fields. We each have our different roles. But, Sister Arwen, Timothy isn't the leader of the house—I am. I raise our children because that's the most important job."

"Uhhhh. Wait, what?" Arwen leaned away from me. She blinked and then said again, "What? Are you not ruled over? Oppressed? Forced to serve men?"

I dried my hands on the towel. "1 Corinthians 11:3, 'But I would have you know, that the head of every woman is Christ; and the head of the man is the woman; and the head of Christ is God.'" I worried I had overwhelmed her with information, so I summarized it succinctly. "We follow the Word of the Lord here."

Arwen put a hand behind her head as if she was thinking hard. I put a hand on my hip impatiently.

"I'm pretty sure that's different scripture than what people, you know, outside are taught."

"Oh, and have you studied scripture yourself?"

"No."

I let her answer hang in the air for a moment. It was evidence enough.

"Now, what's the real problem? You think that I'm trying to marry you to a brute?"

Arwen nodded.

I put the clean dishes on the floating wood shelf my father hung last summer. "I don't know what kinds of marriages you've been exposed to, but that's not how it should work. What about your parents?"

"My parents were partners, they made decisions together."

"But didn't your dad go to fight the demons? Didn't your mom stay with you?"

Arwen tensed and pulled back slightly. I'd debated scripture many times with the other women, but I'd never truly had to convince someone. It was like teaching James why he couldn't bring salvaged junk in the house.

"Yeah, and I always hated that they did that. *He* left to go fight. *She* had to stay and die a slow death of servitude to her kids."

I put my hand gently on Arwen's arm. "Maybe that's what you saw. But your mother was protected by your father's sacrifice. She wasn't left behind. She remained to lead."

It was quiet for a minute before I felt like I could ask the question I'd held on to this whole time. "So, there's really nothing out there?"

Arwen knew what I was referring to. Her eyes went a little wide with exaggeration, shrugged, and gestured wildly, as if there were no words.

"I don't know, Marah, I don't know what else there is to say. There's no one out there as far as I can see. Some of the towns are torn apart, some are filled with ripped-apart bodies, some stand empty. When there's no sign of the Deadlights, it's almost peaceful. But then your back prickles, and you look behind you quick to see what's there. Or you feel the distant power of one of their ships and you hope that it goes anywhere except where you are." She touched her throat before letting her hand drop. "What did you do when they came here?"

I nodded at where the cellar entrance was outside. "We went to the cellar. When the former Elder Sister passed, and Elder Sister Hetta was new, she had a dream. In the dream the demons came and burned everything aboveground. But we were roots under the soil and we survived to grow again."

Arwen's nose crinkled in disbelief. "I mean, yeah, the army used the ol' hide underground on occasion, but it didn't do any good."

I forced myself to smile. There was no reason to be pessimistic. "It's worked so far."

My new friend shook her head.

Arwen peppered me with questions throughout the morning until the boys came back. I set her to churning the butter—she was more clumsy than little Sister Emily at it—while I brushed the boys' hair and double-checked their homework from Sister Rhonda. Gideon had to bring something that started with *G* (we settled on garlic) and James's math homework was impeccable as always.

Sister Rhonda had approached me recently. She said she thought James would be finished with schooling soon. His reading and writing were on par with the other boys in his class, but his math was at the high upper end. She said it was comical seating him with the older girls for math lessons.

Each child finished school at different ages, but generally once boys could read their Bible and work out the figures related to cattle breeding and farm raising, they were ready to move into an apprenticeship. Girls were encouraged to school for another year or two.

The boys were off and I decided to take Arwen on a tour of the community so she could find everything. Arwen was quiet as we toured the shared barns for the horses and the nearby fields. She had lots of questions about the water pump that I couldn't answer. To get some rest from the walk, we had tea at Sister Abigale's house, her plump belly reminding me of what it seemed like I'd never have.

When we left, Arwen asked a strange question. "Marah, where did Abigale get that painting? The one above her fireplace?"

"*Sister* Abigale. Um, last summer some of the men went to a larger city to search for supplies—no, I don't know which one," I said to cut off her question. "Her husband carried that all the way back from a museum." I brightened. "I don't care for the style, but…" I drifted off. "What's wrong?"

"They went to an art museum and took the artwork? God, Marah, do you have any idea how much that stuff is worth? How delicate it is? You can't just hang it over a fireplace."

I didn't personally like the picture, but suddenly I found myself defending it. "It's not like anyone else was using it. The city was empty."

Arwen's lips turned down. "The city wasn't empty. There would have been bodies. But I guess the men didn't tell you about that, huh?"

I shrugged, but I was growing upset. "I don't know, maybe."

"Not maybe. If the buildings were still standing in that town, that means the Deadlight Gardes passed through in what we called extermination. The large cities they demolished. It was worse than a blight, a type of military strike. New York, Chicago, Los Angeles—everything was just flattened. But in other cities, smaller ones, the Deadlight Gardes went in on foot to exterminate. Like they wanted to leave everything as it was but had to root out the pests first."

I glanced around the cold forest. Pine trees towered over us so it was hard for me to imagine these towns full of dead bodies severed at the head, but I didn't like the way this was going. "I don't want to talk about this." Nothing registered on Arwen's face. I could tell from her eyes that she was far away. I tried to draw her back. "Abigale is pregnant with number one hundred and sixty-four…well, one hundred and sixty-five now that you're here." I cleared my throat and awareness slowly reached Arwen's expression.

"Why would she want more kids?" she asked. "She already has three."

I tried to hide my offense. "Children are a blessing. I'd like another one. A girl."

"Okay, but that's not something I'm interested in. First of all, I don't have a partner."

I smiled wide. That was the type of talk I loved. "Well, that first one is fixable. There's four men who are currently single. Would you like to meet them? Brother Marc is very handsome."

Arwen shook her head, irritated. "Second, the world is falling apart. I can't bring kids into this place."

I left it alone. Arwen didn't understand. I rephrased my thinking. She wasn't a baby who needed to be told how things were. She was an eight-year-old, one who thinks she can change everything and do things her own way. Like James. Changing her perspective would take a lot of time.

"So, not everyone out there has kids?" I asked.

"Some do, but it's a big choice. It impacts the rest of your life. And yeah, I knew another soldier that got pregnant. She thought it was her responsibility to further the human population, but her story didn't end so well either."

"So, she wasn't married? But she still had sex?" I stopped myself in time from putting my hands over my cheeks.

"No," Arwen said, "lots of people have kids with a partner, but Harriet just wanted a kid. She was committed to the mission, that is, until the primary mission fell apart. Once it was clear we couldn't fight the Deadlight Gardes and evacuation solved nothing, we were just waiting to be ripped apart. She planned on getting pregnant and then deserting to raise the kid on her own."

I didn't ask what happened to Harriet and her baby. I could guess.

Something occurred to me. "Arwen, have *you* had sex before?" I tried to keep the shock off my face.

Arwen's face didn't go red like I expected. She boomed with laugher.

"Geez, Marah, that's a pretty rude question. But, yeah, of course. I'm twenty-seven years old."

I felt mixed up about what she shared. On one hand, I knew it was important to keep sex between a wife and a husband. Sex outside of marriage was completely taboo. But I still wanted to hear about it.

"So, who was he?"

Arwen laughed again but indulged me. "Oh my God,

Marah, you are something else. But I guess you're working with a limited sample size here. Um, well, okay, my first time was with a guy named Vincent in the refugee camp where I lived with my mom and brother. He was very good-looking. A few years older than me. Then I hooked up with Eterra, that was a mistake. She made my life a living hell when I broke it off—"

"Wait. A woman? You slept with a woman?" I stopped dead in the trail. My face no longer gossiping but earnest.

"Yeah, I already noticed all the partners here are heterosexual—that means with a man and a woman. I wasn't surprised. It was consistent with what I expected coming to a community like this, but you should know men have sex with other men and women have sex with other women. And a whole spectrum in between. I mean, not everybody has to do the same thing."

I couldn't breathe. I couldn't focus on what "a community like this" meant. I literally couldn't breathe.

Arwen's voice came out urgently. "Hey, bend over and put your head between your knees. Marah, are you okay?"

Arwen forced me to bend over and I took some shaky breaths.

The first words out of my mouth were, "Is it a sin?"

Arwen's face clouded over. "No. It's just people falling in love. Or having fun."

"Oh, dear Lord," I muttered. Anything Arwen would categorize as fun was probably a sin. How could I have been so wrong? Or was I wrong? I took shallow breaths.

"Marah…I don't want to cause problems for you. I only came here to learn how to dry berries and make cheese. Obviously, um, you have a very happy life here." She bit her lower lip. "Maybe it would be better if we didn't talk about the outside world."

I was hardly listening. Arwen had given me too much to think about. I always knew people lived differently than Lilium Springs, but for the first time I sensed that right and wrong might be subjective.

When I didn't say anything else, Arwen took a breath and said, "I'm not getting married. You all don't have to build a house for me. I can leave."

"Don't be ridiculous, Arwen. There's no passage in the Bible that says you have to marry someone to get a house." I instantly regretted how dismissive my tone was. I got up and started walking too quickly and was out of breath almost before I started.

"Okay, so, what's going on? What's this all about?"

I turned to her. Maybe that was my only out. My only shot. Tell someone about what I'd done, an outsider who wouldn't judge me. I cast about, indecision plain on my face. No, I couldn't seek solace in Arwen. She didn't know anything about how the world really worked. I put on a smile.

"I'm sorry. It's a lot to take in." I forced a laugh. "My brain feels like the first time I tried to sew a quilt—everything got jumbled inside my head and I was frustrated I couldn't visualize each step clearly." We started walking again. "Arwen?"

"Yeah?"

"Do you think you can find your way back home from here?"

"Of course." She looked around herself to get orientated, but she couldn't get lost on these trails. There were only so many places to go in Lilium Springs.

"Good. I'm going to tell the men to start on a small home for you. Then I'm going to see an old friend." I grimaced and turned on my heel. Rachel should be alone this time of day.

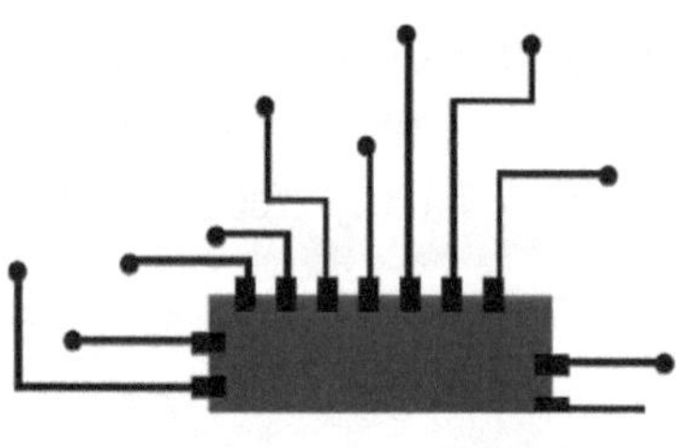

7. Ram's Horn

My house was coming along fine. Rows of rocks marked the perimeter, and at each corner a hole was dug and a large log stood upright within. The men poured cement inside and then took down the scaffolding that propped the logs up when the cement hardened and they stood on their own. The trees looked skinned, branches and bark hacked away. Without my armor, I knew how they felt.

The men were in the process of cutting and stacking logs. Timothy told me they could work on the house only in the late afternoons, because they had to make sure the last of the harvest and slaughter got done. When he saw my worried look, he reassured me that I'd have a place to sleep by the time the snow flew. Timothy had the calm demeanor of someone you could trust. I was grateful for his reassurance—going on a month with three bunkmates between five and thirteen years was getting old—but that's not why I was worried.

I felt like I was putting them out, like I was using them. I wasn't going to live my whole life there, just for the winter. But I didn't want to tell them I planned to leave. I don't know how that would change the tenuous dynamic here, but I guessed it'd be for the worst. If Marc and the others would *show me how*, I'd do the blasted work myself. When I joined in gathering rocks for the foundation, Timothy got Marah to call me off. She needed help that very moment with the bread.

It didn't make sense; it was supposed to be my house, shouldn't I work on it? Learning to do those practical things was the whole reason I came to Lilium Springs.

By now I was a pro at washing clothes by hand, and I had learned to pickle all matter of vegetables in the past week. My hands and hair continued to smell like vinegar even after I jumped in the stream.

I'd explored the community thoroughly. No one thought it was odd that I poked in the supply sheds or walked the trails between houses. Everyone was perfectly friendly, probably too sheltered to be suspicious of a stranger. And, I had to admit to myself, the boon of deference many gave to me just because I was a woman was tantalizing.

Still, I almost couldn't admit it to myself, but the

women made me uneasy. If I had heard about a secret community where women were in charge, I would have thought it was cool. Progressive. In fact, if someone had told me that's what I'd been walking toward all those months, I would have wept with relief.

Instead, the female collective made me feel uneasy. As if *I* was the brainwashed one. Brainwashed by American society and army culture. Brainwashed to see housework and child-rearing as a lower form of labor. Brainwashed to expect men to make the final call. It was hard to admit that that was how I was raised, even after all this progress, even after the end of the world.

I should have been behind the women.

Instead, I felt nervous with the way they drew themselves up in their power, and even more apprehensive knowing where it came from. I had yet to read this sacred Bible but had attended enough church services to know it wasn't my jam. It shouldn't be anyone's jam. Everywhere I went in the community I was reminded of the stark difference between the way these people lived compared to the rest of the country.

Which was what led me to the chilled woods. The oak and maple trees lit up with the embarrassment of losing their skirts among the well-endowed pines. Already there was a layer of crunch on the forest floor. The sky glowed with autumn sun, but for a Southwesterner like me, it was Jesus Fucking Christ cold. Not that I'd say that in front of Marah.

My ribs were packed in fat once again. My ass was

back. It was time for me to get the lay of the land outside Lilium Springs. I was so hungry and weak when Marah led me in, I hardly understood what lay beyond the boundaries of the community. What roads were nearby? Could I find this place on a map? Where were they getting all these extra clothes and salvaged items? How close was the nearest abandoned town? Were there…any towns not abandoned? Was there anyone else out there that'd take me in for the winter besides scary Hetta? These questions ate at me as I lay in Matty's lumpy bed, James seething on the floor near my elbow, waiting for the day he'd get his bed back.

It was time to answer them.

I breathed out into the fall air, expecting my breath to fog up like it did in the movies, but it still didn't, just as it'd been failing me all morning. I couldn't understand how it'd get even colder than this.

I walked fast to keep my blood warm. Despite the cold, it felt good to stretch my legs on a long walk. Everyone walked everywhere in the community, so I was getting plenty of mild exercise, but I hadn't pushed myself for a while. I did push-ups and pull-ups in the barn, but I would have loved to get a punching bag. I wondered what the sheep would think of that.

At the top of a rocky ridge, I heard something: the sound of metal on metal. My senses flew through the roof as I tried to discern more. Was it something blowing in the wind? Men from the community working? A Deadlight Garde?

That cleared my head. Deadlights didn't accidentally make noise. But I knew enough to know that wasn't the only thing I should be scared of in these woods. I slipped into stealth mode as I stalked forward. I heard tinkering again, intentional.

I caught the sight of a red jacket and a thin frame, and I froze in my slouch. Julian. It was my brother. The thought hit me like a bag of bricks slathered in sorrow.

"James," I called, hoping not to scare him with the tremor of my voice. What I would give to find my brother in these woods, a survivor after all those years. But I was being stupid. Julian was older than James, even when I last saw him alive.

Marah's middle child shrank at the sound of my voice. Figuring he couldn't disappear into the dirt, he finally looked back at me. I *didn't* know if he was allowed out there, but once he looked at me that way, I sure did. That kid was hiding something. I tried to look over his shoulder. There was a plastic bin next to him, but I couldn't see what he was doing with it so far away.

"What are you doing out here? It's freezing." I put my hands under my armpits and stamped my feet in demonstration.

"It's only forty-five degrees, thirteen degrees above freezing," James said.

"Oh. Well, it's cold anyway."

"It's not cold," he said. "Wait until January. Forty-five degrees will seem warm." He slipped what he held into the plastic bin and put the cover on. That sneaky devil.

I closed the gap between us. "What are you working on there, James?"

He shrugged. "What are you doing so far from the community?"

A laugh burst out of me, possibly my first real one in months. I didn't expect to be the one on trial.

"There's a difference. I'm an adult."

"And a woman." He sounded resigned. As if I was going to punish him.

We stood for a minute before I realized what I could do. I stepped over to the brown container that came up to my knees. It was all scratched up. James didn't move even as I pulled the cover off.

The smell of metal and rust hit me. Inside were piles of metal plates and old casings of one kind or another. At the bottom was a layer of random screws and nuts and bolts. Though it was garbage to me, I understood I was looking at a kid's lifelong work.

A hiccup of a sob escaped James, and I looked up quickly. I let the cover drop. "Hey, hey, what's wrong?"

A real sob escaped, and though he was fighting it, he couldn't stop crying. I sat near him on the cold ground, both of us waiting for him to be able to talk. When he seemed close, I asked him again what was wrong.

"You're gonna take it away. And then you'll tell my mom and I'll get in trouble."

I glanced at the bin. I didn't understand what was going

on, but I wasn't stupid. James broke some kind of taboo, either by being out here without Marah's permission or by fiddling with the scrap. I guessed a bit of both.

"Listen, kid, it's no problem to me if you're collecting nails. If you should be at school though, maybe we should get back."

"Why? I'm almost done with school anyway. Teacher Rhonda told me I finished with the boys' math book. I asked if I could keep doing school, but she said that was only for older girls."

I was nearly dumb with irony. Where I came from, women fought tooth and nail to be taken seriously in STEM programs, or did, before they all died. It was assumed that men were better at technical thinking and given every opportunity to explore their interests. Here was James, a boy, who wasn't allowed to do math.

I was acutely wary of the life the community had built, but for the first time, I wondered what it was like for a boy growing up in a female-dominated world. What they did wasn't any better than what we did out there. It was the exact same kind of worse, just strangely opposite.

"So, uh, you're done with school," I said awkwardly, "and you wanted to play out here?"

James scowled. "I'm building."

Finally, something we could talk about. "Okay, what are you building?"

It was the wrong thing to say.

James went silent and said, "Dunno," and looked away.

"All right, should I pack all this up and get rid of it? If it's garbage?"

He wasn't fooled, but the idle threat drew him out enough.

"I want to build an invention. One that makes electricity."

"Hmm." My voice went deeper as I tried to show James I was taking him seriously. "Have you seen electricity before?"

"No, but I've heard of it. Brother Logan told me about it."

My own formal schooling broke when I was his older brother Matty's age. There were pockets of schooling in the refugee camp my mother where finally settled me and Julian, but the need for education wasn't as urgent as the need for survival. But in the army I learned a lot, and fast. My understanding of history and the arts was below standard, but I knew enough math and had a good enough hand with technology to survive. And in the army, that was something.

Electricity was taboo in Lilium Springs, and I didn't want to get beaten with pitchforks for getting a simple motor running, *and* I definitely didn't want to bring the aliens down on us, if there was any clout to my working theory that electricity, radar, and that whole shebang called the attention of Deadlight Gardes.

"That's pretty ambitious," I told James. "Why don't we start with simple machines? You have to have a solid foundation for inventing."

James lit up. "Yes. That's what I want."

"Your family already uses a lot of simple machines." I pulled random pieces of metal and old electrical equipment from his plastic tub to demonstrate an inclined plane, a wedge, and a lever. Screw was easy because he actually had one, and he understood the wheel and axle from his family's wheelbarrow. Even the pulley was in use at some pumps.

He grew suspicious of how easy it all was. "Those aren't machines."

"Sure, they are," I said while scratching the back of my neck, swathed in layers of scarf and sweater. "You're just used to them. When technology is all around you, you forget that at one time it would have seemed like magic. Think about what early people thought when they discovered how to make fire."

"God makes fire. She was the burning bush."

I didn't say anything, but I tilted my head and pressed my lips together. Was I going to *tell* this kid that everything his parents thought was wrong? Nooo, I would never. Was I going to subtly subvert everything this kid grew up believing in favor of a rational, well-balanced outlook at life? Yep.

"Hey, I have an idea." I warmed to the notion, even as I said it. "It's something I did when I was a kid in school. I know you want to make electricity, but there's other ways of harnessing energy." I told him briefly about the simple supplies we'd need for a hydropowered experiment: a bottle and funnel, string, a thin stick, pliable plastic sheet, and whatever the boonies' equivalent of wine corks was. James started digging through the bin, but I interrupted him.

"Another time, bud. It's getting late and we have to get home before your mom notices."

He was willing enough to walk back home with me, though a bit cagey about storing his bin back under some fallen pine branches. I could tell he didn't like that I knew where it was. I wondered if he'd move it to a new spot the next day.

A chill was rising in the wind as we walked, conversation halting between us now that the props were gone. I wanted James to maybe think I was cooler than I was—that he'd look and see a type of adult entirely different than he knew. I had just asked him what he knew about the planets when we saw the leg. There was no strong stench of decay, no distant screams. It was one leg—I'd seen much worse. But in that moment, I was on the battlefield, new acquaintances falling around me, a leg sticking out from under a smashed car. I was in the streets of a deserted town, lifeless limbs turning in the wind, body stuck on a twisting rope like a dancer in a music box.

James turned quickly toward me, panic on his face, and I recoiled as I realized I was the adult. I had to deal with it.

I dropped to the ground, taking James with me. We crouched, backs to a tree as I took in the woods around us. James was quiet, more from startled fear than strategy. I felt a tremor move through him. A recently woken owl hooted in the distance, the eerie sound riding the wind.

The leg lay motionless, sticking out from a shallow pile of leaves and straw. It was clearly a woman's leg. The calf was more than shapely and ended in a blue sneaker. My mind raced as I tried to pair the leg with an owner.

I told James to stay and approached cautiously. Up close, the mound of leaves took on the shape of a human body. The limb stuck out at a sharp angle. It wasn't the work of a Deadlight Garde. Someone had pulled leaves across the large body after it was dead for a while—the forest mulch showed no signs of dried black blood. Someone tried to hide what had happened. My stomach welled up and bile rose in my throat as I tentatively brushed the grasses and leaves from the head.

Sister Abigale stared back at me, horror etched deep in her ruined face. Her face was puffy across one side. Blood caked at the neck. Waves of pressure rushed to my head and made my hands shake as they hovered over her dead body. I willed myself to brush the rest of the debris from the body. It was cold, but I could smell the faint rust of blood. She hadn't been dead long. Of course not, she would have been missed.

Sister Abigale—the body—was broken open at the chest. Something had cracked her ribs to eat the internal organs.

Unbeknownst to me, James had crept up beside me for a clear view of the shattered rib bones and empty cavity. Absorbed in my own thoughts and trauma, I only realized

James was there when he spewed vomit down his shirt. He coughed, and I pulled him away from the grisly scene, the smell of vitriol filling my nose.

"Was it…was it the demons?" he asked.

"No, they don't kill like this. This was an animal. She was hunted."

James spit to clear his mouth, and I told him firmly to stay away. I went back to the body and closed Abigale's eyes, my mind on her baby's life, ended before it started.

A knock came at the door and Marah bustled to answer it, even through her sobs. Timothy and a few others had gone to retrieve Abigale's body while I washed my sticky hands in the basin. The smell of vomit lingered in the house as James changed clothes in the bedroom. At the door was a slight, scared-looking teenage girl. Marah nodded at her through red-rimmed eyes and turned to me.

"Elder Sister Hetta wants to see you. I suppose to talk to you about—" She broke out in a fresh wave of tears, and I helped her to the couch and covered her with a blanket. Before I left, I gave James stern instructions to stay by his mom's side.

I didn't go to the church. I went to Hetta's house as directed, the gloom of a late fall evening descending around me. The lantern felt heavy in my hand. I hadn't had reason to be out at nightfall yet.

I saw a rooftop peek through the trees. The way I understood it, though houses were built for new couples, the older houses in the center of the community were reserved for the Elder Sisters and their families. Not that the center acted as any kind of town square. Whoever built those houses a hundred years ago liked their privacy.

Though Hetta's house was old, the paint was smooth and the porch steps were firm. I was sure the men of the community took preservation of their leader's house seriously. It was utterly unlike the other cabins I'd visited. Hetta's house was far from rustic. A huge expanse of windows lined the second floor. The wooden borders around the windows showed serious woodworking craftsmanship. Even before I knocked, I guessed the first floor would have vaulted ceilings.

I heard Hetta shuffling to let me in as I wondered how many people in the world—with the battles and food shortages and disease and displacement and death—lived safely in a comfortable house.

"Come in. You'll miss dinner with Sister Marah, so I set out some food for you here."

I greeted her and took a tentative step in. I wasn't looking forward to this conversation. I'd already shared what I knew—which wasn't much considering James and I stumbled across the body and then immediately left for help. I had wanted to get the kid home in case what had eaten Abigale remained nearby. I told James it was an animal, but I didn't know for sure. All I knew for sure was it wasn't a Deadlight Garde. It couldn't be.

Though the decorations were sparse, the bones of the

house were beautiful. I was right about the vaulted ceilings. Hetta ushered me to a broad wooden table set under a gigantic cross and white lily. I looked away from the flower that echoed my dead sister. I sat where directed and was shocked to see what hung on the opposite wall. A bleach-white skull was flanked by huge but tightly wound horns on either side. Of course, there were bighorn sheep in the mountains, but I thought it odd Hetta would showcase something so sinister. I felt her gaze fall on me as I took in the skull and horns.

"Who built this house?" I quickly asked.

"Our founders. This was originally Sister Wendy Martin's home. She lived here with her husband, Brother Bill, and their six children." She spoke without question of her community's history. "It now passes from Elder Sister to Elder Sister. The Lord has blessed me to live out the last days of my life here."

I frowned in carefully crafted concern. "Are you ill?"

"Oh no, soldier. I just know God's plan for me. I am leader until I die. Then the next Eldest Sister will take my place. That would be Sister Bethany, unless God takes her before me. All in Her will."

In front of me, on the table, was a bowl of soup and a not-quite-a-scone set beside it. Hetta's own seat had no food before it.

She saw me looking and waved her hands. "You don't eat much when you're old. I have a request for you, but first I need to hear what happened to Sister Abigale."

She spoke placidly about the catastrophe. I searched Hetta's features for signs of shock or remorse. I'd known Abigale for only a short while, but I was completely shook by her and her baby's untimely deaths. I took a polite bite of soup to buy me a moment, then relayed how James and I had unwittingly found the dead body.

Hetta made a simple noise of affirmation in her throat and nodded. "My request is that you train our men to fight the demons."

I bit the inside of my lip, mouth full of dry scone, and winced. I automatically put my hand to my mouth but quickly brought it down. I swallowed and felt the lump catch in my throat.

"Elder Sister Hetta, they're not demons," I coughed. "I told you, they're aliens. That is, they came from another planet."

"Indeed, they do, child."

Her quick agreement threw me.

I pushed further. "And what killed Abigale was not an alien."

"No, it wasn't."

My suspicion grew. She didn't even see the body. How could she know?

She slowly licked her bottom lip. "It was a mountain lion."

"A cougar? What makes you think that?"

"They're the only carnivore in the mountains that won't leave their prey under open sky. It's been a very long time since a cat so bold has come so close. And to attack an adult is nearly unheard-of."

I leaned forward. "What would make one suddenly attack?"

Hetta moistened her lips again. I wished I didn't have to watch her tongue snake out again to wet the limp flesh of her bottom lip.

"The beast must have grown desperately hungry. Perhaps something scared away its game."

Something tugged at the back of my mind as Hetta described the hunting habits of big cats. Hetta had yet to show signs of empathy for this gone member of her community, as if these Earthly troubles were below her.

"Regardless," I said, changing the subject, "I can't teach anyone to fight the aliens. My military had grade A weapons and huge numbers and we were casually decimated. The Deadlight Gardes—the demons—are machines and are deadly. It's not like I fought them and won. I'm only here through sheer luck."

"But they've been here a very long time. It seems as if you held out."

I shook my head and wiped my mouth of soup. "For us, the fighting was urgent and catastrophic. For them, they did everything in their own time. Almost indifferently. Attacks would shift to new areas of the planet. We'd hope we finally threw enough atomic bombs to scare them, but they always came back."

Hetta thought over what I said as I ate more of the soup.

It was good, much better than the scone.

"You would leave us defenseless?"

I paused as I wondered if she had guessed at my plans, then figured she meant my refusal.

"Ma'am, if a Deadlight Garde came within ten miles of here, it'd be better for the whole community to split up and run than try to take a stand and fight."

She smiled serenely, and I was aware of how fragile she looked. Her white hair puffed around her wrinkled head like one of Dean Miles's mushrooms. She lived her entire life in a simple corner of the woods. I wondered if it was possible for her to imagine fleeing it.

"The demons have come on foot closer than we'd like." Hetta stood slowly and shuffled to a desk off to one side. Chills began to run down my back. They couldn't. How, then, could these people still be alive?

Out of the drawer, Hetta lifted a piece of metal, one that didn't gleam but deadened all light around it. My breath caught in my throat as she advanced. It looked like the shredded metal part of a Deadlight I found in the water village…weeks ago. Miles and miles ago. How did it get here?

"It's true, you've seen them up close." Her voice was low, husky, as if she didn't want to attract their attention to us now. Back at the table, she didn't sit. She stood next to me, holding the piece out, offering it to me. "It's a piece of metal, soldier. It's not connected, it's not alive. It can't hurt you like this."

I felt abashed and took it tentatively. I had thought if I ever felt the dark, polished substance, it'd be as a clawed limb wrenching my head off my neck. It was warmer than I expected. Not quite as chilled as a solitary piece of steel. It was also much heavier. Much denser than my Titan Suit, the best the US Army could come up with for the masses to push back against the Deadlight Gardes.

I felt the blind spot of my back prickle. "You seem to know a lot about the aliens. Does this look like demon flesh to you?"

"Oh, dear, a name is but a name. We call them demons. You call them aliens. It doesn't matter. They're a deadly species that has come to kill us for one reason or another—doesn't matter. You've lost. What matters is what comes next."

I took the last bite of breaded mass and felt it catch in my throat once more. I took a drink of the water set by my plate. The aftertaste of the scone soured the water in my mouth, but I swallowed anyway to force it all down.

Hetta raised an eyebrow at me. "My people's greatest fear was being taken by the Antichrist and forced to renounce God. They knew the end was coming. What they didn't count on was surviving past the end; being left behind by the end of the world.

"God showed me something recently. The aliens *will* leave. For them, this is one stop of many. To us, they've been here a long time, but to them, it's very short."

I shook my head in disagreement at her overconfident

assumptions, but also because I suddenly wasn't feeling well. My head was hot. Too cloudy. My eyes shifted to Hetta. Was it crazy to think she put something in my water?

Hetta continued speaking but watched me closely. I fought to understand her words. "God revealed it to me." Her voice was utterly serious. "The aliens travel, planet to planet, exterminating intelligent beings, collecting the resources they need to travel the way they do. Not gold." Hetta gave a rasping growl that served as a laugh. "Oxygen. Tiny pieces of matter humans can't even see being taken away. While they're replenishing their supplies, the extermination of the human species is a mere sidenote. We've grown too rapidly while they've been away. They have to cull us back like weeds. Keep us from growing too numerous. Keep us from advancing off our planet like they did theirs." She slashed a hand in the air. "Disable us so we will never be competition to them."

I was no longer eating or drinking. I felt heavy. My limbs certainly but also my mind. Then, something flashed within, a sudden vision, a moment like when you solve a difficult problem but struggle to keep the answer fresh in your head. I *saw* what Hetta was saying. The aliens came to Earth not because they cared about us. We were just beetles in their garden, gnawing too much, devouring *their* resources, destroying *their* things. They committed genocide to keep our numbers down, to keep us from using up what was theirs. They didn't care if a bug or two escaped, as long as we would struggle to repopulate.

So that we would never reach for the stars for ourselves.

I raised my cloudy head and looked straight at the ram's skull. Only a dark sliver of shadow showed of the sockets set on either side of the head, but I saw a flicker. My stomach churned and sweat broke out on the back of my neck. I had a sudden thrill of desire to take off my clothes and let the drops evaporate off my skin into the night air. I wasn't in Hetta's kitchen any longer. I was in the forest, followed, stalked by a ram with a taste for blood. I stood on the tallest tree and looked toward the destruction of a planet and felt a rasping tongue lick the salty sweat off my neck.

Hetta's iron voice spoke. I blinked and was sitting in an ordinary kitchen chair once more. I struggled to focus as she talked. "I want to ensure that my people survive. Else who will go forth and populate the Earth?"

My forehead was sweaty yet chilled. Bile was already in my mouth by the time I realized I was going to throw up all over the table.

8. Under Lock and Key

The breeze lifted my skirts. It would be the last day I wore them until next spring. Though it was cold, I wanted to wrap myself in power. Make it clear who I was and what I represented.

Across the now empty wheat field, Arwen did push-ups with all the men in the community between sixteen and fifty. Thirty-seven in all, I knew without counting. Well, I mused, I had wanted to introduce Arwen around. But this wouldn't connect her with handsome Brother Marc in the proper way. It was entirely inappropriate. I didn't understand why Elder Sister Hetta allowed this. She made the announcement for this training at church. I couldn't remember a time something so unexpected happened in the sanctuary. Even when God performed Her miracles, it happened as it should. This—Arwen mixing with married and unmarried men—was outlandish.

Arwen moved into her own cabin five days ago. I was saddened that the close contact I had with another woman every day would be taken from me altogether. We had found only minutes each day to talk since then. She didn't mention plans for this training and had made herself scarce after church on Sunday, so I didn't hear when the training would take place from Arwen. Timothy, too, could have mentioned it to me that morning but didn't. Instead, I only found out because Matty asked me if he could go hang out with little Jon while the men trained, the two of them being too young to be involved.

No other woman would come with me to the fields. Sister Esther had no interest—she didn't have much of an interest in anything since Sister Abigale died. My mind stumbled on the name and my thoughts rushed on, angry— but Sister Esther was always a vapid one, it wouldn't be up to her to restore order.

I swallowed. *Lord, I didn't mean those hateful thoughts against my Sister. Forgive me.*

The men finished with their push-ups. I saw Brother Marc jokingly flex his arms, as if he was already stronger. I was torn between drifting closer to hear what Arwen said and stomping away.

Rachel wouldn't come with me either.

Our reunion hadn't gone as I had planned. On paper we

were friends once again, but she was as quiet and polite toward me as she was with everyone else. I wanted to go back to how things used to be, but she wasn't letting me in. I didn't know if our friendship would ever be fully restored. *Why did I have to kiss her?*

Even when I talked to Sister Bethany that morning, she wasn't entirely on my side. I could tell she was confused by Elder Sister Hetta's commandment to train the men to fight the demons, and more confused that this newcomer should do it, but she couldn't say or do anything about it.

"Sister Marah, God speaks to Elder Sister Hetta in ways you and I can only dream of until we're leader, God willing. She's doing this for a reason."

"But why," I practically wailed. "The demons aren't going to come here. Elder Sister Hetta isn't going to send my husband and the other men out there, is she?"

Sister Bethany paused. Finally, she said, "No, Sister Marah, I don't think so. It would be folly to move our small number against the Devil's army. That said, we can't know what God has preordained to happen. Perhaps another community will attack ours. Maybe Sister Arwen will pass away this winter and God desires for her to pass on her skills first."

That last idea gave me goose bumps. As mad as I was at Arwen, I felt my overprotectiveness of someone so naïve was justified. I didn't want God to take Arwen from me. She brought so much change to my life. I just didn't want her to change the men's lives too.

Sister Bethany continued, "All I'm saying is that it's not up to us to question Elder Sister Hetta, because that is questioning the Word of God Herself. Understood?"

I nodded, meek like a child, which I was. I had to remind myself that compared to Sister Bethany and Elder Sister Hetta, I was indeed a child. However, Sister Bethany hadn't expressly forbidden me to get involved. There was nothing that said I shouldn't check in. It was correct for a middle Sister to get an update on a new activity.

I picked my way carefully through the stubby stalks, the day's mending I was supposed to be working on growing further and further behind. It was difficult walking in a skirt.

Arwen selected a man to stand opposite her in the field, while the others loosely grouped around to watch. It was Brother Barry Garland. He stood uneasily in front of Arwen. Arwen explained something as she hacked her hand at Brother Barry's neck and groin. I was stunned to see Arwen's hand come within inches of Brother Barry's penis. He was clearly shocked too and there was a break of nervous laughter. That woman was going to turn us all into Jezebels, I thought just as Arwen swooped her leg behind Brother Barry's knee. His laughter shifted to one of panic, and he fell in a wobbly motion to the ground. Arwen pounced on him and twisted one of Brother Barry's arms behind him. Arwen smiled, but no one else did. I didn't like what she was doing, or know much about it, but she was practiced. And savvy. In two motions, Arwen had proved to the men she didn't care who they were and that she'd best them anyway.

"Sister Arwen, that's quite the move."

She flashed me a brilliant smile, and I had to acknowledge how healthy and strong the recent weeks had made her. To me, men had always been stronger, but kept in their place by God. I had never seen a woman who was as physically strong as Arwen. Did that mean she couldn't be strong spiritually? I wondered.

"I'm not much of a teacher," Arwen said as she helped Brother Barry up, "I learned that day two of Basic."

Brother Barry stepped aside more than a little awed. I wondered if he enjoyed what had just happened—if he'd think of it that night. I impatiently brushed a hair away from my cheek, uncomfortable with the thought.

It was time for the women to talk. I didn't mind keeping the men waiting.

"And is that going to help us against the demons, if they were to come?"

"Definitely not," Arwen replied, acknowledging the dubious expressions around her.

I was surprised to hear Arwen admit as such. If she thought that, why was she bothering with training?

"But," she continued, "it's a good idea to be prepared. I didn't see anyone else out there, but it's possible someone could find this place and want to take what's yours. Elder Sister Hetta asked me to train the men up in case the aliens come to exterminate, but I've already explained to the guys here that if the aliens come, we should run."

The *guys*. I looked at my husband, and he lifted a brow and shrugged. I nearly smiled. He was flexible and good-natured in ways I never would be. Stiffness was the price of responsibility. If I ever had a daughter, I'd need to remember to teach her that lesson.

Arwen saw where I was looking. "Actually," she said, "Brother Timothy told me about the wrestling matches the boys do for the spring sports rally. This isn't so different than that. I was surprised sports are popular here."

"Oh sure, Sister Arwen." Brother Barry got his tongue back. "Everyone likes to let off a little steam and have some fun. Get some exercise."

"It's lucky you all are in such good health here. Honestly, you're fitter than many in the army."

"Now why would that be?" Brother Godwin spoke up.

"In the military, there were some whose job it was to do recon on the ground, like me. We trained hard because that training might save our lives someday." Arwen shifted her feet. "But others were trained in technology—fixing our bodysuits, building ships, even detonating missiles from a screen—but never saw real action. Everyone here does so much manual labor. It's clear it's keeping you healthy."

Brother Godwin nodded sagely. "That was one of the reasons our founders came here. To live our lives connected to God and what's important. When we used to go out to collect supplies before the demons came, I'd see how disconnected the people were. Everyone staring at their screens."

I didn't like the line of talk, but it was Arwen who shifted topic.

"Sister Marah," I heard the nuance of laughter in her voice whenever she called me by my title, "it would be good to get the women involved in this too. Build some basic knowledge of exercise and resilience."

I felt all the men look at me, waiting to see what I would say.

"I can't see that being possible. First, Elder Sister Hetta specifically asked the men to train." I kept my misgivings to myself. I'd never undermine Elder Sister Hetta's leadership in front of a crowd of men. "Second, who would watch the kids and teach school and cook while we took a break for fun? Besides, I think childbirth makes us resilient enough."

Timothy was at my side now. He had drifted there during the conversation, and I was glad to have his support by my side. That comfort vanished in a moment. "Now, Marah, it's not just fun. Like Sister Arwen said, it's training."

"Mmm. And that's why you all were laughing?" I purposefully made them recall Arwen gesturing to Brother Barry's groin.

Arwen took it as a challenge.

"How 'bout this, Sister Marah. If I can teach you something in the next five minutes, you'll ask Elder Sister Hetta if the women can participate."

I dropped my voice a bit. "I don't think that would be appropriate, letting married and unmarried men and women mix in this…in this physical competition." I felt my cheeks redden and my ego bruise at losing my composure in front of so many.

But Arwen was already off on her task. I didn't like that I didn't understand what was about to happen, but I tried not to show it.

"Brother Barry! Come on over here and show us some H2H combat."

Brother Barry ambled up. He spread his legs apart, bent his knees, and put his hands up on either side of his jaw. I didn't know what they were all so jazzed about. It looked like the stance the boys took before wrestling. I'd never wrestled, of course. I played volleyball with the other girls.

Arwen nodded at me to follow suit.

I crouched slightly and put my hands up.

"Open your legs more," Arwen said.

I could nearly hear the contained laughter. No, I *did* hear laughter. Keeping my face serious, I slid my legs apart and bent my knees. I balled my hands up into fists of anger. Arwen was making a mockery out of me.

"That's better." Arwen smiled.

I felt flustered and realized I liked to see her smile at me, even here.

"You feel like you can take on the world, don't you?"

"With the Lord's help," I replied. "With the Lord's help."

Arwen crouched and slid in close to me. Before I could think of what I was doing, my right fist flashed out and punched her in the nose.

The Lord indeed.

Laughter broke out again, this time the loudest from Arwen.

"Wow, Sister Marah," I heard the repeated emphasis on *sister*. "I didn't think you had in it you. That was a good punch. Not enough to bloody me but enough to take me off guard. It's better to punch the throat though. It's much softer. If you'd done that, I'd be writhing on the ground and you could make a quick getaway."

"It's only because you're both women," Brother Phil said from the back of the crowd. My, how I hated—disliked—Brother Phil's voice.

Arwen turned to see who I was looking at. Brother Phil took that as a signal he should open his mouth again. "Your pardon, Sister, but fighting between two women is one thing and fighting between two men is another. The gift God gave man was strength. You don't want the women to train with us, and I don't want them to train with us either. It'd be inappropriate and it'd slow us down."

That was Brother Phil's way: always throwing his opinion out there when no woman asked him.

I opened my mouth but Arwen was faster. "Easy there, love handles." All of us, me included, looked around at each other, trying to decipher the meaning. "This isn't a philosophical debate group. It's a little exercise.

"Group up in twos. Try to take down your partner with the leg hook I showed you. No punches, no hands at all. If you need to, grasp your hands together so you don't use them. This isn't *Fight Club*. Did you hear me? I mean *now*."

The men grouped up easily. I doubted Arwen would notice, but they each paired up with another man from their peer group. Brother Barry paired with Brother Marc, and there was bad blood between them. There was so much she didn't know.

I tried again. "Sister Arwen, this seems like a waste of time."

She frowned and stood her ground in the wheat field. The cold weather and exercise had reddened her cheeks. I hated looking up at her. I *disliked*, in the most pleasant way, how hot I felt when she stood close to me.

She spoke with her voice down. "Marah, *your* leader asked me to do this. And yeah, I think it makes sense. I'm glad you all have survived so long out here, but there's going to come a day when you need to defend yourselves. Why is it you're resisting so much? You don't want to feel afraid for the first time?"

She said it all matter-of-factly, but I lashed back. "Don't presume to know how I feel. It was my child that found Sister Abigale in the woods. It was me that hid my kids in the cellar when the demons flew over. But I think all this shows God that we don't trust in Her protection. And the idea of all the men and all the women in the community in physical training together? I've never heard of anything so—"

"Scandalous?" Arwen smiled, but there was a bite under it. She was making fun of me. I'd done nothing but try to help her since I found her—starving—and she was repaying me by disrupting everything.

"I'm going to talk to Elder Sister Hetta."

"You do that."

I turned on my heel and burned my way across the field to the trails.

Lord, You brought her here. You need to keep her in line because You know I can't manage that woman. She was all mixed up and when she should have been getting married to one man, she was out wrestling a field of them.

I muttered to God all the way to Elder Sister Hetta's house. I knocked, and when I didn't hear voices or stirring inside, I cracked the door open. Elder Sister Hetta knew if she didn't want to be disturbed she'd lock the door or put out a tiny handwritten sign Sister Abigale made that said jokingly "In Prayer. Don't bother returning after God does." It was uncomfortable when she didn't answer the door and the sign wasn't up. It was an unspoken dread among the women that no one wanted to find the Elder Sister's body when she passed on.

"Elder Sister Hetta?"

There was no answer. Everything was tidy in the house and no fire burned, despite the chill. My instincts told me she wasn't there, but I made a quick pass through the house to be sure.

My head had cooled, but I was determined to talk to Elder Sister Hetta, alone if I could. I made my way to the church, the list of chores I was forsaking running through my head. Mending Gideon's pants—they were all coming apart in the knees and kid's clothing was hard to come by. I had planned to start knitting our winter socks and measure out the cloth for Timothy's Christmas present. None of it would get done.

At the church, my stepmother's peer group measured out a new curtain to hang behind the pulpit. The great swaths of dark purple fabric were brought in last summer, but there was no time in the height of food production for extra projects. It felt strange to see something so ordinary taking place in the sacred space.

Goodmother Kristy spotted me and came down from the altar. She gave me a happy hug. "Blessed Lord, you look more like your mother each day."

My heart lightened. I always appreciated that Goodmother Kristy spoke openly of my mom, instead of pretending she didn't ever exist. She updated me on happenings around her household and the projects my papa was working on, and I did the same as was polite. Then I inquired as to the whereabouts of Elder Sister Hetta.

Goodmother Kristy nodded as if she saw my question coming from a mile away. "She's on a prayer walk."

"She is?" I felt bad for the question. A prayer walk for the Elder Sister was completely different than for any of us.

My Goodmother leaned in. "We all feel it, sweetie.

Things feel changed around here. Elder Sister Hetta's just getting orders from God." She patted my hand like a little girl.

I said goodbye and returned to the path outside. I didn't know where to go next. Part of me wanted to go home and have my kids huddled around me. I wanted to go back to certainty and safety. I didn't like this talk of aliens or changes to our duties. I didn't want Elder Sister Hetta out on a prayer walk, getting words from God that would disrupt our lives.

But if any of this was going to happen, I wasn't going to be the last one to know. I shivered as I walked back to Elder Sister Hetta's. Cool and crisp already, a cold front was moving in. I didn't expect it to snow, but we were dropping degrees fast. And I'd be waiting for Elder Sister Hetta when she got back.

I sat at Elder Sister Hetta's dining table for less than five minutes when it occurred to me it could be hours before she was back from her prayer walk. I wouldn't get my work done today, but I could make myself useful. I set about cleaning Elder Sister Hetta's already clean kitchen and living room. The only chore that needed to be done was sweeping so I took the broom through the house.

It didn't matter to me that Elder Sister Hetta had the largest house though she lived alone, her husband long dead. I was glad her descendants could gather there for Easter and Christmas. God willing, I'd do the same someday. I felt a pain as I imagined the leadership my own mother never had. Then, I imagined Matty, James, and Gideon gathering in this very home with their children, me in the height of my power. In my vision, there was a woman there, my adult daughter, ready to support me in my leadership of the community. I wondered if that would ever come true.

My head snapped up, but all I had heard were leaves hitting the large expanse of windows. It was darker now, gray and ready to storm. I wasn't worried about finding my way home in the dark rain—I had every inch of this community memorized—but I was dismayed that sometime soon I'd be cold and wet. I considered lighting the candles, but I felt odd about it. I didn't want anyone else coming to Elder Sister Hetta's door, expecting to call on her and finding me all alone, making myself at home. And if I decided to leave, I didn't want the scent of fresh smoke to linger. I sat down in a plush but worn chair and curled up.

I must have dozed off because the next thing I heard was a strange, incessant noise. My eyes flashed open from drowsy sleep. It was a sound unlike anything I had ever heard. I stood quietly, cautiously, as if the noise was going to change everything, like Arwen's appearance had. I knew it was no remnant of a dream because I heard it again. I crept to the closed door of Elder Sister Hetta's study. I knew it was such, though I had never been inside. I had studiously avoided it on my cleaning circuit throughout the house. I paused, wondering what was on the other side of the door.

I shivered in my dress. Typically, someone would have lit a fire in the house for Elder Sister Hetta to battle the wind outside. I hovered at the door, hoping to sense something. What if it was Elder Sister Hetta? But what would that noise have been? What if she had been in there the whole time, lying paralyzed on the floor? And me, sitting in her chair in her house thinking of the day that it'd all be mine while she was trapped.

The door eased open automatically. I was surprised to see my hand on the knob. I peered into the darkness. An outline of a single small window glowed dimly near the ceiling. I heard the noise again and turned toward it. It was so dark I could barely discern the closet door before me. My hand touched the cold metal knob, a tight knot in my chest. I had gone that far. I twisted it.

It was locked. The noise came again. I backed out of the office and made my way to the kitchen where I lit a single candle. Rain struck the enormous windows, filling the house with a soft, rhythmic patter. Then, I opened a drawer and felt with my hands for a jingle of keys. It was a fluke that I knew they were there. Some years ago—three maybe—I had taken tea with Goodmother Kristy and Elder Sister Marie, Elder Sister Hetta's predecessor and Goodmother Kristy's aunt. Someone had come for a shed key and Elder Sister Marie retrieved them from that very drawer.

I moved trancelike through the dusky house and back to the study, armed with a candle and a set of keys of all different sizes and shapes. I tried each one in turn. All the while, the sporadic noise, tiny really, came through the door. It only could have woken me because it was unearthly strange.

The door unlocked at last, and I slipped the keys into my dress pocket. The door hinge caught and creaked, but my candle lit the small space to the back wall. It was a well-stocked closet with shelves on all sides. There, among the clutter and extra Bibles and old sermon notes, was Arwen's outfit, what she had called her Titan Suit.

It lay as if still exhausted from the long journey, propped up against the back wall. A tiny blue light shined from its forearm, brighter than my candle, even though its flame was a tenth of the size. I swallowed as I realized it was electric, something I had never seen alive before.

Breath caught in my throat as I realized what this all implied. Arwen wouldn't have brought her suit here, I knew it. She didn't like Hetta, though—events of the day coming back to my still drowsy mind—clearly Arwen was willing to take her orders like the rest of us. Did someone find the bodysuit and give it to Elder Sister Hetta, concerned what the strange object could be?

I had helped Arwen pack it away when summer skies flew and knew how heavy it was. It was ridiculous to think that Elder Sister Hetta had brought it here of her own ability. The hairs on my arms rose and I looked behind me. It wasn't safe—it wasn't proper—to make assumptions about what the Elder Sister couldn't do; God helped her at every move.

But what was she doing with Arwen's stuff? And where was Arwen's gun? I looked around, but there was no sign of it.

I smoothed my hair with my hand, candle wavering in the other. I set the candleholder down on a shelf and leaned over the bodysuit. In a fit of spirit, I touched it. It felt cold like metal but flexible as if it had been woven of steel thread. I wondered what it felt like on. I remembered the easy way Arwen twisted and stalked in ethereal motion. I lifted the arm and gave the dark a wry smile. I'd never be strong enough to lift the whole outfit, much less walk around in it.

Which brought me back to my first question: How did Elder Sister Hetta wind up with the bodysuit in her home?

I straightened and took back my candle and noticed where I'd set it: a shelf with three handwritten Bibles. We kept Bibles in the church and at the homes of each of our oldest Sisters. Because transcribing the Bible was time consuming for those who acted as scribes, we didn't have many copies. It was the reason we memorized so many verses when we were young.

I took one of the manuscripts down from the shelf, heavy in both arms. I let it slide open and I saw the many different hands it took to write out the entire book. I would give a copy to Arwen, make her read it, make her learn our ways. Then I'd return the Bible to this closet when Elder Sister Hetta was out.

I thought I wanted to give the Bible to Arwen so

everything would go back to normal. I didn't tell myself that I wanted to return and see if the bodysuit was still there or not. But you can know things about yourself and not yet realize them.

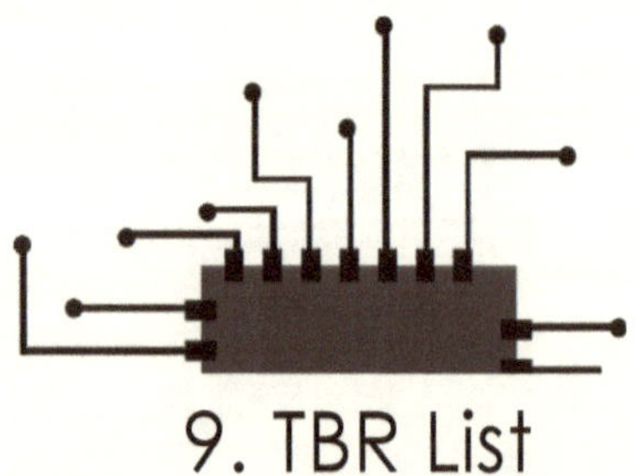

9. TBR List

"Husbands, submit yourselves unto your own wives, as it is fit in the Lord." Colossians 3:18.

The pages under my right hand thinned—I was nearly done with the book. I had more questions than answers about why Lilium Springs was created and why the aliens hadn't blasted their nook of the Rocky Mountains to kingdom come.

Marah delivered the Bible to me one night in a rainstorm with a smug smile on her face. The book wasn't a neat black copy like the ones I saw in a military chapel—those unassuming, mass-printed testaments sent across the Earth. Instead, the Bible Marah brought filled her arms with loosely bound handwritten pages tucked between an enormous cover. I staggered under the bulk of it when she handed it to me. It had to have taken years to write by hand, by several hands from the look of it. Ink of varying shades of black and blue ran into each other. The handwriting at the beginning was textbook worthy, but it was apparent that other scribes were less disciplined in their work.

A water stain marked a section of pages, but it was an old wound, long dried. The rainwater hadn't smeared the handprinted text. When I said as much to Marah, her strange glance at the rain told me she hadn't considered it. She brushed at the wetness of her clothes as if she hadn't noticed the icy fall of the storm soaking her through. I was cold just standing next to her. Before I could understand where her mind was at, she was off with excuses of dinner prep and putting the kids to bed.

I started reading the manuscript that night, but it took weeks to get through. There was a flood. There were lions. As I neared the end, Jesus made an appearance. I liked it when he threw the tables in the temple, not that I wanted to wash his feet with my hair or anything like that.

Between these well-known stories, ominous shadows littered the pages. The uneasiness I felt wasn't due to weird verses about boiling a kid in its mother's milk or problematic stories about women having sex with their dad because they thought the world was over. Though in the current state of things, I was glad the community didn't take that story to heart. It was that I knew from the fervent writing I read that they were more than stories told to pass the time. It wasn't a book of fairy tales. They were philosophy, a way of living via oppression.

I did not like what was being proposed. It was as if they asked themselves, what value did life have if someone wasn't in submission to someone else? And they answered with a resounding "None!"

Plus, I wasn't a scholar of ancient texts, but I was certain about one thing: I'd always heard God referred to as He. Marah's copy referred to God as She.

Any section about wives and husbands was suspect. Without a comparison document, I couldn't be sure, but I believed they changed the original mention of husbands to wives and vice versa. Why else write this damn thing out by hand except to seem mysterious and give people something to do in the middle of winter? It was to change little pieces along the way, I was certain about that.

I shifted in my bed, nearly at the end of another book, little *b*.

As I read, my mind operated at a different level. The Bible was so dense and contradictory that it led to wars between people, each citing the Bible and God on their side, even if all sides were working with a similar translation of the Bible. It's never been unusual for a cult to take that long-standing form and run with it. What about a group that sought to shape it?

Cult.

I let the mammoth tome fall backward flat on the bed. Was that what I was a part of now? A cult? A short grunt broke from my lips, stirring the silence of my cabin.

I had wanted to save my life. Not risk my soul to these crazies.

What made them so crazy? So, the founders changed He to She and Husband to Wife. Yes, someone made these changes to meet their own ends. Did I feel uncomfortable because religious texts are sacred? Or was it because I was predisposed to a certain type of sexism? When I thought Marah Bennett was taking me to a doomsday prepper community run by men, I was completely on edge, ready for the knife to appear. I was walking straight into the patriarchy. When that turned out not to be true, I grew complacent, if largely because I was confused. But was it progressive?

I thought of James, hiding in the woods, trying to teach himself because he was banned from going any further in school. Desperate to learn something real. *That's* what bothered me. They didn't modify a book to make things better. They—the founders, I assumed—simply reversed things to continue benefitting a different group of people.

As a thought experiment, all this would have been very interesting to me. I could only assume Lilium Springs had been started once upon a time by people acting of their own free will. Someone came here looking for a better, more spiritual life. Did they come intending to shape religion to fit them? Or did the women seize power one dark night? And how would they have done that?

It wasn't a thought experiment. If a group of women would go to these lengths to control the people around them, how was my story—the last outsider—going to end?

I had to leave. And soon.

Morning light bloomed at last through my window enough to warrant blowing out my candle. Dawn came later every morning as the Northern Hemisphere descended into gloom.

True to their word, I had my own cabin now. It was a small open space about ten paces across, but there were two closets with shelves. If I didn't light a fire in the hearth, windy blusters blew down the chimney. I figured that was something I'd have to get used to.

I had settled into a routine. I ate simply. I didn't make bread, I just fried pancakes with my allotment of ground wheat. Except for potatoes, I sliced and ate most vegetables raw. Part of the reason for my apathy was it still felt like a blessing—Could I say "blessing" and still remain an atheist?—that I had food at all after my experience in the woods. I received a full one-person share of harvest and occasionally received an allotment of eggs or dairy. No cheese though. Sister Bethany was adamant about that. I hadn't helped make the cheese, so I wasn't getting a share. Nice to know that Christianly love extended only so far into the love-thy-neighbor territory.

It was Sunday, so I had church twice on my social calendar today. In fact, that's all I had on my agenda. Every other day of the week, I had assigned chores around the community or I was given days to stay home and work on projects there. Now that harvest was over, I most wanted to learn to hunt, but instead I was told to rake leaves outside Elder Sister Hetta's house or sort moldy specimens out of the food stores. At home, I was supposed to do laundry or bake sourdough bread for my imaginary family. Celebrate my womanhood, woo woo.

The chores I deemed necessary—push-ups, general eating of the foods, and chopping wood for my fireplace—took only a few hours each morning. I spent some afternoons with Marah when she wasn't encircled by other mama hens. I found when I didn't live under her rule, she treated me more like an equal and I enjoyed spending time with her.

Other days, I explored. I thoroughly surveyed the eastern ridge and the chain of ponds off to the south. The bitter cold made the hiking not nearly as enjoyable as it used to be, and I didn't make as much progress as I would have liked. Some days I met James and we did simple experiments I remembered from school, and he asked me about electricity and tools I used in the military. I still hadn't found the cavern that housed my Kronos L85 and Titan Suit. Every time I mentioned it to Marah, she made excuses that she didn't have time to stray from home to show me.

I closed the thick, worn book and set it on the small table Marah's father crafted for me of dark walnut. The manuscript nearly filled the whole end table. I left warm blankets behind and rebuilt my fire. I proved to be terrible at banking fires and had to struggle each morning with the dry tinder and flint.

Once the fire was going reasonably, I chopped a potato and set it to fry in a cast-iron skillet with some grease. Most of my cooked meals were half-burnt, half-raw. Marah said I moved the tripod around too much. As the potatoes cooked, I washed my face in a basin of water and swished the ice-cold liquid in my mouth. I'd noticed a few community members missing a tooth or two, and I knew I had to develop a better dental hygiene routine or I'd be gumming my food by forty. I set out a small handful of dried raisins on a plate. With a big mitt, I carefully tipped the iron skillet over my dish and sprinkled a pinch of salt on the breakfast potatoes. Some days, I pretended I lived in a historical reenactment village and any minute a tourist was going to coyly grill me about what I used for toilet paper.

I ate quickly. With no one to talk to, mealtimes were a fast affair. I washed up the dishes and got ready for my least favorite activity in the community: church. I didn't take special care with my hair or the clothes I wore, though that seemed like one of the main Sunday pastimes. If men had a suit coat, they wore it to thwart the chilly air. Women and girls were predisposed to wear skirts, but the cold weather meant more wore pants to church.

It was time I forced myself to consider my plans. They brewed through the dark nights of reading, but I was scared what it would mean if I acted on them. I wasn't used to indecision.

Before leaving my little cabin, I packed the most essential items in a backpack I found in one of the storage containers. In a few hours' time, I worried I may be in the position of needing a quick getaway, and I wanted to be ready.

At church that morning, I was going to expose Elder Sister Hetta as a con artist.

"And you're saying there are no trees," Barry said.

"There *are* trees, but they're scrubby little things and few and far between. It's nothing like this dense forest."

Church had yet to start. Sister Esther was at the organ organizing her papers. None of the council was yet on the platform. Thus, Barry thought it was the perfect time to continue a conversation we had started earlier that week at the water pump. He was fascinated by the desert ecosystem that he had only ever read about. I described the way the heat baked your skin and the endless expanse of horizon. After so many quiet days at my cabin, it was unexpectedly nice to have someone listen to me.

"And what do the deer eat in the heart of winter without tree bark?"

"Things grow even in winter. And there's no deer. Well, I don't think." I paused as I tried to remember if there were deer before the aliens came.

"It sounds otherworldly. I wish I could see it."

"Sister Arwen has a picture of it," Marah piped up. I glared in her general direction. She shouldn't be offering out my own business.

A small shadow moved at my elbow and James

appeared. He had come over with his mom. I could tell from his edgy look that he wanted to set up our next meeting time and talk about supplies to bring. I had planned to talk him through the 3-D-printed circuit boards he had collected, but I had no idea what my actions of that morning would mean for our experiments. I shook my head slightly at James. At the same time, I saw one of the sisters' eyes narrow on me. I needed a distraction. And an in for what I wanted to discuss.

"Sister Marah," I said. "I'm ready to report I've read all the way to Colossians."

Marah's face lit up. "Wow, Sister Arwen. We'll make a Biblical scholar out of you yet."

"I don't know about that, Sister Marah." I could afford to be gracious right before I ripped her world apart. "As it turns out, I do have some questions about this Bible. And how it compares to the Bibles we have out there." I tried to layer my voice with meaning.

Barry leaned in, waiting for me to go on.

"I never thought of Bibles being out there in the world before," Marah said. "I assumed people didn't have the chance to read scripture; that ignorance was partly why the demons won so easily. You mean to say they knew about God and still turned away?"

I gritted my teeth. "What I'm saying," I tried to clarify, "is that I think the Bibles here and the Bibles out there are different in some significant ways."

A murmur went through the crowd. James edged away

from me, that little poop-head. He sensed that I was quickly becoming a social pariah.

"And where did you get your copy of the Bible?" The voice creaked behind me like a warped floor, but everyone went silent.

I was expecting her to make an appearance soon. Like a fly to shit, Hetta made it her business to be around in moments like these.

"I heard readings from time to time." I tried to sound casual.

"Sister Arwen, that is not the question I asked. Where did you get one of *our* Bibles?"

I had been ready to go head-to-head with the con artist, but this drew me up short. Marah hadn't yet spoken up, which made me wonder if she was supposed to give me the Bible in the first place. No one spoke as Hetta closed the distance between us. I felt uneasy. I hadn't been this close to her since that strange night at her house, when I left damp and sweaty, suddenly taken in by the flu.

"Soldier, I'm not used to waiting for answers, as I may not have long in this world."

I heard someone chuckle.

"My apologies, Elder Sister Hetta. I brought the Bible to Sister Arwen. I wanted to get her acclimated to our ways," Marah spoke confidently but kept her eyes lowered.

Hetta frowned, an easier feat for her stroke-affected face to take on than a smile. "If you had asked me," her words were designed to bite, "I could have told you I planned to share a copy of our most sacred text with the newcomer later this winter, to allow her time to settle into our way of life before taking up her spiritual responsibilities."

I saw Rachel watching over her husband's shoulder intently, scared for her friend. I'd never seen Hetta look at Marah like she did now. Usually, Hetta and the other three on the council were unwaveringly benevolent to their protégée, a rising leader among women. Now, Hetta looked at Marah shrewdly, calculatingly.

Marah spoke, words halting as she tried to justify her unsolicited actions. "I should have sought your guidance first. I was needlessly careless with the text. I brought it to Arwen in a rainstorm," she said as she drew her brows up in confusion, "but the ink never ran."

This was going seriously off the rails. What did it matter when Marah gave me the book? What did it matter they used no-run ink? I could burn bridges. But I wouldn't do that to Marah's family, and I definitely wasn't about to further their myths.

I interjected, "I'd be very interested in learning more about who wrote this Bible, and why they're different than the ones in my world."

I never understood what happened next. It had to be a fluke, but it was frustratingly perfect timing.

Marah and I jumped as the front entrance of the church burst inward. The wood door banged as it hit the wall and snowflakes flew into the room. It was my first time seeing snow, and I would learn it wasn't a light dusting. It was a full-fledged blizzard. The howl of the blizzard whirled in like a rabid animal. The temperature in the church dropped ten degrees in seconds, and the snow accumulated in thick sheafs of white on the floor and the nearest pew.

Timothy took a few long strides to the door and fastened it shut. The young boys hurried to do their duty and stoke the immense hearths set on either side of the church.

By the time I turned back to challenge Elder Sister Hetta, she was at the pulpit, the three crones behind her. She didn't move or speak. Just stood unearthly still while we mere mortals adjusted to the cold, pulling coats back on and stamping our feet.

My mind belatedly caught up to how dangerous the situation had grown for me. With the arrival of the early blizzard, the window of my leaving had disappeared. I couldn't imagine myself out there stalking southward in the snow, flimsy puffed jacket between me and freezing temperatures. I had enough food in my cabin for the winter, but how could I ever carry it all with me? And even if I found a place to hide out, what then? Could I make it through the winter on my own?

That damn dog at the bottom of the cliff flashed in my mind, but with me in its place. Abigale with her blood-clotted neck smiled at me.

Maybe there had been an opportunity to sneak away, to leave this place with its weird happenings and wayward people, but the snow dispersed that opportunity. For the first time, I realized the immediate danger in my life might not be the Deadlight Gardes. It was the hard place I was stuck in between wilderness and Hetta's control.

Esther started the hymns.

10. Yearn

I kissed little Gideon's rosy cheeks as I dropped him off at school. He was more than capable of walking there on his own, but since James began joining Matty and Timothy for their daily labors, I liked to give some company to Gideon when I was able. I waved to Sister Rhonda as he ran into the schoolyard. I stood, watching my golden boy make his way to a small knot of boys his age. Soaking up these last bits of Gideon's childhood were bittersweet.

It was becoming clearer to me that I'd never have another child. Not only did my monthly flow come with the timeliness of bread rising, Timothy had become neglectful of his marital duties in a way he never had before. There were times I enjoyed sex with him, but mostly it was a pleasantly neutral presleep activity. What I enjoyed most was experiencing Timothy's sheer need for me. The look on his face, the things he'd do to plant his seed, it made me feel powerful; proof that God created men to worship and serve women as women do the Lord.

Yet recently, *I* was the one coaxing *him.* I didn't know if this decrease was part of the natural course of aging. I'd normally talk with Rachel about it, but with our friendship soured since summer, it felt like we'd never be close enough to talk that way again.

I wrapped my scarf more tightly and turned back down the path. It was packed down slick. After the unexpected blizzard, we had a few above-freezing days that melted the snow by day and froze it at night. One quick slip could sprain an ankle. I didn't have time for that.

I rushed through housecleaning that morning. I did the bare minimum: hanging the rugs to dry, sluicing the melted snow out the door, and washing up from breakfast.

I had a mind to visit Arwen that morning. We saw each other at church and occasionally she was assigned to join my peer group for chores, but in front of the others I couldn't talk to her like she and I had when we first met, or when she lived at my house. At the beginning of the season, she was apt to come and sit for a spell, but that had faded as it seemed she'd rather stalk off into the woods than take company with me.

Though I saw Arwen rarely these days, she was often on my mind. In fact, my eagerness to sit next to her at church embarrassed me. I was desperate to hear more about life outside Lilium Springs and her questions about life here amused me. In a community where every year followed the same pattern, she was a novel blip on the timeline.

Sun glinted off the snow, blinding with glare the way a pure, fresh snowfall did. Everyone was still marveling at how early the snow had come this year. It usually didn't snow until the week of Christmas. Or I simply associated snow with Christmas; it was hard to remember thirty-two years' worth of Christmases and winters.

I turned the corner to Arwen's homestead, which was located on the bare outskirts of the community. Past her house was the ice-crusted wilderness. I shivered. Where my family slept, flanked by houses in all directions, was safe. Though, from what Arwen said, if the demons broke through, it wouldn't matter where I was in the community— my family would soon be dead. I shook the worry off. It was unimaginable. God would never let aliens set foot on this land.

I closed the gap to Arwen's cabin, the smallest I had ever seen. I glanced upward. Where was the smoke? Unease welled up in my throat as I took in the surroundings of the house. Footsteps marred the slippery snow, but the tracks were days old except for the well-worn path to the outhouse. Arwen didn't have a barn or livestock—I planned to give her a ewe next spring—but there was little outward evidence of general chores. Panic replaced my worries. Was she not able to take care of herself? Did she get hurt? In my haste, I forgot to knock and shoved my way straight in, pulling dirty, icy snow in with me.

"Sister Arwen? Are you all right?"

The bedclothes bolted upright—Arwen still in them at midmorning.

"Oh, it's you," she murmured and curled back into a ball.

I looked around in dismay as the sour smell of the unwashed hit my nose. I couldn't take my coat off as it was nearly as cold inside as it was outside.

"Are you sick, Sister Arwen?"

"No. And it's just Arwen. And leave me alone."

Hot air issued from my nose as I exhaled deeply. I slipped out of my boots and put on the slippers I brought. I set about to make a fire, but there was no wood. I put my boots back on and went outside to collect some. While there was some chopped wood stacked haphazardly on the side of the house, it was only enough for a few days. If another blizzard struck, Arwen would be in trouble.

Inside again, I made myself busy setting the fireplace. Once a burst of warmth hit the air, Arwen shivered as if her body had only then realized she was cold. I leaned over to feel her forehead. My cold hand felt warm against her body. As much as my own flesh protested, I slipped off my coat and piled it on top of Arwen's blanket. Then I left my slippers on the floor and crawled under the blanket, settling in next to Arwen's body.

"Marah," she said sleepily, "what are you doing?"

"Hush, you're deathly cold. Arwen, you're lucky you're alive. No fire. No wood. Your place is a mess. Just because there's other people around doesn't mean winter's something to sneer at. You've got to take care of yourself."

Arwen shook with cold but lay quiet.

I tucked myself around her, hoping she'd soon warm. I'd only seen one case of hypothermia. It was when little Brother Westly fell through the ice the winter I was fourteen. They got him out of the lake, but he died quickly. I didn't think Arwen had proper hypothermia, but she wasn't well. I hoped she would warm up fast.

"What if I don't care?"

I didn't understand the context of Arwen's question. "Huh? You don't care to be alive?"

"Marah," she said, "have you ever been so severely depressed while suffering an existential crisis that living seemed like too much work?"

"Oh," I laughed. "Is that what's wrong? You're a bit blue?"

"I'm not just sad." She pushed away from me. "My whole family is dead."

"I'm sorry, Arwen," I said much more gently. "I shouldn't have made light of it." I pushed a lock of her hair back. We lay silent for a moment.

My voice came haltingly. "I got very sad after Gideon was born. I loved him very much, but there were days I wondered if my family would be better off without me. I knew it was ridiculous, but I couldn't help thinking it."

I put my arm around Arwen. Her unwashed hair lay like oily snakes, but I felt the pleasant roundness of her backside against me. The sound of my swallow enveloped the cabin. Everything was slowly warming.

"But you're here. You're strong. You fought against the demons," I said with wonder.

Tears burst from Arwen's eyes. I tried to calm her, but she cried until she had to wipe dripping snot away.

"I'm not a war hero." Arwen shook her head in dismay. She rolled away from me as she began talking. "I wasn't entirely honest with you."

I stiffened and she felt it.

"I'm not even sure it would matter to you, but I guess it matters to me." She hesitated, looking up at the ceiling. "Marah, not everyone in my base was dead when I left. The night before I left I had been on watch and I fell asleep. I was deathly tired. I felt like my body was slowly grinding down to nothing. We'd been on alert for what felt like years, and I was just so tired.

"Power grids were out, so we were down to a few manual systems. The beeping of a battery-operated detector woke me up. I didn't know how long the alert had been going, but I didn't turn the system-wide alarms on in time. We should have evacuated, but there wasn't enough time. I ran, barely making it out of the complex when it happened."

I didn't fully understand what Arwen was talking about, but I let her continue.

"The Deadlights didn't send troops in on foot. There

had been a chance to escape. It was a small, highly targeted strike. By the end, the entire western side of the base was smashed, the air hangar and everything else of value was destroyed. So many had died or deserted by this point that there were only a few dozen of us in the whole base. Most of them were killed. But the building I kept watch in wasn't even hit. If I had stayed long enough to sound the alarms rather than run, I could have saved them."

I understood how that would be worse than dying. Arwen touched her throat as if she could feel the dust and smoke still caught within it.

"I tried to help gather the bodies, but Officer Palmer told me to go. That I was dishonorably discharged." It was quiet. Then she said, "I just thought I would tell you."

We lay for a long time as what she told me turned over and over in my mind. So, there were others out there. Some, at least.

As if she heard me, she spoke, "It used to be you could point at a globe and anywhere you touched, people would be there. Then we had to start doing the opposite—map other camps or working bases. There were so few of us left, we had to mark them down or we'd be lost to each other forever."

Arwen took a deep breath and closed her eyes as she let it out.

Eventually she stirred. "Why did you come?" She rolled to her other side until she faced me. She was still very close. Our knees touched, and I wondered when the last time was that Timothy and I lay together in bed in the daylight.

"I wanted to check on you," I said. "I didn't realize you weren't doing well."

"I'm not." She seemed to want to say more but repeated, "I'm just not."

"Let's—"

"Marah," her voice was firm. "I'm not going to pray about it."

I said okay and slipped out of the bed to begin her chores. I set some snow to melt on the fire for the dishes. While I waited, I picked the dirty clothes off the floor. Snow melts quickly, but everything in the entire cabin needed to be washed, including Arwen, so I divided my time between washing and melting more snow. Arwen lay in bed. What thoughts she had; she chose not to share. My stomach rumbled, but I kept at it. Finally, I got out Arwen's large copper basin. Steam wet my face as I filled it partway with warm water.

"Arwen, it's time to bathe."

Under the covers, she took an exaggerated sigh. I couldn't tell if she was being sarcastic or trying to find the motivation to get up. Whatever it was, she folded back the covers. Out of bed, I could see how exhausted she looked, even though she had been doing nothing more than lying down.

In a fluid motion, she had her pants down around her feet and her shirt off. Even when she lived at my house, I hadn't seen so much of her body. I took that as an indication of how little she cared, but I couldn't help but notice the tautness of her legs. Her stomach and breasts weren't like mine, marred by a decade of pregnancy and infanthood. They were still rounded in place. She was lean and muscular and built for some other purpose than my body was. It was as if we had altogether been designed for different lives.

Arwen squatted in the copper tub, water coming up to just above her belly button. She wet her hands, cupped them, and splashed warm water on her shoulders.

I moved behind her and knelt. I tilted her chin up so I could pour water over her scalp. How many times had I done that same thing for my children? But the routine activity was charged. I was doing it for an adult, and I felt strangely soft inside as I washed her hair. I felt needed like I hadn't in a long time. I handed her a cake of soap and a washcloth and she washed her body in utilitarian movements.

I laughed. "Is that how they teach you to bathe in the army?"

"You don't sit down when there's an alien invasion. Bathing for us was basically running through a room fixed with showerheads."

I asked her about showerheads and she told me while I sliced an onion to brown and set barley to boil. When Arwen was out of the bath, she dunked her bedclothes and swished them around. With more snowmelt, she rinsed and hung them to dry over the fire. Stray splatters steamed on the hot rocks as she pulled on clothes from her closet.

It was unusual that I felt so at home in her cabin. When I called on other women, they went out of their way to host and make me feel like a guest. We were burning through the wood I brought in that morning, so I went to retrieve more. When I came back inside, Arwen had the Bible I had given her on the table.

"Marah, I appreciate what you're doing for me, but I have some questions. I don't mean to seem ungrateful for your help, but there's no one else here who I can ask." She licked her lips. "And, if I'm being perfectly honest, you're the one who saw me…before. It's easy for the others to imagine I'm like them, but I'm not."

I nodded and dished the food. I set it in front of each of us and prayed. Then I took the first bite.

She took a shaky breath.

"Okay, my first question is: Where's my Titan Suit and Kronos L85?"

My heart stopped. I didn't want to keep dodging the subject, but if I told her it wasn't where we left it last summer, it would create all kinds of problems. I couldn't undermine Elder Sister Hetta. I also didn't want to ignite a fight between her and Arwen, because Arwen would surely come out sore. I was very careful with my words.

"We left it in a crevice near the hot springs."

"What hot springs?" she demanded.

I couldn't help but laugh. "North of the community." I told her briefly what trails to take.

"So, why am I bathing in this tiny copper bucket instead of there?"

"I don't think anyone goes to the hot springs, actually. At least, not often. It's a bit of a hike, so you're cold and wet on your walk back."

How Hetta had gotten to them was beyond me. And if she hadn't, that begged the question, who did move Arwen's gear?

"Two days ago"—she interrupted my thoughts—"I finished reading your Bible." I didn't like the way she said *your*. "You already know how Lilium Springs operates is very different than how the rest of the world operated."

I nodded. "And for that, the Lord has protected us."

Arwen swallowed a bite but tilted her head to convey her doubt. "Basic communications across the world, across our country, have completely broken down. There could be people twenty miles from here and we'd never know it."

"But you didn't find anyone else." I didn't mention the people she had left behind.

"I've been having nightmares. I never used to when I was just walking, trying not to think, but it's as if now that I have enough food, now that I know wolves aren't going to eat me, there's space in my head to think about this stuff again.

"When I joined the army, I wanted to fight for my planet, make a difference. But we lost. No matter what we did, we lost. Now that I'm here, I feel safe from moment to moment, but every night I'm terrorized by the idea that there's Deadlight Gardes in the woods, that we're next on their list of people to annihilate."

"God wouldn't let that happen to us." The intensity in Arwen's voice scared me. I wanted to shut out the demons too. I didn't want to think of what *could* happen, but what *was* happening. I had to believe we were safe.

"It would be nice to think I've found the only safe place in the world, but that's unlikely." Arwen pushed her plate aside and picked up the Bible—it lay heavy in her arms. She opened it to a scrap of paper she was using as a bookmark and pointed to a specific verse. "I think I've heard or read this before, but the words were different. Marah, has it ever occurred to you that your leaders could be lying?"

That was so wrong I didn't know where to begin. "They don't lie, Arwen. They fight for the truth. Besides, what would they even lie about?"

"You're going to have a hard time believing this, but in most communities, men are in charge."

"Yeah, you told me that."

"I mean Christian communities. Ones that read the Bible. Because their Bible, the widely accepted version of the Bible, calls God 'He' and speaks about women as if they're servants. A long time ago, I don't know when, but at some point, someone in this community rewrote the entire Bible. You're being controlled, even if you think you aren't."

I tried to speak, but she interrupted me. "Can you think of any reason women should be held in higher esteem than men besides verses in your Bible?"

I didn't reply and she continued, "You were told to think a certain way, so you think a certain way. But Hetta and the rest of them probably have been lying to you. And if she can't be trusted, how can I believe that I'm safe here? Hetta knows way more about the invasion than she lets on."

My dander was up. "Of course she does. She's the leader. She needs to make decisions."

"The fucking US Army didn't know what the aliens were doing here. How would little old Hetta know? She thinks they're going to leave soon and you all can wait the end of the world out here, but you can't. I keep thinking over and over that we need to leave."

I tried to remind myself of the huge break that Arwen was facing and dialed my tone back. "Arwen, even if that's all true, from what you said, there's nowhere else to go. Why would I take my children"—my voice broke—"somewhere else? No plan. Just hoping that's the right thing to keep them alive."

"I don't know. I'm trying to figure all this out, but I can't and that's why I've been in bed for two days!"

I looked at my friend critically. No one had ever spoken to me this way before. Sure, I'd debated scripture with the rest of them, but the idea that the world I lived in was a warped, miniature version of the rest of society scared me. But I felt a ring to her words that could be truth. I decided to put myself out there.

"When I got the Bible for you, I was actually waiting

for Elder Sister Hetta to come back from a prayer walk. I wanted to talk to her…about something. When I opened the closet where the Bibles were, I saw your armor."

Arwen went gravely still. "When was this? Why would she want my bodysuit?"

"I don't know. It was the same night I brought you the Bible."

"Why didn't you tell me?"

"It's not my place to question Elder Sister Hetta. It's not your place either."

"It sure is. In fact, it's your responsibility."

I tried to shake my head, but she kept talking.

"You have kids to take care of. A parent needs to protect their kids by challenging leaders, ensuring they're worthy."

I ruffled at the assumption that I would be careless with my kids' future. "My kids are protected here. Timothy and I make decisions to keep our kids safe. We wouldn't be any better out there with no support. You're here, in *our* community, because it is the safest place. And I know you don't, you know, believe in God, but I do. And I think leaving this place would take me away from Her, and I don't ever want that."

Arwen stared at me. The drying strands of hair lifted and curled around her face while the wet underlayer hung in a damp mass. It was a cloudless winter day. The afternoon sun highlighted each flyaway so her dark hair nearly glowed.

"It's nice to see your hair growing out."

She was taken aback by the sudden shift in conversation. "Oh, I was thinking of cutting it, actually. It's always in the way."

I dropped my spoon. "No, Arwen! You can't. You just finished reading the Bible. Didn't you notice all the verses about a woman's head covering? Our hair is a form of worship."

"I get that you've lived in all of this"—she waved her hand around—"and don't know anything different, but that sounds pretty crazy. Like you said, I don't, 'you know, believe in God,' but even if I did, why would She or He care about the length of hair on my head?"

Arwen was finished with the lunch I had made her, but she made no move to get up and bustle around the kitchen cleaning. Instead, she leaned toward me. I could smell the onion on her breath. Or was that me? Her hand reached out and touched my wrist lightly.

"Marah, the way I see it, they're using all of this conversation and debate about things like hair length to distract you from the important things." She pulled her hand away, the soft touch already faded.

"Who's 'they?'"

"I don't know, the founders? Hetta and her circle? Society? Remnants of the patriarchy? If there's one thing I learned fighting and losing, it's that as individuals, we can't change the road society is driving down. But we can get out of the way. And right now, I don't care about my hair. What

I care about is why Hetta would take my bodysuit."

I couldn't sit in the wooden chair any longer. I stood and stacked the dishes to clear the table. I had a hard time resting when there were chores to be done, and an even harder time sitting, pretending none of this talk affected me.

"What you're saying is basically blasphemy. Elder Sister Hetta is in charge." I dumped the dirty plates in her basin. Arwen could wash them herself.

"Then will you go with me and ask her about it?"

I whirled around. My head shook back and forth before I could form a conscious response.

Arwen lifted her chin. "That kind of fear speaks more to me than anything else you've said in this conversation."

"Arwen, really, you should drop this. I've known these people my whole life. We work together and survive. But I've seen things. I've seen the way the Lord can protect a leader in danger. Our Lord is a vengeful God. Do not threaten our way of life here."

Arwen stood and moved slowly to one of the closets. She took something out and, on her way back to the table, I recognized it as the little papers she showed me the day we first met in the bloom of summer. I knew she had to have kept them, but I never saw her take them out at my home. She laid them out on the table—the landscape, the bits of books, the map—with such care I wondered if I had misjudged the sentimental nature of them.

"I know the people who made these things seem remote to you. They're all dead. And for that you think less of them.

But they're like you and me. Or they were. Just because they believed differently didn't mean the aliens targeted them specifically or that the love they had for their kids was any less."

Tears appeared in her eyes.

"Billions of people dead in a decade. And if we don't find a way to survive, humans may be wiped out entirely. Think past your religion for one moment. I'm worried, but I don't know about what. Marah, I have good instincts for this. I don't know how yet, but I think Hetta is putting the community at risk. I don't trust her. I don't expect you to blindly believe me, but when I come to you with proof, I want you to at least hear me out. Okay?"

I nodded.

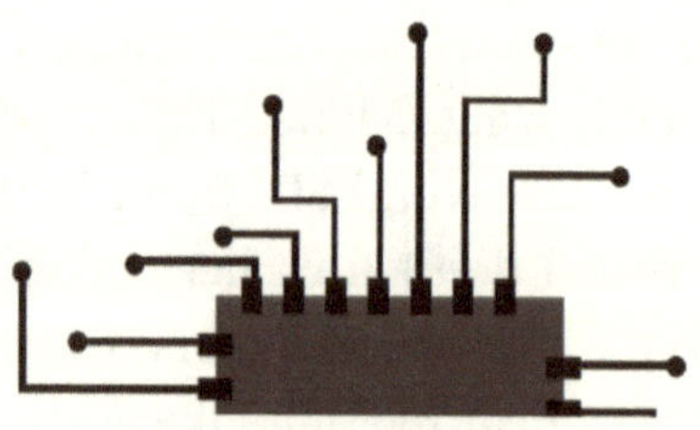

11. The Hot Springs

I'd already admitted it to myself but wasn't dwelling on it: I was scared to go back to Hetta's house. I was a soldier. I'd faced up against the Deadlight Gardes destroying our population. I'd survived three months in the wilderness. And I was afraid of an elderly cult leader. One with white hair and wrinkles.

Which was how I found myself heading north to the hot springs instead of directly to Hetta's house to confront her. The walk was deathly cold. Well, maybe not deathly, but very, very cold.

A woman named Alice had generously sourced warm winter clothes for me. One of her jobs was sorting and disseminating clothing to families and receiving them back as their children grew. Her role wasn't as lofty as food distribution, but she was up there. I'd heard more than one woman approach her at church to beg off extra pairs of clothes ahead of schedule. Alice came across to me as very thoughtful and observant, making sure she gave families what they needed right when they needed it.

As such, my sparse wardrobe was supplemented with heavy jeans, leggings, and bulky sweaters. When outside, I wore thick black boots, red snow pants, a navy down coat, and a hat and mittens. Alice apologized for the mismatched mittens, but I was dismayed most by the red snow pants. The first time I wore them outside, I rubbed them down with dirt. It barely made a difference—anyone within eyeshot would spot me immediately through the forest, making it hard to hunt or hide. Replacing them was high on my mental to-do list.

The brisk cold snapped eagerly at my cheeks. The thought kept coming to me on my long walks that you could grow colder and colder until you died. Winter in the mountains was downright horrifying, but I guessed the same could be said about heat in the South. Heatstroke versus hypothermia. Rattlesnakes versus grizzly bears. Jaguars versus cougars. Aliens versus demons.

I paused, uncertain where the trail was. Marah had given me a thorough description of where the hot springs were and then the hideaway in relation to that, but it didn't occur to me that snow would obscure the well-worn trails. Fortunately, I had been in the area long enough that I could identify the mountains. I had given the peaks nicknames—pointy top, Mt. Doom, the trio. The problem was, I was an insignificant human surrounded by hundred-foot pine trees. I had to maneuver around for an open vantage of the peaks and then correct my course. As it was, I was making bad time.

Though I hadn't seen anyone yet, I had excuses prepared in my head. If I came upon a Brother hunting, I could say I was hiking as per my military training to keep strong. Training had halted because of the weather conditions, but they all understood that I was committed to fitness.

I had yet to secure an invitation hunting or convince one of the men to show me how to make a snare. And since I had no man contributing meat, I received none. If I had a trapline, that wouldn't be a problem. I bet Hetta got all the meat she wanted.

In the white snow ahead, running perpendicular across the direction I was heading, I spotted a set of human tracks. I paused to glance around, listening carefully, but I didn't see or hear anyone. I didn't want to get accidentally shot by a man out hunting, but it'd be easier to avoid that by following behind them rather than circling around. With my mind made up, I approached the tracks. Once I was on top of them, I could see the boot prints were slightly smaller than mine. Okay, not a man, then. I had a good guess who might be wandering the forests unaccounted for by his mother, and I picked up my pace.

Within less than one klick, rocky outcrops popped up among the trees and the incline wound steadily up. I checked each rocky area in case that was the one where my Titan Suit had been hidden until recently. I hoped once I was there, I would learn something to help me frame what was going on. I followed the tracks around one bend where a great steaming pool of water met me.

The steam floated delicately on top of the tranquil pool, fading into the air the higher it went. The pool was flanked by rocks on two sides. I had expected to find the hot springs, but I was taken away by their beauty. They lay placid and smooth in the center of a forest of prickles, pine needles, and jagged rock.

I didn't see James anywhere, but his boot prints tracked back and forth on the ground. I followed a set apart from the rest around the rocks to find an even bigger pond. And there, at the edge, wrapped in ash-colored steam, was James.

As in our first meeting, he was hunched over his work, oblivious to the world around him. He was fully clothed in a parka like me, so I guessed that he wasn't planning to go for a soak.

I called out to him. Ever defensive of his privacy, he flinched at the sound of my voice. His face moved through a rapid series of emotions as he panicked. He glanced back at the water, so I instinctively did the same. Ripples cascaded outward from where his gaze was directed.

"Hi. Sister Arwen?" he asked, though he knew it was me.

"What are you doing up here, James?"

With one last glance at the water, he stood quickly and met me halfway. I looked beyond him but didn't see any tools or play instruments.

"I come here sometimes. To think," he said.

"Do you ever go swimming? That's what people usually come to hot springs for."

James shrugged. "My dad said he took me here once when I was little, but I don't remember it."

"So, people from the community don't come here often?"

"It's a far walk. Plus, I think they're uncomfortable here. Look."

We had fallen in step back toward the smaller pond, and he pointed out a great bubble that came up. It released the scent of sulfur in the air.

"They don't want to come because of the smell?"

He rolled his eyes. "They don't want to come because some people call it the Mouth of Hell. They say it goes all the way down to the Devil."

James and I made eye contact. I guessed he was reading my face for any indication that I thought the statement was true. That poor kid.

I elbowed him. "As scientists, you and I know that's silly, right?"

Relief crossed his face and his mouth relaxed. "Of course, Dr. Arwen." James had developed this shtick where he talked as if we were real scientists. It was a little annoying but also endearing, the way kid stuff is.

"And what in your studies brings you here today?" he continued.

I accepted my role willingly. "Well, Dr. James, I'm on a field hike, looking for particular rock formations. Do you care to join me?"

I felt bad that James spent so much of his time alone. I knew Marah punished him often for skipping his work, and I worried about his safety out there all by himself. After Abigale was attacked and partly eaten, some of the Brothers had tracked the cougar a two-day walk from Lilium Springs. They claimed the cat was passing through to new territories and said it was safe to walk the woods again, but from my point of view there were endless threats.

We were both willing to leave the humid air behind—I felt clammy inside my coat. I had a good idea where the cavern might be. James followed me eastward, stopping to examine interesting rock formations along the way under our pretense. I told him what I knew about how hot springs were formed—that they were exactly what they looked like, pools of water heated from deep within the ground. I wished I knew more about them and hoped that he'd spread the word to the other kids. No wonder no one went there. That must have been why Marah thought it was a good place to store my gear. Who wanted to poke around a portal to Hell?

I asked him just that.

James dropped his gaze to the ground and then darted back up at me, assessing me in some way.

"I found something in the water." He paused. "It was kind of like a fish."

I tilted my head. "A fish? Fish around here don't live in water that hot."

"I know. I think it's a new species."

"Cool," I said.

We walked half a klick more using the rocky ridge as our guide. I wondered what I would say to James if my Titan Suit and Kronos L85 happened to be in place after all, but that turned out to be a nonissue. I spotted the deep but low hole. After so many near misses, I was instantly certain it was the same one. I crouched down and could see all the way to the back. Empty.

Coldness broke over where sweat had built up during the hike. If there was anything I was sure of, it was that Hetta wasn't making this long hike under her own power. It crossed my mind more than once that Marah was the only person who knew exactly where my gear had been stored and when it was put there. But my instincts told me she hadn't ratted me out. I knew she was terrified of being found out to have kept information from Hetta. Though I knew it was uncharitable to my friend, I also understood Marah wasn't concerned with the bigger picture. What she cared about was the day-to-day safety of her family and her standing in the community. As my equipment fell into neither of these categories, I knew she was neutral. The only reason she had helped me hide them in the first place was because she wanted to avoid gunshot first impressions of an outsider wrapped in bizarre clothes.

I suggested to James that we should head back to the community. On our way he talked about Christmas. I gathered there was a lack of belief in Santa Claus in Lilium Springs, but traditions included gift-giving, a pageant that I had already heard a lot about, and a big community meal.

"What do you think I should bring to the meal?" I asked him.

"Huh?" James said, taken off guard. "I don't know. Whatever you want." He was entirely indifferent to the subject.

I smiled, teasing him, "Everyone knows I'm the best cook in the community. What do you think, should I catch a field mouse and BBQ it? Maybe you'd like to help?"

He giggled and we joked back and forth about outlandish dishes to bring to the dinner.

Though my suit was missing, allegedly stolen by an old lady and a mysterious henchman, I felt happier than I had all week. I liked spending time with James. It reminded me of Julian following me around when we were younger. James was the only one in this damn—or blessed, depending on your point of view—community that could think with an inkling of a scientific mind-set. Too bad I wasn't actually a scientist in my former life. I was just a grunt sent out to distract the Deadlight Gardes while better-trained and more-connected individuals launched missiles from control rooms. Not that it did them any good.

I was still standing. That was something. And a kid was

looking up to *me*. I didn't quite understand why in the face of all the terrible loss that had happened and may happen that I could feel happy right then, but I did.

The trails were slippery going downhill, and we both fell on our asses, him more than once. I planned to make sure he got back home, safe under the care of Marah's watchful eye, and then head to my own house to devise a game plan for getting my suit back. Previously, I had visions of barging into Hetta's house and causing a scene, or else sneaking in at night, both ending with my soon-to-follow banishment or fleeing of the community. But in that moment, walking with James, I considered finessing my plans so I'd be able to stay in the community for the rest of the winter, like originally planned. I could ask Marah how to get my suit back in a politically savvy way.

But Marah wasn't home. Timothy was.

We heard him just as he came into view. Timothy was pacing the lot around their house, yelling his son's name. Matty wasn't with him, like the typical shadow he was.

Timothy spotted us, and I could almost see his eyes narrow, though we were half an acre away. Timothy marched forward resigned. I wondered how often this scene played out.

"James, where were you? Sister Arwen, what's going on?"

James didn't respond, so that left me—the responsible adult to answer. "Uh, well…" I had to think quick if I was going to lie or not. "James and I went for a walk in the forest. I'm still not used to the area and needed to be sure where I was going." That was partly true, but damn, did that make me sound stupid.

"And did James not tell you he was expected in his grandfather's workshop this morning?"

I could only shake my head.

"Dad, I didn't—"

Timothy cut him off. "James has responsibilities. I understand your situation is unusual, but Sister Arwen, you can't ask that others forego their duties to help you."

I felt the undercurrent of his tone and wondered if we were talking about more than James.

"Of course. I'm sorry, Brother Timothy."

"Good. Please tell me it won't happen again."

"But, Dad! I don't want to work with Grandpa."

Timothy turned his dark eye upon his son. "Your grandfather has honored you with an apprenticeship. God has gifted you with clever hands, James, but you need discipline if you are to do any good with them. You will go. Apologize to your grandfather and beg that he allow you to continue your apprenticeship."

James started to cry and I felt a strong wave of secondhand embarrassment. I didn't think I could edge away unnoticed.

"I don't want to make dumb chairs. I want to be a scientist!"

I was shocked to see Timothy's mask break slightly. I swore I saw the hint of a smile.

The inkling was gone when he spoke. "Son, go apologize to your grandfather or you will go without dinner tonight." So much for the amusement.

James turned and fled down the path. Timothy exhaled deeply as we watched his son run away.

"Five to one he gets distracted and never makes it there."

"Brother Timothy, I didn't know you were a betting man."

He shrugged his heavy shoulders. Timothy was nearly as tall as I was, but he was thickset, less barrel-chested than corded muscle. "I'm not officially. It's just some of us…" He rubbed his nose with his gloved hand. "Now," he said switching to the issue at hand, "this is the part where you tell me it will never happen again."

I squared up my shoulders in line with his. I liked Timothy, but I didn't like this demeanor one bit.

"James was helping me out."

"But this wasn't the first time." It wasn't a question. Though I had lived with his family, Timothy was always in my periphery. I wondered if that had been a mistake.

"No, but I don't go looking for James. I often find him in the woods. Then we walk back together." My voice was steady because that was entirely true. Then it turned icy. "He says he's not allowed to continue at school. It's obvious he's a smart kid. What else is he going to do with his mind?"

Timothy nodded. The tension dissipated, slightly. "It's true. He's a very smart kid. I often wonder what our community would be like if we let kids school longer. But Sister Arwen, we live in a remote corner of the world. Our focus is on survival."

"And God," I said.

"And God," he agreed. "Listen, I only have a vague sense of what we must seem like to an outsider like you, but it's enough. I've seen the deserted communities. As a young man, I even traveled with my father into them when they were populated. By comparison we're poor. Stupid."

I tried to interrupt, but he waved me off.

"I want a lot for my kids, but the thing I want most is for them to live." He looked me in the eye now. "And for them to live in Lilium Springs, I need to be able to teach my kids to do things a certain way."

I didn't expect the conversation to take this turn. Suddenly, we were talking life or death. I was playing catch-up and tried to read his face, but he was carefully neutral.

"So, I'd appreciate it if you didn't distract James from his duties."

"Sure. He's your kid. Like you said, I'm just an outsider."

He gave a slow smile. "Yeah, but one that Hetta bent over backward to let train with men." Timothy shifted casually to his other foot, but I was acutely aware of the absence of title.

"Where did you and James go anyway?"

I looked northeast into the woods. "The hot springs."

He raised an eyebrow.

"*I* didn't take him there, Brother Timothy. I found him. He was pretending to fish."

Timothy spoke as if he were doing me a favor by giving me some information. "You know, some people think the hot springs are an entrance to Hell."

I smiled tentatively. "So James told me. I obviously don't believe that. James doesn't either. Do you?"

We stared into the woods for a moment. I wondered if Timothy had ever been asked what he believed in, or if Marah always told him what to believe.

Finally, he shook his head. "No. But like I said, it doesn't matter what I think. What matters is what other people in our community think."

"How does it help James?"

"Like I said, my children stay alive."

I was ready to head back to my own house. I was nervous talking to Timothy, as if Marah would walk up and catch us. I also felt bad. Yeah, I wanted James to explore and learn and be a kid. What if instead I had inadvertently led him down a path that would mean he'd never fit in in the only community left on Earth? On the other hand, if I didn't foster his curiosity, maybe that would mean James wouldn't be able to make the hard decisions when he had to. It was making my head hurt and I had to pee.

"I went out for supplies recently." He paused and I looked at him expectantly. "I don't typically go with the groups, I'm usually hunting or working in our fields, but

Brother Logan felt ill so I went instead." He shifted his weight again.

"It's bad, isn't it?" I filled the gaps in for him, reminding him I wasn't someone he had to protect from the truth.

"I was prepared for it to be empty. I wasn't prepared to see signs of a war."

I did my best not to laugh—and I didn't—but I did smile ironically. "Well, we have been in this one for a decade now."

He shook his head. "Not that, I mean signs of violence against people by other people. We found a group of bodies, all with bullets in their heads."

I looked away, as if that would save me from the visual forming in my head. "A group suicide?"

"No, the bodies were spread out. They had clearly been fighting another group. Maybe they were fighting over food. And who knows where the killers are now. Who knows anything about what's out there now?" The intensity of his voice grew. "This might be the only place my kids can live long enough to grow up."

"Okay, I get it. I'll do my part, but go easy on the kid. He already doesn't fit in here."

"None of us really do." Timothy walked away to the path leading out the back of their lot.

I walked in the other direction, back to my own home with plenty to think about. It was a ten-minute walk, but my legs were already tired from navigating the mountainside. I smelled woodsmoke and caramelized garlic wafting from a household as I passed.

Once home, I visited the outhouse and then went inside and left my jacket on while I built the fire. After my breakdown in front of Marah, I had made sure to chop wood regularly and stack it neatly by the door. I was purposeful about bathing and taking the time to cook proper meals instead of eating everything raw or barely seared. Once I started doing those basic things to take care of myself again, I had begun to feel more human. More like I was living and not simply surviving.

There was very little I could do to change the way of life in Lilium Springs. Maybe Timothy had been more like James as a kid than Marah. I guessed he had given up pieces of himself to live here, and I wondered what would be enough of a threat to make someone change who they were—who their kid was.

The cabin was warm enough, so I took my jacket off. The snow I had dragged in had melted and I stepped in the puddle on my way to the window. I stared numbly outside, wondering if I was doing the same.

12. The Pageant

"This is so surreal," Arwen said again for the tenth time. Her eyes were huge as she took in the display on the altar. The back curtain was completely blocked by our homemade creation of Bethlehem. Pretend shops made from fake stone lined the streets of the ancient city. On either side stood separate sets—an outdoor hill with a star-studded black drop and the inside of a home. Everyone in the church was abuzz with the promise of a good show.

"We do this every year," I said patiently. And we had. I was in the Christmas pageant as a child. First as various barn animals, including one-half of a camel, then as a Wise Woman, and finally, in the coveted role of Mary herself.

"Yeah, I bet you do. But Christmas last year I was thirty

feet underground with sixty-some other soldiers in between battles."

"Hmm." I didn't want to encourage this kind of talk at church, but I made a mental note to ask Arwen what that was like being underground. I knew Arwen felt like we lived in a different world, but to me, the world she came from was the different one. Here I was, stomach plump from the Christmas feast and ready to watch my youngest in the play. For me, it was this way every year. It wasn't a substory of the apocalypse. Her world was gone. Mine remained.

Sister Esther bustled over in her winter coat. "Merry Christmas," she chimed. "Sister Marah, I noticed your new hair clip. Is that a Christmas gift?"

I smiled genuinely at the question. "Yes, from my father." He had ingrained a pattern of flowers in the soft wood. All those years out of his house and he still gave me a gift at Christmas.

Sister Esther turned her attention on Arwen. "And do you celebrate Christmas where you're from, Sister Arwen?"

Arwen deadpanned, "Sure, I put up a Christmas tree last year while fighting the demons."

I snorted, but over a room full of chatter Sister Esther didn't hear me.

"That's nice. It's important we take time to remember the birth of Jesus, even in times of tribulation." Sister Esther turned to greet someone else.

I nudged Arwen in the ribs, but caught a glimpse of Rachel a few pews over, her hair in a lavish fishtail braid. It sent a pain to my heart. I was acutely aware of what we had missed that holiday. It was traditional to give gifts to immediate family members, but in addition to my father, I had still given gifts to Rachel, until that year. It started when we were kids. I bolted out of my house one Christmas morning determined to give her my homemade gift and, unbeknownst to me, she had done the same. We met halfway on the path, breathless, gifts in hand for each other. It felt like it was meant to be. I knew from then on that we were destined to be lifelong friends. We had reenacted it every year since, save this one.

The only mar on my Christmas Day was the worry that Rachel had gone out on the path and found it empty. I hadn't made her a gift this year and I definitely hadn't taken the chance to stand outside in the cold only to be rejected. I desperately wanted know if Rachel had gone looking for me, hoping against everything that I'd show up. But I thought it unlikely. Things were peaceful between us, but we were hardly talking. How could we exchange gifts?

The lanterns in the back of the church dimmed and people found their seats. Timothy sat next to me, Matty and James at his side. They were too old to be in the pageant, which was only for school-aged children.

Young Lacey played Mary, and I covertly (a word I had learned from Arwen) eyed Matty to gauge his response. She was a Godly girl and, Lord willing, one of my top choices for Matty. I couldn't read anything from his bushy eyebrows in the dark though.

I was always moved by Mary's story. She felt like a kindred spirit—chosen by God, gifted a son, not a daughter, who against all odds changed the world.

The scene of the three Wise Women opened on the hillside with a flock of sheep made up of the littlest performers. I spotted Gideon pretending to eat the green carpet that served for grass. His golden hair trembled as he took to his role with unusual seriousness and vigor. I took it as a mark of maturity in the face of responsibility, but it also made me sad. My baby was growing up.

The play was generally the same from year to year—there was only so much creative licensing one could take. Next to me, Arwen stiffened during Mary's dialogue. I hoped she was moved by God, but knowing her, she was stifling some kind of wisecrack.

The Christmas pageant closed to thunderous applause. Within moments, Gideon, my little lamb, came hurtling down the aisle toward me and Timothy. James gave his little brother a pat on his fluffy wool head. It was a happy moment but tinged by sadness. I felt time passing too quickly. How many more years would Gideon participate in the play? And then I'd be further removed from another important part of community life. I didn't mind growing older, leadership harkening at the end of life, but I mourned any change to life with my little ones at home.

Some families had already left to get home ahead of the night's deep, biting cold. Sister Rhonda and the other teachers tidied the props and costumes. The bulk of the set would be torn down by a group of Brothers ahead of next Sunday and put into storage until next year.

Of the people left, there was a rush of chatter, everyone hesitant to go home and thus end the Christmas season. I watched Rachel pack her children into warm jackets. She didn't look my way once, so I didn't try to make eye contact.

Brother Barry held Arwen in conversation. I wondered if Arwen knew what he was considering—her. Though Arwen held fast to her solitary home, I knew it was only a matter of time before the few single men in the community put their bids in. Lightly, to see how it went, but then more seriously as the playing field of suitors was established.

As previously arranged, Timothy bundled up the boys and headed home with them. The Christmas feast in the side room had already been cleaned up, but Sister Bethany had asked that I lock down the church. I had recently taken the role on at the end of church services, and I was delighted to receive my first key. To me, the key was a symbol of the leadership and power I was amassing in our community. I thought of the tangle of keys Elder Sister Hetta had in her drawer and quickly backed away from the thought, remembering the uncomfortable evening at her house.

It took a good long while for people to leave. Those with sleepy kids were long gone, but the older couples were happy to chat. Brother Barry lingered. I circled the room, making last goodbyes as people headed out.

"Sister Arwen, could you help me out with the last of the cleanup? Sorry to interrupt, Brother Barry."

Arwen quickly agreed and Brother Barry left on a promise to teach her how to make a snare. Was that what they were talking about? I was disappointed.

He left with the rest and I turned to Arwen. "Snares? As in hunting snares? I thought he was interested in you."

"Oh, he is for sure. It's all in how you turn that interest around. He's going to teach me how to build a snare and Brother Marc promised earlier this week to make me some fishhooks."

I leaned in. "And are you *interested*?" I emphasized the last word.

Arwen grinned. "Yeah, in the fishhooks. I'd like to try ice fishing."

I shook my head. "Come on, help me check the doors and put out the lanterns."

We circled, turning off lanterns. Arwen broke apart the fires in the fireplaces and I double-checked that the side rooms and back office were all tidy and darkened. Though the sanctuary was nearly dark, it wasn't yet cold in the wake of the press of bodies there a moment ago. I looked around for Arwen and thought she had left when I spotted her on the altar. I made my way over.

"I always wanted to visit Bethlehem," Arwen said as she fingered the stage props.

"Really?" I brightened.

Arwen's teeth gleamed in the darkness. "No. That is, not specifically, but I did want to visit the Middle East when I was younger. I thought it'd be neat to see deserts like mine, but ones that felt entirely foreign."

I didn't know where that was and said as much as I drifted up the stairs to the altar, feeling the thrill of a slightly bent but unimportant taboo. Well, I did have to check that everything was secure, didn't I?

Arwen continued, "The way I heard it though, most cities looked the same. I never left the country, of course, but it sounded like cities across the globe were just skyscrapers and shops and roads. The only difference was the language on the signs."

"That can't be true."

Arwen shrugged. "We'll never know." She walked the stage. "It must be strange being in those cities now. All burned-out and quiet."

I waited for her to say she'd never know that either, but she didn't. Instead, she went in the little barn that sheltered Jesus's manger.

Her voice boomed through the sanctuary. "Lord, my Mother, Giver of Life, thank Ye for this babe. But could Ye not have made he a she?"

I recognized her satire of Mary's monologue and Arwen smirked at me. She knew I hoped for a girl baby and thought me frivolous for it. For once, I didn't care. Arwen settled on the edge of the stage, legs dangling over the very spot in which I knelt in prayer on numerous occasions.

As if she heard my thoughts, she said, "It feels a little naughty, doesn't it? It's been a long while since I felt like a teenager. Not that my mom said much was off-limits."

"How's this for off-limits?" I stood and retrieved the bottle of communion wine from behind the pulpit. I laughed at Arwen's shocked face. I laughed some more and then winced as spit flew out and landed lightly across my hand. I hoped she didn't notice.

"Oh, it's fine, Arwen," I reassured her. "There's nothing sacred about the communion wine or bread. It's a symbol. I've had leftovers before."

"That's surprisingly progressive."

I sat by her on the edge and proved what I said with a sip. When I offered her the bottle, she took a great gulp. When the bottle left her lips, she shivered.

"Marah, why do you call me by my first name? Isn't that improper?"

I shrugged but kept eye contact to gauge her response. "I guess I thought we were more than neighbors." I didn't have to hesitate long to find what I was looking to say. In a lower voice I said, "You're not of this place. Some days, I still wonder if you're an angel of the dark sent to torment me. Make me question everything."

She grinned in response, teeth shining from the remaining candle. It reminded me of a wolf, lip curled back in thought, debating if attack was worth the risk.

I leaned in, felt Arwen's breath on mine where they mingled in the dark. She smelled of roasted vegetables and savory ham. Arwen wasn't like the men I knew but not like the women either. My kiss with Rachel was soft, if unwelcoming, and I wondered what Arwen would feel like.

Taste like. I swallowed and knew she heard it, knew she heard my assessment. Arwen didn't move a muscle. She didn't draw away either. Neither did I.

I leaned in and touched my lips to hers.

Lightning flashed in my stomach. Her lips felt hot and parted under mine, the way they were supposed to. I couldn't help but compare the kiss to the one I had shared with Rachel when she pushed away from me, or even Timothy and the way he always pushed forward, wanting more, pushing past the kiss to take me in bed.

Arwen's tongue darted into my mouth, and I reached out and pulled at her shoulders, pressing my chest against hers. When we finally broke, she stayed close to me, her lips only an inch from mine. My mouth tingled; a bloom of soreness stretched across my lower lip.

The dark shadows that enveloped us stirred at her voice. "Marah…you're married."

Was that an improvement over "Marah, you're gross?" I wasn't sure. I took a shaky breath. She leaned back while I gathered myself, studying her face in the dim light cast by candle and weakening coals.

"Sometimes I feel like I don't fit in here."

A shadow came over Arwen's face that I couldn't read. She pulled back and ran a hand over her face. "That doesn't change your obligations to your family. It's not fair to Timothy. You should talk to him about it."

"I'm not supposed to voice doubts to my husband," I said, fighting against my anger. "I'm supposed to lead my family. If I were to cause anyone to backslide, they would spend eternity in Hell because of me."

Arwen took a deep breath through her nose, all amorous intent gone.

"I've tried to describe to you the dangerous nature of this cult you live in. I'm sure it seems completely ordinary, but one group of people shouldn't be holding power over another group of people. It's sexist."

She'd already described that word to me—treating someone differently just because of their sex—but I didn't understand how that could be a bad thing when it was what God told us to do. Men were not spiritually fit to lead the house. Women were created in God's image. She gave us the power.

"You should know, Marah, cheating on a spouse isn't okay out there either. If you made a commitment to another person that you'd be exclusive, you should honor that. If you feel differently now, you should talk to him."

My face bloomed with anger. I didn't understand how things got so off track in the matter of minutes. "Timothy doesn't make decisions for me. I make decisions for him."

"Oh my God, what was I thinking?" Arwen stood quickly. "It's like trying to reason with a bully, but the bully looks nothing like you expect them to so you keep forgetting that you can't reason with them. Then I remember this whole place is warped and you're another victim of it. And even Hetta's a victim in some way." She made a guttural sound in her throat. "But you're all grown-ups. Even if you've never seen anything else, you should be able to *reason* your way out of this."

I stood up too and pushed in toward her. "Stop, Arwen. You think you know everything. You know what's right or wrong, but how could you? Oh, that's right, you're special, magically born with the knowledge of good and evil." I waved my fingers around to hit home with the sarcasm. Then I pointed at her in accusation. "*You're* regurgitating what *you've* seen out there, and guess what, *they're all dead.*"

In an instant, I knew I had gone too far. I was talking about her parents. Her brother and sister. They were dead. And I had rubbed her face in it.

I thought she'd storm out, but instead Arwen froze like I'd never seen before. She didn't freeze with shock. She crouched slightly, tensed for an incoming punch. Her expression went so flat it was fierce. I felt my stomach draw up as I watched her respond to some unseen threat. She slowly put a finger to her lips and grabbed my arm tight to keep me from moving.

I cocked my head, straining to hear someone else moving inside the church or at the front door. I should have been home by then but there wouldn't be a problem unless someone actually *saw* what we were doing. Or heard. Damn it, how loud was our argument? How could I be so reckless?

Then I felt it before I heard it. Terrible buzzing rang through my bones, nearly as distinct as when the demons had come months ago. Arwen let go of my arm, the release of pressure causing sensation to flood into my hand. She walked soft-footed to the only window on the western side. She didn't hide around the edge and look outward, she crouched down and looked up.

I yanked on her arm and shouted, "We need to get to one of the cellars, quick."

Arwen spun toward me, eyes blazing. "Marah. Shut. Up."

The now-audible buzz zoomed somewhere above our heads, not quite over our stretch of woods. She shivered with fear and I felt my heart stop. I wanted nothing more than to be home, my children safe and sleeping in their beds. If I must hear such an unearthly noise, I should only do it while praying feverously over my children.

I didn't know if I could move as quietly as Arwen, but I couldn't just stand there. If the face of the Devil was in the sky, if I could finally see what we were up against…I had to see it for myself.

It felt like it took minutes for me to make my way quietly to Arwen's side, heart pounding in my ears. I crouched down next to her.

She whispered to me, near silently, mouthing the words in the darkness against my ear. "Take me up to the steeple."

Every ounce of my body resisted that idea. Go up there? *By them?* I didn't know what was going on, but I had to trust Arwen. She knew these things. She was alive after all this time. She followed me, her hand gripping my arm again in the pitch-blackness. For the first time that night, I felt cold.

Tendrils of icy freeze clawed at my exposed neck, which had flushed with the heat of desire and anger moments ago.

I led Arwen through the labyrinth of rooms, trying not to trip. I couldn't hear the noise anymore, but the silence was equally oppressive. I felt as if the dark and the silence were smothering me. Arwen shook my arm and I realized we were at the door to the steeple, me dazing in front of it. I slid the latch open and held the door for her. Arwen moved ghostlike up the stairs. I didn't want to go, but I couldn't stand to be left alone.

I followed the spiraling stairs up, Arwen already out of my sight. I caught up to her at the top. There was hardly room for the two of us on the tiny platform. She stood pressed against the railing, as if terrified of touching the rope tied to the bell tongue. I too was abnormally fixated on it and slid against the sides. I looked in the same direction as Arwen.

There, a light, tinier than I expected, in the distance. I had always associated light with God, but I was eager for the wide night to swallow that light whole.

"It's a scout ship," Arwen whispered to me, or maybe to herself.

"The ones that passed by before were much larger. They shook the whole house."

The light stopped north of my home. I watched it hover in the air, miles away.

"What is it doing?"

Arwen shook her head. "I can't say for sure. Sometimes

it seems as if they're collecting information. Or, if they stay for a time, they're usually off-boarding a squadron of Deadlight Gardes."

The light moved swiftly away and I felt a shift in Arwen's stance. We stood together, watching the light recede westward until I was all but certain that the pinprick I stared at was fully imagined.

I was near frozen to the bone yet sweat stood out on the back of my neck.

Arwen turned to me, her face cloaked in shadows. For the second time that night, I felt her exhalation of relief hot against my cheek and she took my lips unto hers. I yielded under the power and heat of her mouth, barely sating the bloodthirst of the animal within me.

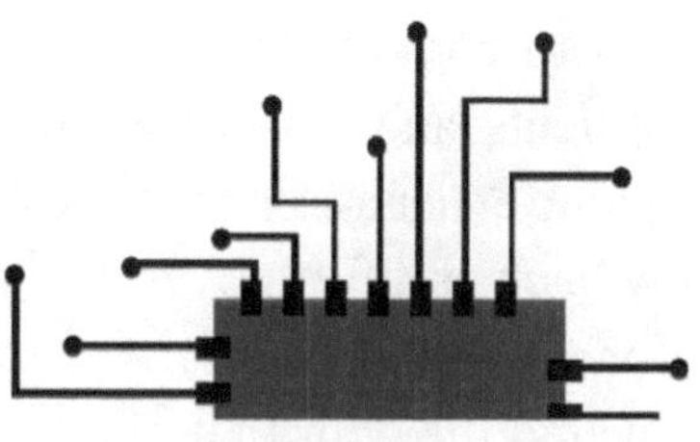

13. Tête-à-tête

Hetta's living room was designed for comfort if not class. The couches were decades old but engorged on fluffy batting and springs. They were low enough for an aging leader to sit in with a ramrod straight back, giving a cold shoulder to all that comfort. The fire crackled pleasantly and homemade tea—a blend of fragrant flowers and grasses— was served alongside tiny, iced cakes, but I was entirely uncomfortable amid the four Elders. I'd rather be in the middle of a battlefield on my own terms than in Hetta's arena of carpet and sweets.

It was the third time I'd been to Hetta's house in the two weeks since Christmas. The first was the night I left the church, completely panicked. I banged on Hetta's door until she woke up—I wasn't worried about the noise; the Deadlight Garde ship was already too far away to hear my human skittering. I was more worried about the future. Days, weeks, hours, I didn't know when they'd be back, but in this world it only stood that eventually they'd root us out. I had to make Hetta see that. She needed to get rid of the idea that we'd be able to fight off even a single Deadlight Garde. I wanted to convince her to immediately limit her people's movements and activity to remain hidden, then start talking about evacuation plans. I didn't like that the scout ship flew back and forth over the woods to the north, as if looking for something.

Hetta answered the door that night with clear eyes and disheveled hair. Her thin white locks spilled down her shoulders in a tangle and she shivered in her cotton nightgown, but her cadence told me she'd been awake. That was good, she had to have heard the ship hovering over this sector of the Rocky Mountains.

"What is the meaning of this, Sister Arwen?" She looked upon my form in the darkness, not with fear but annoyance.

"The demons. They were here."

Hetta's right eye, the stronger of the two, glanced upward to the sky, but quickly, as if she couldn't help admitting she was worried about them too, and then back down at me in examination when nothing was up there. I held firm in her doorway. I was not going to my own house until we had settled a few things. She allowed me as far as the roomy foyer but made clear I was being a nuisance. I wondered which was worse: Christmas at Lilium Springs or the one the year before at the base. At least then I had allies and a common enemy.

"You're mistaken, Sister Arwen. I've been awake, praying, this whole night, and have heard nothing. You probably had a night terror."

"No, I didn't. I felt the ship's velocity. Marah and I *saw* the ship's lights." I tried to explain what we saw, the flight pattern, the ship type, but like a bulldog with a bone in sight, Hetta licked her lips.

"You and Sister Marah? What do you mean?" she questioned.

I paused. The explanation of the aliens' behavior was ready on my tongue but I was thrown by the intensity of her question about Marah. As casually as I could, I said, "I was helping Marah lock up the church. We both saw the ship. She'll tell you what she saw. I can go get her."

Just as easy as pie, Hetta's attitude shifted. "Perhaps I heard a disturbance too." Hetta patted her wisps of hair back. "My hearing's not what it used to be."

I cocked my head, trying to figure her out. Then it hit me in a bloom of anger. She was gaslighting me. She pretended the faint vibrations hadn't happened—because life would be easier if they hadn't—until she knew there was evidence to support my statement.

She must have seen the conclusion on my face, because she quickly stated that we'd talk about the matter in the morning. The only acquisition she made that night was she'd give the command to silence the bells over the church. There would be no more ringing on Sunday mornings or at noontime. I had a list of other demands I thought would keep us safe—well, safer—but she refused to make any concessions, citing the freedoms of her people as God-fearing women and men. As if I was more of a threat to their way of life than the alien ship that had come perilously close to the settlement.

After a second failed conversation with Hetta that bordered on rudely short, I was driven to query each household in the community. Did they hear anything that night? Did they see anything? When was the last time they saw something unusual in the area? I made myself very unpopular very quickly with claims that we were not as safe as they all felt. Rhonda's husband sent me away, saying I was scaring the children. And I never got those fishhooks from Marc. I wondered if he counted me as a narrowly avoided misstep.

All of that cost time. It was a relief that Deadlight Gardes hadn't arrived to slaughter us all, but I didn't relax in the passing days. I kept at it until I heard Marah's stepmother Kristy mention that the four Sisters were in conversation at Hetta's house, and I made myself at home in their meeting.

Which was why Bethany fixed me with a cold look as she stirred a great glug of cold milk into her tea, utterly nonplussed through my account of what I saw and heard. I explained in detail how I had helped Marah close up the church when we heard something strange, rushed up the steeple stairs, and saw the lights disappear to the west.

At this point, the council of four didn't have a hard time believing that what happened had happened. They just didn't care. My only chance was to stare down the elderly. I was the one who had seen the monsters kill. I knew what their technology could do. But as always, the old biddies picked the wrong leads to follow.

"What I don't understand is why you were at the church so late that evening," Hetta said. "The Christmas pageant was over. It sounds like when you heard this faraway sound, the rest of us were in bed."

I had been through it a hundred times in my head, wondering if someone had seen us, if anyone could have possibly seen us kiss, but I was certain there was no opportunity. It was dark. I could hardly see what was happening. Unbidden, the feel of Marah's mouth against mine came back to me.

I swallowed before speaking. "I was helping Sister Marah close the building and I asked her some questions about the play. We got to talking about the performance. The story."

Bethany peered over her glasses, not unfriendly, but I could tell she cared about the truth. Unlike Marah with her warped understanding of her responsibility to others—I still hadn't sorted my own feelings out.

"I'm curious what a former outsider like you thought

about the story of Mary's unlikely motherhood. Tell me one of the questions you asked and what Sister Marah's answer was."

In unison, the other crones turned to look at me. I wasn't fooled. This was an interrogation, plain and simple. I only hoped the Sisters hadn't talked to Marah privately beforehand and, if they had, that Marah stuck close enough to the truth to give me a chance to corroborate her words.

I sighed, hoping it sounded more like I was impatient to move on to other topics than scared. "We talked about Bethlehem." That was true, even if only a little. "I asked Sister Marah if she knew where it was located—she did not. You may want to get a world map up in here.

"We also talked about Mary, and how she was called to give God a son when God could not birth a human son Herself." That last bit was a remnant of a former conversation, but I hoped I did well enough with the lingo to make it convincing.

Before they had the chance to continue questioning me in that vein, I shifted the topic. "Brother Barry was one of the ones who reported to me that he had heard the sound as well. He said it chilled him to the bone." He had also said it sounded like the laughter of a thousand demons, but I didn't think that would help my case.

"And Sister Alice was returning from the pit latrine and actually saw the lights." This last sighting was particularly damning. Alice lived on the farthest western edge of the settlement. I could only deduce that had she been seen by the ship we'd all be dead.

I saw Sisters Candace and Jackie share a glance. Alice was approaching service on the council herself. From what Marah told me, Alice was an honest woman and well respected—not one who you would expect a demon to get close to.

That must have been enough to scare them because Hetta nodded and said, "That settles it."

"It does?" I fought to keep the shock off my face.

"Yes. The demons came perilously close to us, but God's hand protected us. She always does." Her words were slow. Labored. It seemed to me that she wasn't well, but if the other Elders thought Hetta's inability to speak without gasping was worrisome, they didn't show it.

"Due respect, Elder Sister Hetta," I began, "but God has not protected the rest of the Earth. What is less than two hundred people"—I gestured to the forest outside her windows—"in the face of the annihilation of our species? I'm not going to fall into the trap of thinking we're safe simply because this area is remote enough not to have been attacked yet. We don't know what the Deadlight Garde was doing here or why they sent a scout ship. They weren't simply flying over—they were looking for something."

The crone shook her head. "You have it wrong, soldier. God told me She preserved other holy establishments like ours." She breathed heavily as she looked at each person in turn.

I wasn't usually this close to her and I felt clammy as

memories of the dinner I had with Hetta came back.

"God has promised the demons will depart once they collect the rest of the sinners. We shall inherit the Earth."

"We shall inherit the Earth," the others echoed.

I was seriously spooked. Hetta was going to set all this pesky talk about the end of the world aside and declare that she and her people had no need to fear because of God's invisible force field. And on top of that, the world and all its winged fowl, creeping things, and beasts of the Earth was going to become their own regular Garden of Eden.

My blood boiled and it made me bold. And hopefully cunning. "Elder Sisters, when I arrived here, I left my possessions at the edge of the parameter of Lilium Springs. I worried I might be harmed or misunderstood by the people here, and I chose to leave my possessions behind in case I had to flee an attack. Forgive me, I did not know this was sacred ground."

Bethany's eyebrows lifted. She looked at the others to read their responses. Candace and Jackie looked tired as always. Hetta was perfectly neutral, though spittle gathered in one corner of her mouth.

"I've since returned to the place," I continued. "My possessions were gone. However, Sister Marah told me they are here in your house, Elder Sister Hetta." I hated bringing Marah into this, but I was partly counting on her clean reputation to help me out.

The other three looked to Hetta. So, they didn't know about my Titan Suit and Kronos. I felt vindication rise at outing Hetta and catching her unawares. I specifically wanted to broach the topic in front of witnesses, ones Hetta was at least partly beholden to, to try to force her wrinkled hand.

Instead, Hetta nodded slowly, as if she expected this. "The Lord our God came to me in a vision. She told me of the weapons you had hidden. She said if they were left unaccounted for, a child would bring harm to themselves with them." With her speech, the spit lengthened into a slimy rope.

I realized with a shock that Hetta must have had another stroke. Her symptoms weren't simply due to age, they were progressing much too quickly. Bethany reached over with a cloth and wiped the side of Hetta's mouth. She looked at me, challenging me to say something about Hetta's state.

I wouldn't be pulled off topic. I refocused. I knew how heavy that bodysuit was. "I left my supplies in the vicinity of the hot springs, more than an hour's hike. They're very heavy and cumbersome to carry. Who moved them?"

Bethany looked at Hetta in interest. Hetta looked wary. I could tell I had touched a nerve.

"It is not for you to question the Elder Sister," Candace barked. "Thank the Lord Elder Sister Hetta received the vision. You never should have brought outsider technology anywhere near our community. It's taboo."

I ignored Candace's outburst and stared into Hetta's eyes.

"I want my equipment back." My voice was steel.

"Your request is noted. As leader of this community, this matter is under my discretion. You left your…supplies for a reason, so that God could give them to me. The weapon is too dangerous for one such as you to wield. Not that it seemed to have done the war effort any good."

I heard a gasp as my brow darkened. I felt the confines of Lilium Springs tighten around me. No more. I'd break into her house tonight, take my suit, and run. This place was no longer safe. And Hetta was growing more damaged than ever.

"Your supplies are not here anyway," Hetta continued. "I had them taken far away from the community. There's no need for them here."

"You had no right," I said. Red anger grew behind my eyes. I stood, looming above them all.

Jackie swiveled in my direction. "You will not question the Elder Sister's actions. She is the leader of Lilium Springs. She had every right to act as she did for the betterment of us all."

A bang and a gust of wind came from the front door. Marah staggered in, snow falling from her boots. She had a desperate look on her face, her ears painfully red. Wherever she came from, she hadn't thought to dress against the cold.

She wasn't looking at Hetta when she spoke, but she spoke to me. "James is missing."

I took half a step back. "What do you mean? He's probably out exploring."

Marah fell to the floor and Candace spilled lukewarm

tea all over her dress. Instead of drying herself, she gaped at Marah. Marah shook her head and looked down. The door was still open and, though the wind was light, the fireplace flickered.

"Last night we had a fight. James said he wasn't going to apprentice with my father any longer. He said he wanted to go back to school. That if we didn't let him, he was going to leave." Marah knelt on all fours, mouth gaping. "Timothy shouted himself hoarse and James cried himself to sleep."

My heart broke for James being ostracized by his family for something so simple.

"But what makes you think he's gone, Sister Marah?" Bethany spoke with such deliberate care, that I wondered how many young women she'd comforted in her long lifetime. How long had it taken her to perfect cutting to the core of the problem?

Marah looked up, face swollen, snow shining in her hair. "I walked Gideon to school this morning. James was supposed to be with Timothy all day, but when I got back, Timothy was there looking for James. He had snuck away. All his stuff was gone. His clothes, his little notebooks. It's all gone. My baby is gone." Great racking sobs took over Marah's body.

I closed the gap between us and put a caring but platonic hand on Marah's shoulder. I shouldn't have done that. She turned and fell into my legs, sobbing and murmuring prayers all the while.

Hetta was silent. I watched her out of the corner of my

eye as I tried to calm Marah. Bethany was the one who took charge. She ordered Jackie to have Godwin collect the men to meet at the church.

"Tell them to dress with care and bring a bag of supplies," Bethany shouted to Jackie's disappearing frame.

Hetta nodded her agreement. "Just so."

Jackie was the youngest of the four, but she wasn't fast by any means. I knew why Bethany hadn't sent me—I was untrustworthy. All the work I had done to find safety and security within Lilium Springs was gone in the span of one conversation, if it had ever existed at all.

I crouched down by Marah. I whispered, "I think I know where James is. I'll go now."

She gave me a pleading, wordless look and pushed me from her to make haste.

I threw my coat on and grabbed the hat and gloves I would don on the way. I didn't know if I could find the place on my own again, but I'd travel faster without the bureaucracy in attendance. Any time lost equaled steps that took James farther and farther away from the community and into the wilderness of the Rocky Mountains, into the barrenness of a deserted world, into the territory of the demons.

But I guessed James would make one stop before he left for good. I had a suspicion that whatever brought James to the Mouth of Hell would bring him back one last time.

14. Left Behind

I'd been praying to God ever since I came home and Timothy asked where James was hiding. When I answered the obvious, that he wasn't with me, that I didn't know, Timothy thought I was protecting my little boy. I should have protected him more.

Gideon was at school, completely unaware that anything was wrong. I told Timothy to take Matty to Sister Henrietta's and make the boy swear to stay there until I or his father came for him. Once my other children were secure, I ran, faster than I had ever run since I was a child myself. My breath was gone and my body was slick with sweat underneath my winter coat by the time I arrived at Elder Sister Hetta's. I told the one person that could bring

James back to me. My burden not yet absolved, I raced to Rachel's. I didn't care if we were fighting or not friends any longer. I needed her help.

She answered the door, at first with glad surprise, but when the words tumbled out of me, she looked around in fright. I could see her counting her own kids. Never mind that it was mine that was missing—it was a mother's instinct to project any terror she hears of onto her own brood. The realization that the mishap hadn't yet happened to one's family is always bittered by the knowledge of another way to lose your family—one that always existed in the world but that you weren't privy to. I saw the moment Rachel cleared her mind. She had to. I didn't care what thoughts seized her. I didn't stop talking. The pleas spilled from me until she agreed to gather Gideon at the end of school. She promised—I made her swear to God Herself— that Gideon would stay with her until I came for him.

I did my duty. My two accounted-for children were safe until I or Timothy retrieved them. My Eldest Sister would direct the search party. And the only woman in Lilium Springs who could go searching, the only adult that James would talk to, had promised she'd go. Every man would drop his tools to comb the woods. For me, there was nothing more to do but pray. The most important job, but the least fulfilling. Not for the first time, I resented the obligation that kept me home. What good was it to be God's voice if I couldn't be Her hand? It would be someone else who would find my boy, gather him in his tears. I—his mother—would be the last to know he was found.

I felt overcome with my own presence—a presence in that moment that I fully detested. I grabbed a pillow off the chair and battered it against the wall. Once. Twice. Again and again the dull sound of padded cloth on wood resonated through the cabin, pathetic as my own incompetence.

I couldn't stay in the house. I pulled my boots and coat back on. The temperature hovered above zero degrees all week, which was cold but not so cold that James would freeze. He knew to keep moving, to shelter from the wind while he regained his strength.

My worry was not that he'd die out there but that he'd escape from me forever and be damned to wander the Earth alone. He was truly gone from my life. I was blinded to the truth until now; my little boy was ten times more capable and determined than most of the Brothers. By trying to avoid his eventual banishment, I had stifled him to the point of seeking the punishment on his own.

Outside, the winter sun cast muted glares off the dull snow. We hadn't had fresh snowfall in over a week. The ground was tracked over with many layers of boot prints. I knew Timothy was out there trying to follow James's tracks, but it might not be possible. What did I know of tracking anything, even my own child?

I set off on the trail. If I had a chance encounter with James, it could be the only opportunity I'd get to make things right with my son.

Along the edge of the barley field, I found Brother

Godwin trudging down the trail with his own pack on his back. His great jowls were turned down in solemnity and I could feel him take in my red eyes and tearstained cheeks. I didn't like appearing weak in front of him, but wouldn't any woman cry if her child was missing? Why was I concerned in that moment with how I appeared to others?

Brother Godwin paused as he neared me. "I'm on my way now, Sister Marah. Don't you worry, God will help us find your boy."

I nodded but had no words to utter. He reached out and brushed my shoulder briefly. Maybe I shouldn't have stood so close to him, but the comfort was welcome. I had so often disregarded Brother Godwin, and here he was, ready to meet the dangers of the wilderness to find my boy at a time when the entire community was unnerved by the recent demon flyover.

He nodded back and continued on his way.

As I walked, last night's scene ran through my head— James crying that he hated his life; that he was better off dead than living here with us. It had hurt to hear but I hadn't worried too much once he faded into sleep. Every young person goes through phases of pain and searching. As he slept, I sat with a cup of tea in my lap, thinking of my own woes. I was taken with my own needs instead of my child's.

I severely underestimated James's resolve to live on his own if that meant he could live the way he wanted. It was silly, really. What did that boy think he could do all by himself away from his family?

And now Timothy, my wounded life partner, was more scared for me than angry even though I had betrayed him. Had I risked banishment, or worse, for a few fleeting moments of pleasure?

"Oh, dear Lord, forgive me," I whispered. I put my hands to my head. Moments ago, I felt completely devoid of life but now tears slipped down my ice-cold cheeks.

Timothy ran one hand down his own face, pausing at the edge of his bearded chin. We stood for a moment in silence. I could see the tug of the search pulling at him, and yet he stayed as I racked my head as to how I could make everything go together, fit together again.

"Marah, I don't say this lightly," Timothy's words were shaky. I could tell they didn't come naturally to him. "You know in this moment what it is like to lose a child. I pray, I pray we can get James back and build a better family. We can all do better." He looked me dead in the eyes. "But, if you continue with Arwen, you will have no family left to you. I would be entirely within my rights to tell the Elder Sisters about what I saw and what is going on between the two of you. And Marah, I don't know what they would do to you. All I know is, you won't have the children any longer. And you may not even have your life."

Timothy stepped past me on the trail and walked on.

Again and again, I was the one to be pushed aside. I was supposed to be a leader, *I* was supposed to be the difference. Instead, I was treated like a child.

Watching him race down the trail, his steps quick to get

started on the search for our son, I felt bitterness. I was distraught by the problems I had brought down upon myself, but for the first time I asked myself if they had to be problems at all. James ran because he didn't fit in. Arwen expressed disgust and disbelief at every new insight into our community. Rachel held the power to destroy my life, and it was only through her benevolence that I still stood. Perhaps it wasn't any of us that were the wrong things, the broken things. Perhaps it was Lilium Springs itself.

And still, Timothy's words struck fear into my heart. I started on the path back home, where I would wait, hoping someone else found my child, hoping simply for another day with my family.

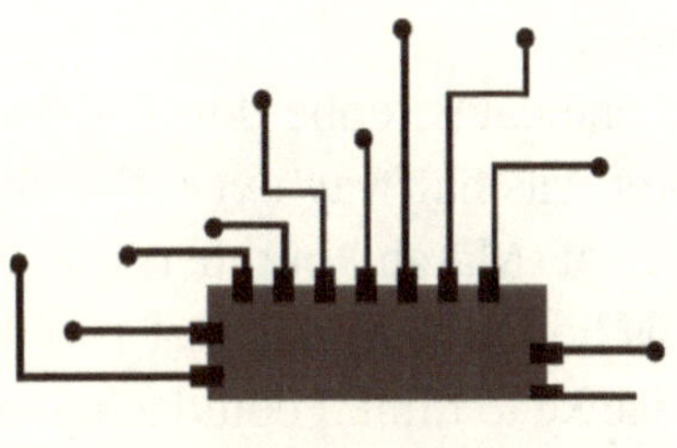

15. The Secret

I had moved through the past several months in a swaddle of provided food and easy warmth. I had given up so much, risked so much, for those comforts. Lilium Springs had stagnated my brain. It was easier to find clarity in moments of urgent crisis. I had been trained to shut everything out and focus on staying alive, keeping others alive, taking out the enemy if possible—a box I'd never been able to check despite my long service.

The last time I went to the hot springs, it had taken an hour. The urgency of my mission hastened me as I ran through snow and ice. If I had my Titan Suit I would have covered the ground in half the time. Damn Hetta to Hell for hiding it. When I got back, one way or another, I was going to make her tell me where it was. Though I'd gone months without its protection, I sorely felt its absence in that moment.

When I found James, he would come with me, I was sure of that. If I couldn't make him see how silly this all was—I couldn't survive on my own out there, how could a scrawny little kid?—I'd carry him back, an easy feat even without my suit.

And then, one catastrophe down, I'd get my stuff and head out. Winter was halfway over. I'd take my chances. I felt…protective of Marah, but her life was here. Mine wasn't. She was bound to things that I couldn't let encircle me. It was a mistake to think I could adopt a way of life that wasn't my own. It was time to cut my losses and go.

As the incline rose, my body slowed to a jog. I broke through a snowdrift, glad I had changed into my red snow pants. The trio of mountains rose in the distance and I kept the long ridge to my right as I headed north. Snow clung in heavy lumps to the branches around me, muffling every sound, even the falling of my footsteps. I strained my ears for any voice or movement. The silence didn't ring back but washed over me in soft, muted waves. In a forest this calm, this pristine, it was hard to imagine someone's world was falling apart amid all that peace.

I spotted the rock formation I was looking for. The Mouth of Hell was near.

I slowed to a walk to catch my breath. I didn't call James's name because I didn't want him to hide in some crevasse or run away. The wind shifted and the egg stench of sulfur hit my face as I moved stealthily through the last trees. My back was already clammy from the run when the steam off the hot springs hit me. There was some relief in the warmth, but I knew it would chill me yet today.

I stopped. The smallest spring was in front of me. The waters were placid but no longer alluring. I didn't know if it was the stories I'd heard since I first saw the place, but the waters looked darker, more sinister. I could believe something lurked within, bubbles of poison gas and mist escaping from its mouth.

My steps fell softly save a slight crunch of untrodden snow as I edged the side of the pool. I followed the smooth, towering rocks nearly as tall as the church steeple Marah and I had stared out into the darkness from. I took them all the way to the larger of the two hot springs. If only I could find what drew James there in the first place, maybe I'd have an idea as to his current state of mind.

Then I saw it, tracks leading to the water's edge from the other direction. He went straight to the large pool. What interested him was here, but what truly startled me was there was only one set of tracks leading straight to the hot water. None led away.

I sped to the dark pool, peeling my gloves and jacket off as I ran. At the side, I sank to my heels and peered over into the depths. My heart sped in momentary confusion when a great breach erupted, violently disturbing the smooth water. Warm waves splashed my face and clothes.

Even as I tried to take in what I saw, I felt the warmth of the water dissipate in the cold air.

"James!" I shrieked. I staggered into the water fully clothed. I made a grab for the boy as he disappeared under the water, thrashing. The water was all the hotter on my cold, chapped hands. My pants and fleece zip-up were quickly soaked through.

Another step and suddenly the stone floor disappeared underneath me. Thoughts of a never-ending hole to the center of the Earth spun through my head. My drenched clothes grew heavy as my feet fought for footing. My head went underwater.

It was the first time I'd been warm since the last day of tempered fall.

I thrashed with my fleece, its zipper moving all too slowly under the water. I opened my eyes in the too-hot liquid, the last of my breath caught in my throat. I realized I hadn't taken off my boots in the panic and they were filled with water. I kicked them off and felt the buoyancy of freed feet—my head cleared more every second with full control of my body once again.

I spotted James ahead of me and I frog-kicked until my fingertips brushed frantically at the lapels of his coat, even as we drifted downward in the water. My bare feet, one still in a stocking, touched something hard—whether the pool bottom or a single shelf stretching from the side, I'd never know. I clenched James, bent my knees, and pushed and kicked until we broke the surface.

I kept my gaze forward, intent on reaching the edge of the rock. I heard James sputter and his body bucked with coughing. My eyes stung from the steaming water, but I kept them fixed on the nearest rock. It was a struggle to roll James's body over the edge. Once he was up and safely out of the water, my heart collapsed. I was hit with a sudden wave of fatigue after the strenuous rush of terror.

I shook myself out of the reprieve and hauled myself up out of the hot spring, giving up my boots for a lost cause. James lay on his side, facing away from me. His body jerked slightly. I pulled on his shoulder and rolled him onto his back.

My recoil was instant. I didn't know what I looked at, but I knew it was wrong. A piece of murky-colored flesh rose up from James's face. The gelatinous mess quivered. What I thought was a strand of seaweed pulled itself purposefully out of James's left nostril. I let out a low noise of panic and disgust. I was paralyzed by the same revulsion that keeps one from stomping on a many-legged centipede. It wasn't an animal I'd ever heard of. What was it?

It came back to me in a wave. James bending by the water. James hiding something from me. James saying he had found a new species of fish.

It was no fish. The abomination finished reeling in its thin tentacle from James's nose and portrayed an agility and intelligence at odds with its appearance. It rolled off James and toward the water.

I lunged for the animal, but I was too late. Once in the

water, it slid fluidly down the dark abyss. The rounded blob billowed out into sheer waves of fin. I hadn't caught sight of any scales, but the creature didn't fit the bill of an eel or squid either. It was more like a many-layered jellyfish, though that description didn't feel right either. It had tentacles, but it wasn't transparent. And though graceful in the water, it wasn't nearly as delicate as a jellyfish.

With the creature out of sight, I turned back to my friend. "James, are you okay? Wake up. Are you okay?" I was back at James's side shaking his shoulder.

He blinked, eyes huge, but he wasn't shivering. That worried me. He erupted with a great sound, not quite a belch but guttural and desperate. Water dribbled out of his mouth as I held his shoulders and head off the ground. His body took over, heaving, and I pounded his back. Relieved not to have to perform CPR, I left James's side for a moment and peered again into the edge of the pool where James almost died.

The strange thing out of sight for good, I turned back to James. He was curled on his side and no longer heaved but blood streamed out of one nostril. I crouched down by him and put my hand on the top of his head to smooth his dark, wet hair back. Another trickle of blood ran out of the other nostril. The wound was deep in the nasal cavity or farther up. I lifted him by his shoulders. With my other hand I pinched his nose and tipped his head back to staunch the bleeding.

James shivered in full force. He looked at me for the

first time.

"Sister Sarah?"

Nope, that wasn't my name. Not even close.

"It's Arwen. Hey, are you okay?" I let go of his nose to rotate his head from side to side to peer in his eyes. He didn't make eye contact, only gazed vacantly over my shoulder. I pulled an eyelid up. His pupils were huge.

"I'm going to get you warm." It was a promise, but I didn't quite know how I would fulfill it. The midwinter sun was already setting. I debated whether I should carry him back, but I figured his clothes would freeze long before we made it to Lilium Springs. I had to get him out of the wind. I struggled to take calm breaths as I outlined my priorities: get him out of the wind, build a fire, undress him, and dry his clothes. My mind processed the situation logically, but my physical body was far behind. I was shivering so much from cold and adrenaline that I could hardly pick James up. I managed to place him over my shoulder. My one sock squashed as I staggered forward.

I muttered to James partly to reassure him but mostly to keep my brain and body synchronized. I was exhausted by the past two hours. It was hard to believe I had sat in Hetta's fluffy living room near the warm fireplace a short while ago. What I would give for one of those little iced cakes.

James shivered but didn't speak.

I paused, asking myself where I was going. We desperately needed a fire, but I couldn't start one. I was as wet as the pond itself. I didn't have a lighter and I was worthless at the longer methods. The severity of our situation finally broke through my clouded head. We could die from hypothermia.

I couldn't look that far ahead. If we were going to survive past the next hour, I needed to act fast before we were overtaken by the emergency we found ourselves in. I untied James's boots and wondered again why he went in the water with his clothes on.

It hit me—we needed to get warm and there was hot, steaming water right next to us. But what about the animal that had attacked James?

Suddenly James went limp. He tried speaking but his words slurred. I saw the panic deep within his unfocused eyes. I thrust my numbed hand to his throat and didn't feel a pulse. He was having a stroke.

I spread James on the snowy ground, ripped the waterlogged jacket away from his chest, and began performing chest compressions. "James," I shouted. "James, stay with me. You're going to be okay," I reassured him even as he approached death.

He took a shallow breath, and then another one. He swallowed and looked up at the sky, his eyes glassy.

With shaky hands, not knowing if what I did for him was enough, I dragged him to the smaller pool. There, I stripped James of his clothes and propped him up on a submerged rock so his freezing torso was in the water, and propped his arms and legs out the best I could. If his limbs went under, it'd encourage the cold blood to pour back into his heart and lower his temperature even more.

Then I started on myself. The wet, warm air was welcome on my face, but it was a physical struggle to get free from my damp clothes. Once I was naked, I splashed the hot water on me, then wrung out our clothes and laid them to dry in whatever fashion they could, before sitting down like James.

I eyed the water for any sign of the fish creature. I didn't know how the pools were connected, but it stood to reason that they were. I just didn't know how far down. I did know, without a doubt, that the fish was why James kept returning to the springs. He wasn't alert enough for a conversation, so questions piled up in my head. Balanced on the other side of my brain was our plan forward. It could take hours for our bodies to fully warm and our clothes to become bearable to put on. By then it'd be dark. I wondered if the search crew would come this way, if Marah would tell the others of my hunch and if they'd listen. It'd be wise not to expect it.

We sat for such a long time that I allowed James to put his legs in the water, and I did the same. He babbled and I cried. He rested with his eyes closed and I shook him awake.

"Arwen."

My heart lifted. I looked James in the eye and found him focused and clear.

"Do you remember what happened?"

He didn't have the energy to nod. "Some," he fought to

say.

"To be clear, you ran away from home and I came to get you. But that's not what we're going to talk about right now." I set my expression as he drew back. "What was that fish?"

He looked down. "It's not a demon."

"But what is it?"

"It's a new species of fish." A bit more life came to his eyes. "I discovered it."

"Gah, *that's* what you've been coming to see? Why were you in the water with it? Did it attack you?"

James paused, uncertain. He said he didn't know. "But it's not *bad*."

I cocked my head, furious but relieved that he was well enough to argue. Blood came back to his cheeks.

"It's not," he insisted. "Besides, Elder Sister Hetta comes here. She would never go somewhere that was bad."

My forehead tightened. "James, what do you mean Hetta comes here? You saw her?"

My intensity startled him. Just as his health seeped back, it flooded away again. He nodded slightly, scared of the outcome. I quickly questioned him. James had started coming to the springs to work on a secret project—he thought he could make electricity. He knew that if he hid his supplies there, no one would find them because no one went to the Mouth of Hell.

"Why didn't you talk to me? You don't have to do everything on your own, you know."

James shrugged in response. He thought I'd say no. He went most days and twice saw Hetta leaving. The second time, he discovered and named the Rocky Mountain Tentacle Fish, or tenfish for the number of tentacles it had. He had seen it only from a distance, gliding through the water. The time I happened upon him was the closest he'd gotten to the tenfish up to that point.

As he described the story, I got the shivers despite the warm water. The idea that the tenfish could be anywhere in the pool creeped me out.

"I want you to stick close to the edge, okay?" I repeated myself when he didn't respond.

"Yeah, okay. I know."

You save a kid's life and he still treats you with disdain.

I got out of the water and the shock of the air made me clench my teeth. James looked in the other direction. Our clothes were stiff with ice, so I beat them on the rocks to break it off.

"I wish we had some flint—"

I looked around while speaking, searching for the dull black rock. What I found turned my blood even colder. I didn't speak but held up a hand to James to quiet him. Not that he'd see it.

There, fifty yards away, was a Deadlight Garde. Watching me. I almost wished it were night—then I wouldn't have had to watch my death come. The ink-black metal made a dark hole in the shadowy forest as all light that touched it died. The Deadlight Garde stood with eerie stillness. At any second I expected it to launch into a charge. Deadlight Gardes weren't projectile machines—they were close-combat fighters. Close-combat fighters trained for something much hardier than our puny human bodies. My puny, naked, shivering human body.

I glanced at James, but he was still looking in the opposite direction of my immodesty. The Deadlight Garde took a step forward.

I launched myself at James and knocked him into the water. It felt like déjà vu, but this time I was the one dragging James in. I'd take the tenfish over the Deadlight Garde any day, but my expectations were low. I'd never seen Deadlight Gardes go through water, but I had heard they slid through like sharks. Like most things in evolution, it seemed as if the top predator had it all.

Still, what could I do but haul James by the neck into the only safe house we had, flimsy as it was? He thrashed weakly against me as I looked all around us for any kind of cave or sheltered cliff. My hand clenched firmly over James's mouth. He took deep breaths through his nose and tried to elbow me into letting go of him.

My ears rang and I swiveled my head desperately to catch a glimpse of the Deadlight Garde. The alien no longer stood under the trees. I looked wildly around.

"James!"

Shallow shouts came through the trees. The rescue group. If I called back, would I lead them into a massacre?

James bit my hand and I dropped it, already letting go.

"Back here! We're here!" He gave me a strange look when he finished shouting.

"There was a, uh, bear in the woods."

I lowered myself in the water. Why did the Deadlight Garde leave? If killing us was on its mind, it'd kill us all. If it had other business, why would it stop and stare at us? I'd never seen a Deadlight Garde look at someone with intention but without acting.

James swam to the side and clambered out of the water. I almost called him back. Shouldn't he rest after having two or three near-death experiences and a stroke?

The stroke.

Hetta's ruined face came to mind.

After James had wrestled with that fish, he had a stroke. Hetta had a stroke in the months before I came here and again since then.

Why would Hetta have been climbing into this Hell pool? Would she have been wandering the woods at her age? Someone came here to get my suit. As if they knew exactly where it was. The amphibian fish monster. The Deadlight Garde that didn't attack. I got the cold feeling that Hetta was somehow connected to them. Which meant that this so-called tenfish was somehow connected to the Deadlight Gardes.

I couldn't organize my thoughts. I was running on fumes and didn't understand what had happened, but I thought it was possible that I had learned more about the aliens that day than anyone on Earth had in the past year.

The Brothers were in sight now. I saw Timothy in the lead, his face strained with shock, eyes set on his son. I wanted nothing less than to start the arduous task of watching these men build a fire to dry my clothes, suffer through the stolen glances, and explain all that had happened, just to return to that damn community.

But running away was no longer part of the equation, not when there was a secret to uncover that could impact the entire planet.

I waved my hand in the air and shouted, "Over here! We're over here!"

16. Disintegration

I added more wood to the fire to keep the broth simmering. Inside the blackened pot was a full chicken carcass. The cartilage and tendons were so soft the skeleton, whole when it went in, broke apart. Vegetable peelings floated at the top of the scummy yellow surface. But my, it smelled good. Once strained, it'd be fine eating. Bone and vegetable broth was something I made often when we had the right ingredients on hand. Usually, I would add dumplings and chopped veggies. I only ever left it as broth when one of my kids were sick.

And my kid was sick.

For a full day, James lay under the pile of blankets.

Physically, I thought he was okay. He could walk to the outhouse on his own and bathed when I told him to. It was something deep within him that was exhausted or broken. If his spirit was cracked, only God could help him, but some broth wouldn't hurt.

Hours after Timothy and James arrived back, Rachel had called on me. Timothy had gone to her house to fetch Gideon and told her all that had happened. She was a welcome help. With little Charlie at her heels, they took care of some of the housework I had fallen behind on while I settled my son. The air was less stiff with them around. Rachel stuck to safe topics, like talk of the upcoming sugaring. It was a different kind of relief when they left.

As the soup simmered once again, I knelt to clear Gideon's blocks from the floor.

"How you doing, darlin'?" I called behind me.

"Fine." James's voice came from his bed. I considered rousing him out. He'd been strangely compliant since coming home, which was not like him at all.

When I first saw him in Timothy's arms, lips blue, skin white, I thought he was dead. For a moment, I was too. How could a mother stay on Earth without one of her children? Even if the other children should need her? Shouldn't God strike me dead for the unholy act of living past my child's last breath?

My tears came when I saw the shallow beat in the side of his neck. They were tears of relief and gratitude.

I hurried Timothy into the house where he lay James on

the table. Brother Godwin ushered Arwen in. I could tell she was affected by the same thing that hit James—The cold? Was there trouble?—but in her case it looked less like a rescue operation than a summons. The other men hovered outside, uncertain how to help. I snapped at them to get Arwen some shoes, Lord knows where hers had gone. I didn't know until later that it was Brother Barry who had gone to notify Elder Sister Hetta of their arrival back.

When the initial work of warming and cleaning and resting was over, Arwen sat, words pouring out of her like water from a broken cup. She eyed Brother Godwin to see if either Timothy or I objected to his hearing, but we didn't. Secrets made poor bedfellows.

Arwen told a story about childish experiments she and James had conducted through the winter. She taught him what she called physics. When Timothy asked how she knew where our boy was, she said she'd seen James by the hot spring before, working on a project on his own. This time James fell in the hot spring in his clothes and she barely saved him from drowning.

It haunted my heart to think that if she had lingered on the path with me, if she had been even two minutes later, I would no longer have three sons. The price of a stolen kiss was too high.

My feet carried me to the doorway of the boys' room. Already James was sleeping since his quiet response.

I let the broth simmer and sat to mend socks, which sprouted holes in midwinter the way flowers bloomed in the summer. I wished Gideon was underfoot so I could take my mind off myself, but Timothy had taken our eldest and youngest outside so James could rest and I could focus on his care. It was a thoughtful gesture but needless. I could manage my children and home on a given day. I understood, though, that it made Timothy feel like he was doing something at a time when neither of us felt we could do enough for our troubled little boy.

The needle pricked my finger along the edge of the thimble. I winced but was only too familiar with the feeling. I set the tan sock down—mindful not to let a drop of blood fall on it—and put my thumb in my mouth and sucked on the side. The light, salty taste washed over my tongue. I could no longer smell the broth, only fragrant rust. I felt more delicate than I had in a long time. I cast the mending on the floor and put my head in my hands to pray— something that had not come easy recently.

A knock sounded on the front door and I jerked my head up. The silence stretched and I hoped whoever was there would go away. I didn't want to see anyone. They couldn't help us.

Footsteps crunched in the snow. I stood in time, obligated to pretend I was heading to the door when a head appeared in the window. Arwen waved. I nodded and opened the door for her. I didn't know how I felt about Arwen coming into my home after so much had happened, but the cold air was welcome. I hadn't realized how stuffy the house had grown with the fire running to simmer the broth. I took a breath of fresh air and felt my head clear and my brow relax.

"Is he sleeping?" Arwen murmured. She peeked toward the kids' bedroom—the room she had slept in when she arrived last fall.

I nodded and gestured to the wooden chairs by the window. Our voices wouldn't carry so much there. And the chairs were comfortable. My father had invited Timothy to build them with him when we were first married. I sewed the cushions with my mother, one of the last projects we did together. The chairs and cushions were now well-worn, but the easy incline of the chair made it a nice place to sit in conversation. Early in our marriage, Timothy and I spent many winter afternoons perched there, discussing the Bible and the stock and our children's future. Of late, it was a place for me and Arwen to learn about each other's lives, both regarded as highly unusual by the other.

"How's he doing?" she asked.

I settled myself before answering, "Fine, I think. He's warm at least, though if it were only hypothermia, he should be out of bed by now. Do you think—" I paused, unsure how to ask the question without sounding sentimental. "Do you think his heart is broken?"

Arwen's eyebrows went up. "His heart? Why do you say that?"

"That huge fight we had before he ran away. He's back and safe, and that's good, praise God, but none of the issues that made him run away have been resolved."

Arwen sat back fully in the chair and rested her left ankle up on her right knee. The pose made me think of Timothy. No community woman would sit that way.

"By not 'resolved' you mean that James wants to learn and he can't because men are seen as lesser in this community and maybe he feels out of place and like no one understands him so why stay?"

"I meant," I said through clenched teeth, "his disobedience."

Arwen leaned toward me quickly. I was thrown by her sudden close proximity, but I didn't lean back. There was a current of fire between us but not like when she had kissed me. It was the energy of a challenge. I had to remind myself that Arwen didn't play by my rules.

"I'm sympathetic to what you're facing as a parent. Personally, I think you should let him be a kid and show him that he's important, no matter who he is or how different he is from what you expected." She ran a finger over a dry lip. It was peeling at one edge. Windswept red peeked from under the dead white flakes. "But I came to talk about something else."

I was eager and nervous to hear what she had to say. I always liked talking with her—I liked simply being with her, but I felt the wedge growing between us just as I had Rachel back. Maybe I couldn't manage more than one friendship at a time.

Arwen let out a shaky sigh. "The story I told you, when I brought him back…that wasn't the whole story."

My brow furrowed. I stilled.

"Everything I said was true," Arwen noted, "but I left a few details out. Big ones. I wanted to tell you earlier, but I didn't think anyone else should hear about it. I did have reason to think James had a special interest in the hot springs. There's a, um, fish."

I was impatient. "Fish don't live in water that hot."

"No." She glanced around her. "They don't."

We stared at each other for a moment. "Lord help me, Arwen, get to the point."

Arwen took a deep breath, a startled, unsure look on her face. "James has been trying to make electricity. He hid his experiment at the hot springs, and a jellyfish he named the tenfish attacked him. I think the fish is an alien."

A laugh escaped my lips before I realized how serious she was. "I've heard the stories of the hot spring too, and Arwen, you should know, it's just stuff that kids make up. I thought you didn't believe in the Mouth of Hell. Why would a demon be in the waters?"

Arwen grasped my wrist. I tried to pull away, but she held tightly. "I *saw* the fish. It was unlike anything I'd ever seen. The creature was doing something to James under the water. There was some kind of tentacle that went up his nose—toward his brain, Marah."

"Let go," I said it once, then stared until she released me. "This doesn't make any sense. James didn't say he'd been attacked by an animal. What was it, some kind of water snake?"

"No, you're not listening. This animal was *doing* something to James. I dove in and pulled him to the surface. I don't think it liked being out of the water because it let go and slid back down. I didn't see it again after that. But this huge gush of blood came out of James's nose. We were both dripping wet. I thought we were going to freeze out there. Then he had a stroke—his heart stopped and he wasn't breathing. I revived him." Arwen closed her eyes and took a breath. "Then—I saw it. A Deadlight Garde."

My hands clenched together and went ice-cold. I made myself release them and rubbed them together slowly.

"But they don't come here."

Arwen shrugged. Her face was calm, but I saw the quiver of blood in her neck as her pulse raced. I understood how terrified she was. "It was acting funny. I can't really say how. All I know is if it had wanted us to be dead, we would be."

"Did you tell Elder Sister Hetta?" Arwen's terror was contagious and I wanted the assurance that someone was taking care of the situation.

A dark shadow passed over Arwen's face. She shook her head slightly.

"Why not?" I demanded.

Arwen leaned even closer. Her familiar breath touched my reddened cheeks. "I think Hetta is compromised."

The tension in my shoulders dissipated. As usual, Arwen had no idea what was going on.

She saw my disbelief and glared back. "You yourself

said Hetta started acting strange just before I got here—that she had had a stroke. And since then, she's been off, confused."

"She's an old woman. It'd be strange if she wasn't acting like it." I said a silent prayer of forgiveness for questioning my Elder Sister.

Arwen kept pushing. "She's got my gun and gear. How did she get that? The things she told me about the Deadlight Gardes—even if she was making things up—how would she know enough about them to spin such a story? And why is she so callous about the world ending?" Arwen's voice rose.

"Shh. I need to think."

We both leaned back in our respective chairs. None of this was as strange as Arwen made it out to be. Elder Sister Hetta was marked by God. God communicated through her the things we needed to know to keep Lilium Springs safe.

Even as I justified everything away, I resisted. I'd been having doubts about Hetta's leadership, but I was terrified of what that meant and didn't know what I could do about it.

My main worry was James. I had just gotten him back, and Arwen was telling me a cup of broth wasn't going to reset our situation. Maybe it would be worth sending a group to the hot springs to look for anything amiss. But if a Deadlight Garde was there…

What it came down to was how much I could trust Arwen. And, as much as I had longed for this stranger, she herself had told me she'd abandoned her people to the south. Her arrival had disrupted everything and had put my son in great danger.

Arwen broke through my thoughts with a declaration. "I'm going to tell Hetta we should evacuate. Go farther north."

I startled. "That's a bit extreme, Arwen. After all," I said bitterly, "we don't actually know anything. It'd be incredibly dangerous trying to move kids and old people at this time of year. A late winter blizzard could kill us all."

"I don't intend to hang around and complete a detailed risk assessment right up to my death. I intend to live. Maybe one day I'll be able to do something with these new clues about the invaders."

She was serious. I crossed my arms. There was no way I was going to tear my family from their home and banish us all to the wilderness on the hunch of some outsider. We'd die.

I shook my head. "No, you're not going to tell Elder Sister Hetta anything."

Arwen cocked her head, straining to see something in my face. I didn't care what she was looking for. Indulging her had been a mistake. I had let it go this far and nearly lost a child. Arwen had done nothing but attack our way of life since she had arrived.

"Arwen, go home." The sun went behind a cloud and a winter chill creeped through the glass windowpane. I glanced at the fire. It crackled, but I was cold. "I'll talk to

Elder Sister Hetta."

"You will? You'll tell her about the Deadlight Garde? Convince her we need to evacuate?"

"I'll tell her everything," I promised.

Arwen smirked. "You'll go now?"

I nodded.

"We're going to need my Titan Suit. You have to convince her that it's more beneficial to the whole group to have it with us. Nothing stands up against the Deadlight Gardes, but if I'm armed, I can be helpful in other situations."

Arwen stood and peeked briefly into James's room. I knew she'd see his small body under the pile of blankets, unmoving. She nodded to me and stepped out the front door, all business, no goodbye. Once she was gone, I pulled on my own coat, grateful for the extra warmth. I'd wake James so he could watch the fire while I spoke with Elder Sister Hetta. I needed to tell her that Arwen Cruz was about to pull everything apart.

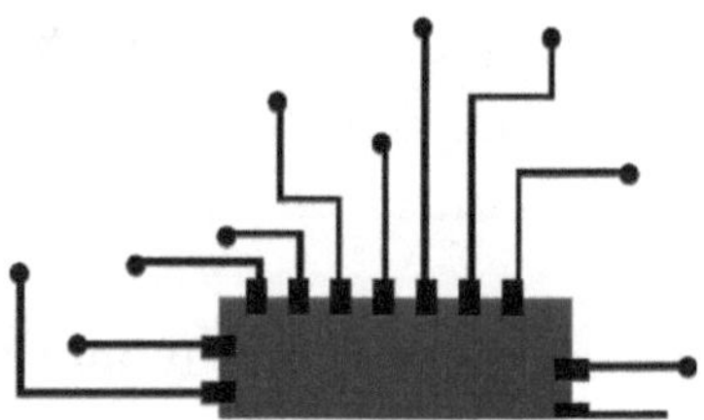

17. A Pragmatic Approach

I sped along the path from Marah's house to my own. I didn't know how long it would take to convince Hetta we needed to evacuate, but I would have my bag ready as soon as I could. Then I would help others pack. I still had to take care with my steps, the snow was icy. Sister Esther had told me the last of the snows would end soon but then would come the great melt. Mud I would take. We wouldn't freeze to death in mud. My plan was for us to head north. I couldn't imagine we'd outpace the onslaught of spring.

On the verge of an exodus, I started to visualize each step. I estimated a third of the community was either elderly or under five years. If I was smart—and no one had ever called me such—I'd take off on my own. Let that mass of human bodies distract the Deadlight Garde in the area as I slunk off.

I pursed my dry lips. A crack in my top lip reopened and I licked the paper-thin cut. I tasted a wispy, sharp drop of blood and kept walking.

No, I couldn't leave people to die. That was why I had signed up with the army in the first place. Just because the military was decimated and didn't want me anymore didn't mean I was no longer accountable to the survival of my species. Plus, if I needed a pragmatic approach to convince myself, I needed only to consider why I had come to Lilium Springs in the first place—I was starving and possibly going a bit loony.

This community was an entire ecosystem filled with specialists in child-rearing, woodworking, farming, and animal husbandry. If I left them to die, what skills would go with them? Even if I eked out an existence on the land by myself, what would the point be if it all disappeared when I did?

I reached my house and took a last look at it. Inside, my fire smoldered in the hearth and I took precious time to build it up. There was no sense in going cold when I'd be sleeping in a snowbank soon enough. As the air in my small cabin warmed, I stripped my coat and gloves. I set my boots upside down near the fire to get the damp out of them, but not so near that the plastic would scorch. My stomach rumbled and broke into my thoughts. I took out the foods I thought would be most cumbersome to carry with me, two potatoes, to wash and steam in the fire.

While the potatoes cooked, I sorted through the foodstuff in my cupboard. I packed the most densely nutritious items in my pack—nuts and seeds and dried meat. I had a tiny amount of dried berries and herbs but plenty of root vegetables and withered apples. After careful consideration, I decided my instincts were correct. Though plentiful in vitamins and fiber, I didn't think potatoes were worth carrying, except maybe as seed. I wouldn't take the apples or carrots either because they were mostly water. I took some time to visualize what I would eat between tomorrow's lunch and midspring when early shoots would come out. If I wanted to move quickly and stick to the essentials, I couldn't take all of my stored food with me. It felt terrible even contemplating leaving perfectly good food behind—I reminded myself I would *actually* leave it behind soon—but that was what the situation required. I wondered how hard it would be to convince the others of the need to streamline their bags to favor speed and discretion. I groaned. Marah's dad flashed in my head. It was going to be hard to convince him to leave everything in his shop behind.

I ate the potatoes piping hot with plenty of salt. I tossed some burnt skin into the fire. I wasn't an especially mindful eater, but it was one of the last meals I'd take in what I thought was my home, however unlikely.

I looked out the window. The afternoon wore on, but there was no sign of Marah. I was fairly certain she would come after speaking with Hetta. For some reason, as much as we angered each other, as much as our feelings convoluted against the realities of daily life, we still sought each other out.

Once Marah talked with Hetta and I got my Titan Suit and Kronos back, a lot of problems would seem much smaller. My bodysuit wasn't built for this winter climate, but I quickly decided that I'd bring only a hat, a jacket, and underwear with me. If I needed to put on civilian wear for some reason, I'd scavenge articles of clothes then. It was a relief thinking about wearing my bodysuit once again. Despite the severity of the situation, I smiled. I imagined how many questions James would have the first time he saw me and what the others would think. If Marah thought I was an angel of darkness the first time, then the others had a shock coming.

Indeed, it would be good for them all to broaden their minds as we traveled, to see how differently others lived. Maybe even *find* others living differently. After all, there had to be other communities out there that survived. Just a few days ago, I had thought that kind of connection lost but maybe not. I couldn't help getting ahead of myself. That was how I had stayed alive so far.

The last item to stow in my pack was the little packet I had of pictures and book pages. My diary. I gave a wry smile. Though I had each item memorized, I shuffled through it. I had nothing from my former life, only a mere shadow.

I was ready. I'd go and help Marah talk to Hetta. They were probably discussing details. I grabbed an apple—I'd eat all I could before leaving our stores behind to put on some extra weight—and put my coat on, apple in my mouth. I took a mealy bite and stepped out my front door onto the slippery ice.

My clearing was small—just enough openness to create a circle around my house and pit latrine. Brother Barry had told me that he'd help me fell a few trees that spring in preparation of an herb garden. Afternoon shadows spilled across the worn snow and in the shade stood six Brothers, Timothy among them, talking low about the current proceedings. Good, we could get started.

"Hey, there. I'm glad you're here." I started their way. It was cold in the shade, and I shivered slightly.

Barry leaned against a tree but straightened at my approach and said, "You are?" He looked incredulous.

"I'm not glad for the circumstances," I clarified, "but I'm glad we can get started on changing them. How far are we? What did Elder Sister Hetta tell you so far?"

The men gave an uneasy glance around the circle. A tingle ran up my back, and I took an instinctive half step back. Godwin and Phil stepped casually behind me, and in a matter of seconds I was circled.

"What is this about?" I asked, fighting to keep my voice level.

"Arwen"—as much as I hated it, the lack of "Sister" alarmed me—"you're under arrest for conspiracy against

252

the elders, for endangering a child's life, and for making sexual advances upon a married woman." Godwin swallowed hard at that last part, but I wasn't laughing.

"What the fuck are you talking about?" I turned, looking Timothy in the face. "Brother Timothy, we need to evacuate now. The invaders are here. I saw a Deadlight Garde when I *saved your son's life*."

Marc replied, "That's a tall tale if I ever heard one. If you had seen all that, why didn't you tell us when we met you at the hot springs?"

I shrugged lamely but fought to shift my feet carefully away from them. "I wasn't sure what I saw. I was almost dead with cold myself. I wanted to talk to Elder Sister Hetta about it first."

"Well, we just came from Elder Sister Hetta," Timothy finally said, "and she had a lot to say too. We're here to arrest you." He took a step toward me. His knuckles were white around a knot of rope. "Don't make this hard on yourself, woman."

I dropped quicker than they expected and rolled between Timothy and Marc. There was a surprised shout as Barry realized I was no longer standing among them. I barely made it off the ground, intending to run full force, when I was hit from behind. I shifted and jabbed a hand upward at someone's nose, which immediately broke in a wash of blood. I scrambled. Godwin grabbed at my leg and I wrenched free only to take a kick to the gut.

I rolled to the side and staggered up. Someone grabbed

me by the shoulder, and I used the momentum to kick at them. I made contact but didn't look back to see the damage. I took off running and made it two steps before someone heavy tackled me from behind. Timothy's stocky frame overwhelmed me and we fell to the ground, my left leg bending awkwardly underneath me. In a matter of seconds my hands were tied behind my back, and they had grabbed me by my shoulders to stand me up.

"You really don't know what you're doing," I tried. I felt blood run hot from a gash on my forehead. "The aliens are *here*. They will come, and Hetta can't protect you. We need to leave this place." I was just a stranger with bad news. Who would want to listen to that?

"Why should we leave?" Marc demanded. "So someone else can swoop in after us and take our land? You gonna tell us who sent you?"

"Deep state," someone murmured.

I shook my head in disbelief. "There is no one else." I tried to put weight in my words but they were shrugged off quicker than wet gloves. "Fuck you," I finally settled on. "You're all acting so tough." I was more than a little dazed from a knock in the head I was just starting to feel. "…tie up innocent people," I murmured and blinked hard

I expected to be gagged. They didn't, but they also didn't listen as we walked the paths either.

I saw Esther come out of her house in a thick shawl and I screamed for help. Her face wrinkled in fear and she hurried back inside. Logan was on the path ahead. I called out to him. Someone shoved me from behind.

My brain was still playing catch-up to my current state, and I was finally coming to understand how much trouble I was in. What was the penalty for endangering a child? That couldn't be much. Expulsion? That'd be fucking fine with me. What about conspiracy? That probably wasn't so good. And sexual actions outside of marriage? That definitely wasn't good. Damn Marah. Damn her to Hell. All I did was help her. And *she* came on to *me*. The whole thing was bullshit but that didn't matter.

What mattered was I was being frog-marched to God knows where and didn't have a single friend among my jurors. Or would they skip straight to a good, public hanging? I didn't have to worry about dismemberment by the aliens anymore. The last of my own species would take care of me.

At last, we came to Hetta's own house and walked up the porch stairs and in the front door without knocking. Hetta was nowhere to be found. The men made short order of their boots. When Phil commanded me to slip my snowy boots off, I told him what he could slip. He shrugged and wrenched my boots off. I had a clear view of the giant cross in the dining room and remembered what stood opposite.

The group hauled me down stairs I'd never taken before. None of the other cabins I'd been inside had a basement, but of course Hetta's house was something in and of itself. We passed two shut doors. I wondered if they were storerooms or other prison cells, for that was surely where we were headed. Funny enough, I never expected to be taken as a prisoner in the war. For so long, I expected to die, so I hadn't devoted any headspace to the unlikely scenario of being captured.

The last door looked like any other manufactured door, a little grimy-looking, but there was a breath of awe as Timothy twisted the handle. I got the sense that the men knew it was there but never used it. I wondered if Marah knew there was a jail in her perfect community. Inside, there were no windows, just an upright, solitary cell made of metal rebar. The walls of the room had a layer of thick padding for soundproofing.

I realized I was no longer talking, but it was likely time to make a last appeal. "I understand you think you're doing the right thing, but if you lock me up and follow Hetta's lead on this, we're all going to die." They pushed me forward. "I am a private of the United States of America and this is an unlawful abduction."

"That's one thing you never understood, Arwen." Timothy made eye contact for the first time since I was tied up. He didn't even look mad. There was no bloodlust in his eyes. "Your laws don't apply here."

Phil opened the cell door. I couldn't help it. I had to try. I headbutted Barry, who was closest to me. I didn't even make it to the hallway before I was caught and thrown ass-first into the iron cell, head doubly woozy

The door clanged behind me. My vision spun from the headbutt, but I scrambled off the ground, lurching forward.

I was too late. The lock latched. I rushed to the bars as the men left the room, unwilling to look at me. I had one last opportunity. I was the only one in possession of knowledge that might further our understanding of the aliens. If that inkling of an understanding died with me…

I called out, "Ask James about the tenfish!"

The white door swung shut, and I heard it lock from the outside.

18. The Sugaring

I smelled the air, trying to decipher any sign of burning, but all I smelled was the subtle scent of oak and the more robust sweetness of sap. I didn't envy young Sister Johanna at her post. Stirring the watery, bubbling mass of tree blood was a hot, difficult job. The cast-iron cauldron hung from a branch suspended between two stout logs. It was difficult to stir the pot without trotting on the fire. Stirring really should have been a man's job—the extra height and long arms would make all the difference—but ever since I was small, women tended the fire and the bubbling mass while men hauled buckets of fresh sap from the forest.

As for my part, Rachel and I supervised the small army of teens. The young women always flocked around Rachel, as if they could sense her goodness. I didn't spend much time with them, my own boys falling into the younger category of children, but soon Matty would be a part of the teen peer group. Perhaps Timothy and I would chaperone group picnics or an outing to the lake and watch on as the young people rolled up their pants and splashed each other with the clear water in the summertime. My foot stuck in the damp ground. Spring was coming, but summer was a long way off. The change in temperature was a relief.

I looked across the way at Rachel who was bandaging a burn acquired due to short stature. Our friendship had been renewed over the past few weeks. It seemed that Arwen's leaving was all it took for things to return to tranquility.

James dutifully attended Father's workshop most days. Last night he shyly showed me a trick, one I remembered well from when I was a child: a wooden ball nestled impossibly inside an uncut, wooden cage. I knew the secret was to soak the wooden brace in hot water so it expanded enough to let the ball slip through, but I didn't let on. I told Timothy that night he had chosen well for our boys. He saw in Matty the need to be outdoors and apprenticed him to Brother Henry for farming. And he saw the crafty nature of James and apprenticed him to my father. We made love that night for the first time in months and since then there was once again a closeness between us.

The pots boiled merrily along, so I headed to Sister Alice's home to warm myself. Though it wasn't very cold, it was unsettling leaning over the steaming pots only to walk away humid and chilly. I could afford a short break.

Sister Alice's home was the closest to the grove of maple trees. They were sporadic throughout the forest. Over a hundred years ago someone had the foresight to plant them heavily near our community. I felt grateful to our foremothers. I often wondered what actions I took would benefit my decedents in three generations.

"Hello, Sister Marah, come on in." Sister Alice loved hosting the sugaring. I didn't think she minded being on the edge of the community due to the essential role she played once a year. She was older, and I wondered if she would feel sad when it was time for her to move near the Elder Sister.

"Oh, it's so warm. That feels nice," I said. There was a delicious smell of ginger and cinnamon in the air, but I didn't comment on it, for it would look like I was inviting myself to her baking. I settled onto a hardwood bench next to Rachel, who came in with a gust of early spring. Sister Alice came bustling over with a pale biscuit. A swirl of dark dotted the middle.

"What's this, Sister Alice? I'm always amazed at the way you make up new pastries."

"Oh, to be sure, it's nothing."

I took a nibble. "That's not true, it's delicious, and it's nice trying something new every once in a while." Personally, I thought Sister Alice spent all winter experimenting with her cooking so she would have something new to present at the sugaring.

Sister Alice and Sister Esther traded notes on baking, and Rachel leaned toward me. I could smell the cinnamon on her breath.

"It's good, isn't it?" She looped her arm in mine. "How are you doing?"

I was startled by the sympathy in her voice. "Quite good, thank you."

She looked at me, as if she didn't believe it, but Rachel was never one to share her mind in front of so many others. She turned away to watch the fire and soon picked up her mending.

Sister Alice left to go check on the girls, and Sister Lacey read aloud from the Book of Psalms while the rest of us sewed. She was a good reader, and I thought again how good of a match she'd make for my Matty. Sister Esther was making a quilt for her daughter's hope chest, not that there was any need for hope—she'd be married off. I was working on a pot holder. I sourced some very strong fabric from one of the sheds the previous summer but was just getting to the project.

The afternoon felt so proper and entirely appropriate, that the one dark spot stood in harsh contrast. I worried that I was simply playacting at my work. Really, since she had left weeks ago, my mind was constantly on Arwen, but I had to pretend otherwise. Though I thought Elder Sister Hetta was entirely correct in batting down Arwen's idea of evacuation, I was brokenhearted that Arwen felt she needed to leave and only said her farewells to the Elder Sister. I had never experienced the departure of a person from my life unless through death, where they would be greeted by God. Arwen was out there, wandering the wilderness. I wondered how often she thought of me.

"Sister Marah," Sister Esther repeated. "I said, do you want more tea?'"

"Oh no, thank you. I'm fit to bursting." I waved away the offer with my thick sewing needle.

"What are you thinking about so intently anyway?"

I worried that my cheeks were reddening and fought to keep my voice neutral. "I was actually wondering about Arwen. Where she might be now…" I faltered, trying to explain myself as conversation in the room dropped. "I mean to say, it would simply be interesting to know what the land looked like from her point of view right now. What curious thing she was doing today."

I caught a look between Sister Alice and Sister Esther that I did not like one bit. I had to remind myself they didn't know about the kiss. They didn't know Arwen's wild ideas about fishes. They didn't know anything, I told myself—but it seemed as if there was some knowledge in that glance I wasn't privy to.

I forced a shrug and laughed. "The random things we think of in a day."

Conversation picked up again, but I knew by the stiffness of Rachel beside me she was thinking, and thinking hard. She was naturally quiet and even shy, but for her to go completely motionless like that, well, she was hiding like a little mouse.

We passed the rest of the afternoon, and I was only too happy to take my turn outside and check the boiling basins. I lingered with the girls out there, not because I was especially interested in guessing when the first crocus would appear, but because I felt uncomfortable among my own peers.

It wasn't until Rachel and I gathered our sewing projects and left to walk home that I could pounce.

"What?"

Rachel turned to me, hazel eyes intentionally blank. "Hmm?"

"You all know something about Arwen. Or think something about me thinking about her. What is it?"

Rachel dropped the careful look. "Yes, Marah." She looked off in the trees, which was worse than her pretending.

My stomach dropped at her admission.

"But if you don't know, Elder Sister Hetta must not have told you for a reason."

I fought to keep my voice neutral. "Did she tell you directly?"

"No." She raised a thick brow at me. "Henry did."

We both stepped off the path to bypass a mire of mud. "Then it stands to reason that you only know because Brother Henry knew, and I don't know only because Timothy doesn't. So, tell me."

Rachel sighed. "I think Timothy *does* know. I'm sorry,

Marah. You're the one wrapped up in this. I don't feel right saying anything."

My curiosity was ablaze, but more than that, shame and guilt rushed to my face. After Arwen told me she wanted to evacuate the community, I went to Elder Sister Hetta and told her about Arwen's worries and expressed my own trepidation that fleeing would undermine God's protection. I didn't want Arwen stirring things up. I knew Elder Sister Hetta would set everything right. She asked a lot of questions, most of them off topic, but I knew she would calm everything down.

When she told me that evening that Arwen disagreed with her decision and had decided to set out on her own, I had to nod and pretend everything was all right instead of breaking down. I stuffed those feelings down fast, but what Rachel was saying threw everything up again. Worse, I realized there was something going on that I didn't know. And if I had put Arwen in any kind of uncomfortable position…

We stopped at the fork in the path, and Rachel broke my panicked thoughts. "Honestly, Marah," she said, "I didn't know you didn't know until today."

I sniffed and brought a hand up to wipe my eyes. "Is she okay?"

Rachel looked at me in shock and absently tidied her hair. A fresh wave of tears spilled over and I hiccupped. Rachel reached out to touch me but stopped at the last second. "You care about Arwen a lot, don't you?"

I brought my hands to my face and covered it. I nodded. When I uncovered them, Rachel was gone, already lost to the dark trees. I cleared my throat and dried my tears before finding my resolve.

At home, I cooked dinner and swept the kids off to bed with astonishing success. Most nights were drawn out because there was no real urgency in getting them off to bed, but I could pull out the works when I wanted to.

Timothy sat close to the fire with his back to it as he opened a jar of beeswax and oils, a paste for red and chapped hands. He had spent the day tapping trees and making sure the boys hauled wood for the boil. I took a thumbnail of the paste and rubbed it into my hands to warm and soften the wax before applying to his. Neither of us had spoken since the kids went to bed.

"Why didn't you tell me about Arwen?" I kept my eyes down to massage his hands. I felt them tense under mine.

"Elder Sister Hetta forbade me to. Marah, I thought you deserved to know, but I couldn't. Did she tell you today?"

"I found out just this afternoon," I said weakly. "I feel a bit hurt to be kept out of the loop, but I guess I understand why she did it. I've been busy enough with James as it is."

Timothy nodded and withdrew his hands from mine to vigorously rub his together. I smoothed the excess into my own hands and the scent of summer filled the air. The paste left a soft, silky feeling, but I knew if I smoothed down my hair or brushed my hands against my lips, it would feel the tiniest bit waxy.

We sat quietly and I waited to see if he'd say anything else.

"The date's been set."

"For what? I didn't realize…." I tried my hardest to sound natural, but I had no idea what I was playing with. If I didn't give him a lead-in, I'd never get more information. But if I seemed too unknowing, he'd clam up.

"For the execution."

My head went light and I fought to hold still and blink and breathe. I struggled to find words and breath with which to say them.

"Oh, I didn't think it would come to that."

"I don't like it either. But there's nothing that can be done. Elder Sister Hetta can't be questioned. And it would be hard to send Arwen away knowing she could return at any time, maybe even with others. I don't think our household should get any more involved than we have to be. They won't do it publicly, of course. It'd be terribly upsetting for the children. James especially would be disturbed."

"When?" I asked.

His mouth twisted as he watched me carefully, but I knew he couldn't see inside. He never could.

"Sunday," he said and stood to get ready for bed.

I left him to crawl into the cold sheets without me and stayed by the fire. I was shocked Arwen was in Lilium Springs, and more shocked that she was going to be executed. She was supposed to have left weeks ago. Elder

Sister Hetta must have completely misunderstood the concerns I brought to her that day. I had no reason to think that she'd slap a punishment on Arwen for wanting to leave.

I froze. Had Timothy told Elder Sister Hetta what he saw transpire between Arwen and me on the path that day? With that information, Elder Sister Hetta could decide what she wanted.

The thought struck me again.

Elder Sister Hetta could do whatever she wanted.

I felt like I was going to break apart at that admission. It was a soft, raw spot I dared not touch. I stood and moved away from the hot fireplace. I was too flushed and overcome with heat and thoughts of Arwen's death. And hate. Oh God, Arwen must hate *me*.

Why me? I didn't even ask to go on that prayer walk. I was sent. Arwen was just there. Would it have been better for her and me if I had quietly slipped away?

I couldn't control any of it. And it all might end with Arwen's death and the aliens coming and blasting my family away or whatever it was they did. It was all because of Elder Sister Hetta. Hetta didn't want to be challenged. Hetta wanted to pretend the aliens would never come here. Arwen had only tried to protect us and I had exposed her.

I found myself pacing and made myself sit down and rub my hands together, warming them, wakening them. When I rose that morning, I was powerless, I just didn't recognize it. I suddenly had more power, more choice. What had I learned since that morning?

The first was that Arwen was captive nearby. I knew the church inside and out. There was no place there to keep her. Arwen was a brawny woman. She must be restrained somehow. Perhaps she was in someone's cabin, but I doubted it. She was likely in one of the Elder Sisters' homes, probably Hetta's. Earlier that day, I had imagined Arwen out in the wilderness when in fact she'd been kept secluded and restrained somewhere in my own community for weeks, set to be executed.

Though close enough to the embers, I was chilled. What was I convincing myself of? Obviously, enough people in the community knew about Arwen's captivity and considered the punishment just. I couldn't go up against all of them. What I had was guile. And when I was willing to put that on display, Satan Herself couldn't stop me.

I checked on the boys and made sure all four were sleeping before wrapping myself tightly in scarves. I pulled my coat on quietly, checked that the fire was banked, and slid out into the darkness.

I had no lantern, but thirty-two years in Lilium Springs meant I had every path memorized. My feet stuck in the mud, but I barely noticed the mess accumulating on my shoes. My only goal was to get to Hetta's house. My cheeks shined with cold by the time I arrived.

My knock rang loudly across the dark clearing. There was a faint flicker of light through one window. I went in only to find a dying fireplace. The house was cold, colder than outside. I moved quieter than a bobcat through the founder's mansion and checked the Elder Sister's room. Her bed lay briskly made up by the girls who did the morning chores. Turning back, I realized I had tracked mud through the house, but I didn't care. I peeped downstairs, but it was quiet as well. An aged woman wouldn't be in the cold basement anyway. But then, where *was* Hetta? I left the office for last, apprehensive, recalling the last time I was in there.

I knocked softly but called even quieter, "Elder Sister? Are you there?"

Upon no invitation or rebuke, I swung the door open. Empty as well. Could she be at Sister Bethany's perhaps? That would do no good. I couldn't beguile two Elders in one night.

Before I left the study, my feet carried me to the closet. My heart sped as I searched the darkness, but I was disappointed. Arwen's stiff clothes were not there.

I left the large home more than a little disturbed and with no new information. I didn't like that Hetta wasn't home in the middle of the night. I especially didn't like that Arwen's belongings were missing.

I stepped off the porch and onto the trail, lost in thought.

A hand as cold as ice and as strong as newly forged steel slid over my mouth. Before I could grunt in protest, my feet flew from under me and I was no longer in control.

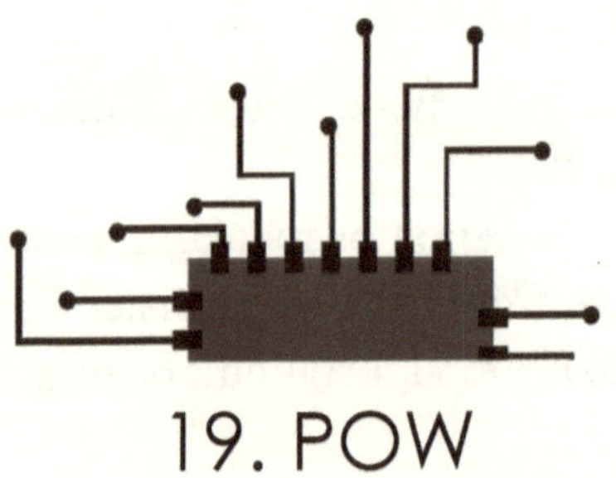

19. POW

I listened to the footsteps above recede away. They weren't Hetta's. She had an off-beat stride that centered around the living room. The footsteps weren't any of my other regular visitors either. I had memorized them all in the long weeks of captivity. I had finished my second and final meal of the day hours ago, so I knew it was night. Brother Phil came to bring me food and empty my chamber pot. Surely the entire community knew I was being held captive—enough men were involved and the basic act of keeping me alive required some support from the Sisters.

I listened intently, straining for any clarifying detail. The steps crossed over my prison twice. I guessed it was someone combing through Hetta's entire house. I thought about calling out in case it was Marah, and even opened my mouth to yell, when it occurred to me it could be the Deadlight Garde I saw at the hot springs. They moved stealthily, but surely the simple presence of weight would create some noise. I no longer thought I understood their ways. A decade-long war had been thrown into new perspective when I had saved James.

What else would enter Hetta's house when she wasn't there? I had heard her leave earlier.

I stood in the exact center of the cage, ready for what, I didn't know. Then the tiny creaks stopped. After a while, my heart slowed. I curled up in the ratty blanket. It was cold down in the basement, underground with no fire. I could feel my strength fading daily though I walked and ran in place and tried to do push-ups in a cell where the footprint wasn't big enough for me to properly stretch out in.

I lay awake for a long time and finally slept.

I woke when I heard steps in the hall. The creeper was back. I barely had enough time to right myself and stiffly stand when I heard the lock in the door jiggle. A sliver of candlelight flowed through the cracks. A woman entered and my heart lifted for Marah, but it was someone else.

Rachel stood in the doorway, dim light flickering upon her face, shadows rounding the curves of her shape. Her brown hair floated around her shoulders in waves. Her nose was straight but not too long for her heart-shaped face. Though she had birthed…whatever, some number of kids, she didn't carry the evidence in a thick torso. If I had to say,

Rachel was probably the most objectively handsome woman in Lilium Springs.

She was the last person I expected to come. I knew she hadn't come to dust the cell or fluff my pillow. I tilted my chin up in confidence, though truth be told, I was tired.

Rachel looked apprehensively into my den. I couldn't imagine how it smelled, but I kept my chin from falling and stared at her face, willing her to be uncomfortable. Finally, Rachel looked behind her and softly shut the door, determined to see through whatever idea she had. She slid the keys into her coat pocket and set the now-dripping candle onto the floor so her fingers wouldn't burn. The underlit shadows on her face became severe, but she was still beautiful.

"I know what you did with Marah. She tried the same with me." Rachel's face shifted from apprehensive to venomous. "I think it's—"

"Yep, totally do not care, Rachel. You didn't come in the middle of the night to clear your mind."

She frowned. "The Elder Sisters decided to execute you. It's set for two days from now, Sunday."

I swallowed. I expected some such thing. To them, I was a waste of resources and things did not get wasted here. Besides, I bet the group had been waiting for some likely lamb to come along and remind them why they had separated from society in the first place. I'd had a lot of time to think it through. My only hope was that I'd be hung. I didn't want to be nailed to some cross as a reenactment or burned to death. If I got to pick, I'd ask that they leave me tied in the wilderness to die from exposure. There'd be some poetic justice, a closing of the circle, in that. Maybe I'd end up as wolf shit still.

"And that revelation brought you here in the middle of the night?" I challenged.

She had the drawn look of someone who had worked all day and stayed up half the night so as to not miss her opportunity.

"I'm going to help you escape," Rachel said neutrally. She flicked her eyes up at me to read my expression. I didn't know what she hoped to find there. I was surprised, but she wasn't going to get gratitude. Rachel moved as if automatically. She pulled the mess of keys from her pocket and tried several before one slipped into place. The lock clicked and the cell creaked open loudly. I glanced upward, terrified of who might hear it.

"There's no one here. Just go." She stepped away, out of reach, face still blank.

I stepped outside the cell willingly enough, keeping the candle between me and Rachel. I felt the wonderous stretch of full steps and freedom.

Rachel looked at me warily and forced herself to speak. "It would be an unjust death. God would not approve. Go." She backed away.

"They're going to know someone let me out." I emphasized my next words. "And they're going to assume Marah." And then they'd want to kill her. Was Rachel trying to put Marah in harm's way?

Rachel shook her head. "No, she doesn't even know you're still in the community. She thinks you ran away."

My heart sank at how quickly I had been erased from Marah's life.

"They'll know someone released you, but they won't know who. I'm doing this because I *owe* Marah. She's my sister and I haven't treated her as such for a long time. Please go now. There's a bag of supplies in the hall." She looked down as she blinked. "And don't get caught. I think you can do that well enough?"

I nodded and turned to the door. I let her take a breath of relief before I spun on my heel and forced her bodily into the cell, hand over her mouth. I snaked the keys out of her pocket and threw them toward the door.

"Why are you doing this?" I growled. "You don't care if I live or die. And if Marah doesn't even know I'm here, you're not doing it to spare her grief."

Rachel quivered but pushed back hard. "Just go if you know what's good for you."

"Tell me or I'll lock us both in here and you can tell Phil all about it in the morning." I was bluffing. Dear God, I was bluffing. There was no way I was spending another night in a cell.

Rachel's resolve faltered and the words came out in a rush. "I had relations with Timothy."

My hand dropped. It was slightly hypocritical, but I stepped back. I didn't want to touch her.

"You're having an affair with Timothy?"

Tears leaked out of Rachel's eyes. She nodded and her chin wrinkled trying to hold back her emotions.

I put my hands up and backed away. "All you people are crazy." When I reached the door, I found myself with one more question. "Rachel, your mother's a scribe. Why didn't the ink in the Bible run when Marah carried it through the rain?"

Rachel swallowed. If blurting out her affair with Timothy was painful, this was more so. She finally shook her head. "They rub the covers with wax every year to preserve our ancestor's script."

"I see. And you couldn't have cleared things up when you had the chance." I just about rolled my eyes. Instead, I parted with sarcasm. "Have a nice life, Rachel. Hope you get that love triangle thing figured out."

I was out of the door in seconds, keys on the floor where I left them. True to this at least, there was a bag in the hall. I swooped it up and made a show of my footsteps receding upstairs, then slunk back down and tucked myself inside one of the doors. I waited silently for nearly two minutes before I heard Rachel's sniffs and steadfast tread carry her upstairs. When I heard the front door close, I went up myself.

I paused in the dining room, eyes of that damned ram's skull on me. I took a deep breath as I determined my next move. Then I spotted it, mud on the rug. Little flecks of now-dried dirt were littered throughout the house. Someone else had been through there and made the noises I had heard earlier. They had taken the opportunity of Hetta's absence to search for something. I followed the trail into Hetta's bedroom, which smelled like lilies though they were a season away. Or were they? My body panicked at the question of how long I had spent in the basement. But no, there were traces of snow gleaming in the moonlight through the window. As in every room in the house, a white lily hung on one wall.

When I had first arrived, the lily in the chapel made me think of my sister. I didn't yet know that the lily was the sign of the Virgin Mary. Perhaps if I had known, I would have realized the community displayed her symbol the way others hung crosses. Of course, they were less interested in Jesus than his mother. Since I realized the reverence they put on the flower, I felt weird whenever I thought of my sister's full name in my head. I didn't want to think of Lil in connection with those weirdos. Fuck, if only my family had stayed together then I wouldn't be in this mess.

I continued on, moving room by room, following the trail of mud, which ended at the closet in Hetta's study. The door was already open. I pushed through it apprehensively. It was a closet with papers and Bibles. But I had gotten good at finding hideaways while ransacking abandoned houses and found a fake panel inside the back of the closet. In my many hours locked up, I had deduced my equipment must still be in Hetta's house. I knew she was someone who didn't easily part from power.

If I had my bodysuit, I could have pried the panel open, but I began to suspect that was just where my bodysuit was. I passed through Hetta's room again—checking the back of a magnificent painting for a taped-on key and fluffing her pillows for hidden openings—but nothing.

Then it struck me. There was one object that stood out in Hetta's house. One thing that betrayed her need for secrets.

My footsteps were quiet, carefully placed as I approached the bighorn ram skull and horns that hung on display over her dining table. It had struck me as odd every time I saw it. The lily and the cross: understandable iconography. But the pure white skull? Something pinged at the back of my brain. When I had read through the Bible, there was a particularly grizzly story about a man about to sacrifice his son. At the last minute, a ram appeared as a substitute, horn tangled in the thicket. Was Hetta's ram skull just a piece of local fauna? Or something more?

I slid the heavy but fragile skull off the wall. My skin crawled under the rippled texture of the horns. I pawed blindly at where the brain used to be and felt a key. I understood then that Hetta would sacrifice whatever she thought necessary to protect her beliefs, her rule.

Without thinking, I threw the skull against the wall. It crashed and clattered to the floor, thin bone split across the face, horns forever parted from their twin.

I carried the key to Hetta's closet. It slid in smoothly and there, inside the fake panel, was my Titan Suit. If I was ever going to feel grateful to God, that was the moment, but I wasn't so I didn't.

After weeks of confinement, I was already winded from searching the house. I laboriously peeled off my filthy clothes. Pulling the suit on was ten times harder than I remembered. The stiffly woven cloth was difficult to navigate. The tiny light at my wrist blinked once. I felt my sprits lift; my suit was charged. Then my stomach plummeted. How did that happen? There was no electricity in Lilium Springs. The absence of advanced technology was supposedly the only factor keeping the community safe from Deadlight detection. How long had my suit been charged? Had its signals brought the Christmastime flyover?

Combat-supporting suits were charged in proximity to wireless chargers running throughout military vehicles and bases. I dug into the hidden cupboard again. There was a locked safe, a musty text, and dated screens up the back. I didn't see them on first glance because they were lifeless, but I searched until I found the old-school controls and flipped them on.

"Holy shit," I mouthed silently to myself in surprise.

There were four screens in all, all depicting places around Lilium Springs. I didn't recognize two of them—the homes of Candace, Jackie, or Bethany, I wondered? The other two were obvious—the side room of the church and the sanctuary itself, right where I kissed Marah.

Not only did Hetta have access to the very thing she

forbade her flock to have, she was using it to watch her people. To control her people. She wouldn't have installed the security system—they were much too old and I didn't think she'd have the competency—which begged the question of how many Elder Sisters tapped into the surveillance of their community and how often?

I was completely disgusted and shook my head, willing myself to keep moving. I needed to leave Lilium Springs right away. I put my helmet on. I didn't turn on my headlamp, but the room sprang to life around me, bathed in night vision. I tried the radio.

"This is Private Arwen Cruz, I'm a survivor of the Army Base in Yuma, Arizona. Is anyone out there?"

I didn't hear any voices. I'd try again once I got the fuck out of there. I left my dirty castoffs. Better for them to know I was armed and protected. It might make them think twice about coming after me.

I picked up the bag Rachel left—I wouldn't check what was inside until I was far away—and tramped to the front door. I didn't need to keep quiet. I wasn't defenseless anymore. I stood inside Hetta's door, concealed until I picked a direction. My head was cloudy and I was weak. I'd normally have my mind made up in seconds, but I just stood like a total dummy behind that door.

"Ah, fuck," I whispered.

When the shadow of a ship hit a neighborhood, people had about five minutes to get the fuck out before the buildings came smashing down. In combat with my regime, the Deadlight Gardes slaughtered us when they deigned to look our way. Why wasn't any of that happening here? I *saw* a Deadlight Garde. They communicated with each other. Surely, they could sense the heat from our tiny bodies, and apparently the theory that advanced technology attracted them was out. The invaders had to know Lilium Springs existed.

No, if the community still stood, it was for a reason. Somehow the tenfish was involved.

I remembered the disgust on my platoon leader's face as I was dishonorably discharged. I imagined bringing back information, real information, concerning the aliens' decade-long siege on our planet.

There was an anomaly, a mystery. I couldn't leave it behind.

20. What's in a Name?

"In the name of the Mother, the Daughter, and the Holy Ghost, be gone," I said in my deepest, most authoritative voice.

Nothing happened. I remained in the death grip of a demon. It didn't hang me over its shoulder or cradle me like a baby. It grasped me in its arms facing outward. The lower half of my body flopped like a fish with every step the damned thing took, but its limbs clenched my torso so hard I could barely breathe. As far as kidnappings went, it was most undignified. The only reason my feet didn't drag was because the demon was ten feet tall. I would much rather have disappeared in a plume of smoke.

Either no one could hear me or they were all dead or

they weren't coming to help me. My throat was raw from screaming, and it turned out you can't scream incessantly. I only hoped my impending death would be quick. My legs were starting to feel numb, either from shock or poor circulation. Snot bubbled out of my nose, but I didn't have a free hand to wipe it.

The metal demon carried me farther into the forest, impassive to my threats, banishments, prayers, and repentance. Its lower limbs were long but wide-splayed at the foot, if you could call it a foot. I had no idea where we were going. Would it walk like this for days? Or take me to a ship? I could tell we were moving faster than a human, and not only because of its size and the length of its legs. The entire thing was ethereal. Even in my state, I couldn't help but notice the beauty of the precise, gliding movements, the efficiency of travel. I was simply a frail case of meat with bad knee joints and a propensity for falling. The thing was built for power.

Arwen said they were robots and I understood the basic nature of the things, but I didn't really understand until I saw it. It wasn't organic. It was made. Nothing real was this perfect.

My fear was not passing but shifting lower on my priorities as it seemed I was not going to die that very minute. What was left was fury. I was angry that I hadn't taken my family and run when I'd had a chance. I was angry with God and Hetta. How could they let this demon walk on sacred ground? And Arwen. How could that wretch not have told me how *huge* these things, these Deadlight Gardes, were? Maybe if she had impressed upon us what we were up against we could have done something. I'd always pictured demons as wispy and dark. Terrifying, yes, but ready to disappear in the face of the Lord's name. This was something else altogether.

"Put me down, Devil. In Mary's name, I rebuke you back to Hell."

The monster definitely wasn't a demon. I'd never heard of a demon kidnapping someone. Possession? Yes. Carrying them through the forest in an uncomfortable and undignified manner? No.

I wriggled again—knowing it would make no difference to the metal arms but believing I had to keep trying—when it dropped me. It was only a two-foot fall to the ground, but I wasn't ready for it. My ankle twisted badly and I fell square on my tailbone. I yelped and it took me a moment before I knew I could move.

I kept the Deadlight in my sights, but it wasn't watching me. Though there were no eye whites or light shining through, the face was slightly more transparent than the rest of the body. The body was opaque and all in one piece. I didn't see gears or joints or anything resembling a traditional machine. It was unsettling to look at.

It was the first time I could really look at the robot and I noticed a bloodless, gaping wound at the back of one arm. I stood slowly and brushed myself off. The robot didn't move so I continued pretending to brush my pants while I looked at the hole in its arm. It was fearsome. Not gory but horrendous in that the smooth, continuous outer layer ended in torn inner layers of what I could only comprehend as metal muscle. I couldn't imagine something taking a bite out of this Deadlight Garde but clearly something had.

I took a shaky breath. I backed away slowly. It was a hundred times worse than when I met a grizzly bear in a berry patch, but I could only respond the way I had then. The machine swiveled its head in my direction, not because it realized just then I was getting away, but that it was simply time to deal with me.

I put my hands up. "Let me go. There's no reason to keep me. Dear God, please, you have to let me go." I was crying again. The giant closed the gap in a second.

It bent down. For the giant, that meant its head was level with mine. It lifted its uninjured arm. The strange hook of its hand effortlessly broke into digits, like butter melting into a new shape or jelly spreading on toast.

I took a breath in shock as it reached one digit out toward my mouth. It alighted softly on my lips. The skin, if that's what it was, felt radically different than the hard outer plate that had gripped me recently. It was soft, like me.

This was the machine's first attempt to communicate with me. I could only assume it wanted me to be quiet. Was it trying to hide us from a search party? Or was the thing that chopped its arm up in the vicinity? Either way, I was damned if I was going to make a noise. A search party from the community could do nothing against a beast so fierce, and I had no desire to meet anything stronger and more fearsome.

I put my hand up to push the alien digit away. Instead, my hand rested on its hand. I was struck by the power radiating underneath its skin, the terrible potential resting there. It could crush me with one false movement.

When I first found Arwen, sleeping like the angel of death, thoughts of dreadful deeds came unbidden to me. I understood instantly that she could do terrible things. I was in awe of her.

I felt awe bloom inside me again.

We moved our hands away, simultaneously. The Deadlight Garde started walking, slower than it had while carrying me, but I had to run doggedly at its side. It was unnerving the way I only came up to where the lower limbs joined the torso.

The incline was difficult for me. More than once, the machine waited at the top of a cliff for me to catch up. I didn't often go north of the community to the harsh steps of the mountains, and I was always sluggish at the final edge of a winter trapped inside. We came to a cliff face, and I looked around in confusion. There was no path upward. I turned to the Deadlight Garde.

"I can't climb that."

I didn't know if it understood my words or simply saw the pathetic nature of my human body, but it knelt, hand placed upward on the ground. I took a tentative step forward and looked up. Of course, I found nothing in the face to be read. I wrapped a shaky arm around its shoulder and stepped onto the hand, now neither split into digits nor curved in a rough claw. The hand was mostly flat and wide enough for my feet to perch on. The Deadlight Garde stood to its full height as soon as both feet landed.

A silly sounding *eek* came out of me, and I clung as hard as I could to the arm. The thing climbed the cliff face one-handed. I would think climbing that way would be difficult but perhaps only if your strength was limited. The Deadlight had arms that never tired and two feet to balance on, nearly like hands themselves. In contrast, I was an entirely frail body at the mercy of something entirely merciless. I knew that much from Arwen's stories.

At the top, pine trees closed in on us. The Deadlight Garde placed its hand down low to the ground and I hopped off of my own accord.

The quality of the night had changed since I was first taken outside of Hetta's house. The sun hadn't properly risen, but everything was gray rather than black. I looked up but couldn't spot any last stars through the thick canopy.

The Deadlight lowered itself to all fours, changing shape slightly as it did so. An icy tinge of shock grew in my stomach as my body responded to the sight. The machine suddenly looked more animalistic, more beastly, than before. My head was at what would be the withers of a horse. I imagined the Deadlight springing on me, ripping at me with a newly grown mouth. It crept forward like a cougar, treading lightly on each foot. I walked behind it, much more noisily than cat or machine. I was nothing so majestic or mystic. Even in the rising darkness, even in such proximity, I had difficulty spotting the ink-black metal ahead of me under the trees. My neck was clammy as the sweat that broke out cooled on my skin. As the early dawn wind blew and turned the wet spot on my back to ice, I shivered.

I realized where we were when I saw all the rocky outcrops. I grew sick as I imagined James in that very place by himself. I could only hope all my boys were safe at home. Or better, evacuating from the area with their father and Arwen. I knew that was a far distant hope because of my own actions.

I was about to round the path to the steaming pools when the giant gave its wordless signal. Still mostly horizontal, the machine pulled me onto its back. Before I had time to protest—it wasn't holding me, my weak arms were the only safeguard I had—it was climbing a much steeper face of rock. A whine broke from my throat. I clamped on with my legs as well as my hands.

I prayed, lips mumbling in silence. I thought briefly of when Satan took Jesus to the mountaintop, offering the world below if only He would kneel.

That cold morning there was no discussion of kingdoms or glory. On one sheath of rock, the giant simply swung me down carefully. It occurred to me that the machine knew to be careful only because it knew how very breakable we were. How many of us had this one killed?

It stood neither like a man nor crouched like a cat but squatted with its knees nearly to its ears. I guessed it didn't have to hide often, though the dark metal was advantageous.

Back pressed against rock, I stayed well away from the edge. I looked in the same direction as the Deadlight Garde and gasped. Dawn had arrived. And with it, I could see Hetta, lying prone in the pool of water, naked. Her clothes lay folded neatly at one side of the hot spring. With my leader's nakedness displayed before me, my stomach turned with shame. Something obscured her head from view. It was fleshy and pale, the exact opposite of the huge, rough beast that stood before me. I shook in terror as I realized it was the creature Arwen spoke of, the one that had attacked my son.

I watched, trembling, as the blood stilled in my cold ears and I became aware of Hetta's moaning. Again, I felt my stomach turn at the inappropriateness of my predicament, for it wasn't a moan of pain but pleasure. Bile rose sharply in my throat as I contemplated what Hetta and the fish were doing that could cause her to make those base noises.

I looked at the machine for the first time since spying Hetta. The Deadlight Garde wasn't watching the fish and Hetta as I expected.

It was watching me.

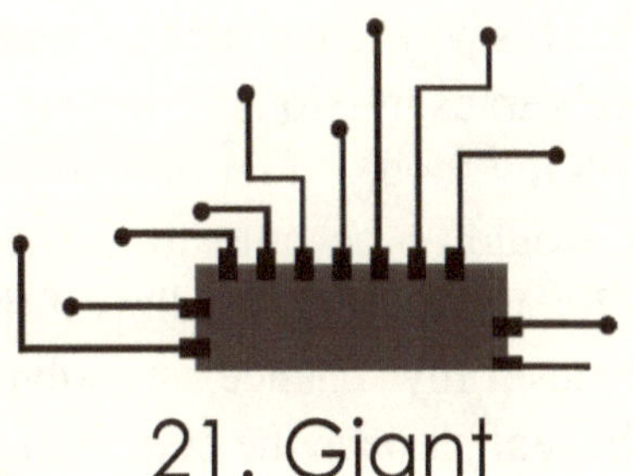

21. Giant

I stepped out of Hetta's house, undecided as to what I should do. Light broke over the trees. It was already dawn and my body was tired and weak, not ready for what the day ahead would bring. Though I had eaten the night before, I was hungry, all the worse because I knew no one was bringing me food that morning. I was back to barely surviving again. Everyone in this community was. They just didn't realize it yet.

My fingers traced the thick casing around my thighs. I took comfort in having my bodysuit back. I didn't know where Hetta was, but she'd return to her house eventually. I made my way to the back of the house, keeping to the shadows. The suit and my gun felt heavy. I was unused to carrying the extra weight, and I felt ashamed that I had grown so weak.

I picked a covered spot in the still-gray woods and hid myself. My mind churned as I settled in for a long wait. I had an unobstructed view of the north path, but the south was shaded by heavy pine branches.

Henry turned onto the south path without a glance in my direction on his way to the fields. I wondered if he knew about his wife's transgressions. I already decided if I saw Phil come with my food, I'd let him go in, then I'd escape in earnest. I wouldn't be able to waste any more time plotting how I could help these idiots if they were coming for me. I'd lose my chance at solving the mystery concerning the tenfish once the community roused itself to hunt me down.

Pink stretched to the sky when I saw her on the path. My mouth went dry at the sight of her. Marah. She walked toward Hetta's house, looking back twice in the time I watched her. My instincts screamed that she was coming for me. I crouched and traveled as quietly as I could through the brush and slush.

I called her name softly. She jerked like an electric shock struck her and looked in the direction of the trees where I sat. With another quick look behind her, she left the trail. I rose and met her in the gloomy shadows.

"Arwen? You're okay. How did you get out?"

Without talking about it, we settled in for a covert conversation by crouching down to the ground. I realized she hadn't blinked twice at the appearance of my bodysuit. I anticipated that she'd be shocked, maybe not that I had it, but that I wore it openly in the community. Instead, Marah seemed to barely register where we were or that she was talking with a convict.

I shook my head. "There's no time. I'm looking for Hetta. I'm going to kill her."

A strange, dark look came over Marah's face.

"You don't understand. She's *dangerous*. She's been watching you all with cameras—she has hidden screens—to make it seem like God told her information when she's actually watching you all. She has the power to control every life here and she refuses to act. I need to know what she knows about the Deadlights and how, so I can evaluate what's going on here. With her out of the way, the people will go. I know you don't understand—"

"I do. She needs to be eliminated." Marah's face was steel and her words sharp.

This time it was me who looked stunned. "Marah, what's going on?"

"I saw Hetta at the hot springs."

That was the first time I heard Marah say the name of her leader without the formal title. The angry animal in my chest flexed and purred. This was good.

Marah continued, "She was in the water with what I can only assume was the creature that attacked James. But, Arwen, Hetta did it by choice. And when the tenfish crawled off her head, she sat there in the water, washing the blood off her face."

My head went up at this last admission as I scoped the trail. "And you beat her back? She'll be here in a matter of minutes, then."

Marah shook her head. "Listen, Arwen, I need to show you something."

"No. My top priority is capturing Hetta. You need to convince this town they need to leave this area. Don't you see? The tenfish is connected to the aliens. To the demons. Everyone's in danger."

"After all this, you still want to save them?"

I gestured around me, though there was nothing to gesture to. "These could literally be the last living people on Earth. Of course, we have to. But Hetta stands in the way of that. You need to think of a way to convince these people. I need to interrogate Hetta."

Marah looked at me impassively. Finally she said, "You're a good person, Arwen." She stood and brushed the remnants of icy mud off her pants. "Follow me." She left without checking to see if I was.

I was stuck between the terrifying idea that the town was going to burn me at the stake, the need to evacuate all these people, and the mystery of the tenfish, but Marah was acting just weird enough. I followed her for a short distance, noticing her no-nonsense attitude and fast stride. Something had changed. She ignored or had replied the negative to all my questions. Finally, I gave up and followed.

Then she stopped and squared her shoulders to me.

"Give me your gun."

Until then, my Kronos was hanging off my back, safety on. At that point, I flipped my gun up in front of me.

"No." There was only one reason somebody would want to take another person's gun. She wanted to kill me, kill someone else, or keep me from killing someone. Okay, three reasons. But they were all bad.

Though my gun was now aimed at her, she leaned into me, careless of death pointing her way. "How do you think I knew to go to the hot springs this night to see Hetta?"

I shrugged and she answered, "Someone told me. Someone who knows a hell of a lot more than we do about all this. And I'd rather you not shoot at them and get us killed."

She nodded to the tree behind her. "Hang the gun and you can come meet them."

My interest was piqued, but Marah was behaving like a nut. I scaled the tree higher than she could reach and hung my Kronos L85 securely on a branch by the strap. No single community member posed a threat to me. In my Titan Suit, I had an even greater advantage. But I didn't want someone thinking they could swipe my gun in the process.

I dropped down, taking enjoyment in the heavy jump and secure landing the suit gave me. I smiled at Marah, expecting her to be impressed, but she looked at me dispassionately. Something was wrong. If it was her family, she would have said so straightaway. It wasn't them. It was her. Something had died within her. She turned on her heel and walked into the dripping forest. There was no sign of other footprints. Marah stopped abruptly and turned me by my shoulder.

My joints tensed automatically, bending in preparation of fight or flight. My heart sped and I felt the familiar but exotic redistribution of blood that comes in the wake of an adrenaline rush, but no rush would save me.

"Run, Marah," I screamed.

I backed fast, keeping the Deadlight in my view while I backed toward where my gun was. Then I went down hard on my ass. Marah had stuck her foot out to trip me.

"Are you crazy?"

"No," Marah said with force. "For once, I am not crazy. I can finally see things for what they are."

It was the worst time for Marah to snap, but she was snapping faster than a rubber band.

"Arwen, meet Giant. Giant, Arwen."

I hadn't taken my eyes off the enormous Deadlight Garde. It must have been nine feet tall. Its black armor neither shimmered nor stirred. It was like it sucked in the very air around it. When light hit the Deadlight Garde, it died. It simply ceased to exist.

The Deadlight settled down in a manner of crouch, blank face intent on me. It wasn't the closest I'd been to a Deadlight Garde, but the closest I'd ever been without it slaughtering the people around me I was trying to rescue and evacuate.

I tried to glare at Marah while not taking my eyes off

the alien robot. "What the fuck, Marah?" I hissed. "You have no idea how dangerous this is."

"I know a lot more than you think. Get up, Arwen."

I stood, tentatively. My asshole was still clenched shut, like that would do any good.

"What's going on here?"

"Giant took me to the hot springs."

"Giant? This is a highly dangerous, sentient, AI robot from another freaking galaxy. A single Deadlight could kill everyone in Lilium Springs in less than an hour."

"But it won't. This morning I was terrified when it took me from the community. These things have propagated the destruction of the human population, but in this moment we have a common enemy, two of them. Giant can't communicate with us, but I think it wants the fish dead. And I want Hetta dead. And you're going to help us accomplish that."

I folded my arms across my chest, well-aware of how ridiculous I looked. To Marah, I was pouting; to the Deadlight Garde, well, crossing my arms would do nothing to save me should it choose to attack.

"I'm not doing anything until I find out what's going on here," I snapped. "And then I'm making a decision for myself. I'd rather die than help this blasted robot."

Marah's eyes unfocused and she took a small breath through her mouth. "I know the oppressed when I see it. I don't know why, but the Deadlight Garde is controlled by the creature at the springs."

"These *things* aren't some poor little weaklings that need our help. They've decimated our entire world. If it wanted the fish dead it would, you know, *do that*!" Then I noticed something. "What's that?"

Marah looked where I pointed. "It looks like an injury, doesn't it?"

I looked away as I thought. "That would match the scrap I found in the water village, the one Hetta had. But how could that have happened?" I answered my own question. "Either it was attacked by another Deadlight Garde, or it ripped a chunk of its own arm off. Maybe to remove a tracker?"

The military never gathered any information that Deadlight Gardes could understand us, but this one touched the mangled area of its arm tentatively, as if it still hurt.

My brow furrowed. Though my extremities felt numb by this point, my brain took over. Why was the robot wounded? And how was the tenfish connected to the alien invasion?

"Marah, what made you think the Deadlight Garde is controlled by the tenfish—the creature that attacked James?"

In a moment, the fierceness drained out of Marah's body. Left standing was a flawed woman who wanted to protect her kids.

"It struck me that in the pool was Hetta and the tenfish, communicating with each other somehow. And Giant and I stood, unable to intervene, unable to act. It made me think of the endless flow of power. God tells Hetta. Hetta tells me. I tell my family. Well, maybe it's the same. The tenfish tells Giant what to do.

"And the ship we saw that night"—she blushed and stumbled over her words, even in that moment. "What if Giant and the tenfish aren't supposed to be here? What if the aliens only came this close because they were looking for something? And what if Giant wants to go back? Think about it, it has the power to go anywhere, do anything, but something is holding it back. The fish wants to be in that pool—it was probably brought there by Giant in the first place. They've been laying low, not attacking, not doing much of anything—hiding. Somehow, it's communicating with Hetta and the Deadlight. I think that's how your armor came to be at Hetta's house."

Could that be possible? The jellyfish thing wasn't Earthlike at all. Could the true aliens that came really be weak, frail water creatures with an advanced robotics army at their disposal? And if that were the case, was this pair on the run? I felt a thrill of terror as I considered how the Deadlight knew where my gear was. Had it followed me and Marah that first day? How many other times had I been alone in the woods, stalked by this creature?

Marah saw the resolve on my face. "Go get your gun, soldier."

I couldn't wait to be out of reach of the Deadlight Garde, not that any distance would do me any good if it decided to kill me. I backtracked quickly and scaled the tree to retrieve my Kronos. I doubted that I'd come back to a dead body, but I was surprised to see Marah and the Deadlight Garde standing there, just staring at each other.

After a final, silent goodbye, Marah came to me and the beast took off south on four legs. Chills ran up my spine as I watched it, impressive every time I saw one. Marah turned to watch the strange Deadlight until it was out of view, then took deep breaths as if she had been holding herself together out of sheer will.

"Marah," I said utterly astonished. "How the fuck did any of this happen?"

She looked me in the eye. "I don't know, but I don't think it was God."

22. Revelations

I never wanted to see the steam of the Mouth of Hell again. My head buzzed and my limbs moved slowly. Dawn was far gone, but I still moved as if I was sleepwalking. I was exhausted, scared, and my entire world view had been plucked down to the bleeding skin.

As Arwen and I walked, I tried to hang on to what I knew was real: I loved my sons. My sons brought meaning and purpose to my life. The rest of it—God, the community, what Giant was—I didn't know what to believe in anymore. But I didn't need to think about that now. All I knew was the tenfish didn't deserve to live. That fish had an agenda and I knew it. So did Hetta.

I looked to my left where Arwen stood, locking her

helmet into place. The mechanical clips sounded out of place in the natural space. She removed the long strap of her gun from around her neck. I couldn't see her face anymore, but I had seen the anger in her eyes before they were shaded from view.

Arwen handed me the gun. I took a step back and shook my head.

"No," I said, "I've never even fired a hunting rifle."

"You probably won't need to shoot it. We both saw the…the thing. It's only flesh."

"And Giant was afraid of it." That was enough for me. I crossed my arms. "If I shoot, I'm going to miss. And that's if I can even figure out how to make the gun work."

"Marah, take a deep breath." Arwen walked me back from panic and showed me where to put my thumb. She put hers next to mine and a tiny light flashed.

I jerked back, but Arwen was satisfied.

"There, now you have permission to use the gun." She shoved it into my hands and I brought it up.

"Whoa," Arwen shouted. She maneuvered quickly behind me, put her arms around me and lowered my aim at the ground. "Keep the gun pointing down until you need to shoot, not that you're going to need to." She raised my arms, pointing the gun at a tree. Even then, I liked the feel of her around me. She maneuvered me around again, showing me how to aim and mimicking pulling the trigger. She stepped away too quickly and my back became cold to the air.

"Wait, what are you going to be doing?" I asked.

Her helmet looked at me impassively and hauntingly, like Giant.

"I'm going to get the tenfish."

Arwen walked purposefully to the water's edge. She stared into it for a moment. I approached, mindful to keep the gun pointed down and my finger off the trigger.

"And the suit will protect you?"

She moved slightly and I assumed it was a nod because the next thing I knew she dove into the water. The hot springs were clear, but the pool was so deep it faded to black. Then it bloomed with clouded light from Arwen's helmet. I hoped she could hold her breath for a long time. Or did the suit provide oxygen? I didn't even think to ask how she was going to pull this off.

I strained my eyes looking for a dart of orange flesh. Of course, if the tenfish didn't want to be found, it would just go down. From what I had heard, the pool was a never-ending abyss. Did I believe it went all the way to Hell? No, but it sure gave me the creeps.

Arwen kicked her legs to propel herself deeper. I leaned over the edge, watching her legs disappear into the blackness. I stood upright again and looked around. I felt utterly alone.

I thought if only someone from the community could see me now. Timothy would flip if he saw me holding a gun. It wasn't taboo—my grandma was a good shooter—but it was completely out of character for most of the women.

I saw a sudden flash from Arwen's light. I leaned far

over, anxious that she was having trouble. At that moment, I felt my foot go numb. I lost my balance and slipped into the dark water. I barely had time to take a sharp breath before the hot water of the spring enveloped me.

I thrashed, reaching for the crest of water. Images of the Devil pulling me to Hell flashed in my mind. The water was so hot it was uncomfortable to open my eyes, but I forced myself to just in time to see the gun sinking downward. A bloom of orange shimmered in front of my eyes. The creature drew up, smooth and powerful in front of me. Its layers and fins radiated out and swayed in the current. It reached a long tentacle for my face. I kicked my feet and fought to cover my nose.

Then Arwen was there, gloved hand clenched around a sheer skirt of tissue. It looked delicate, but I realized how strong it must have been that Arwen could grip and pull the tenfish away from me without the flowing fin ripping. Free from the creature, I kicked up to the surface. My head broke water and I took deep, gasping breaths. My motions were jerky with shock as I scrambled for the rocky sides. My jacket was soddened with warm water. Thank God I wasn't wearing my full winter gear. I had to stop and breathe before I could haul my upper body out of the water.

I heard a splash behind me. Arwen no longer had hold of the fish. Instead, her hands groped for the sides of the pool as the creature wrapped her in its tentacles—some tightly winding around her body, others over her helmet. The tenfish was small, about a quarter her body size, but stronger than either of us had realized. One specialized tendril had a sharp hook, like a fingernail, and hit at the face of Arwen's helmet repeatedly. I spasmed, looking for the gun before I remembered I'd dropped it; it was halfway to Hell.

A sharp crack broke through the air, and I heard Arwen cry out. The tentacle flowed quickly into the dark glass. Arwen sputtered as water rushed in at the same time. I left the safety of the side and splashed toward Arwen. I grasped firmly on the tentacle and tried to pull it out from Arwen's helmet. The outer layer was slippery, like snot, while the core of it felt as strong as chain links. The three of us went below the water again, and I tugged hard on Arwen's shoulders and kicked toward the side.

I was desperate to wedge Arwen on a rock so she wouldn't slide down into the dark depths. Above water, the noises I heard from Arwen sounded nothing like what Hetta made. The thing was treating her roughly. It flashed in my mind to wonder what noises James had made. I didn't know if I was crying, my face was already so wet, but I was stumbling out of the pool, struggling to drag a thrashing Arwen behind me.

"Help! Someone help us," I screamed. I looked around. The only thing I could find was a stick, which I picked up like a spear when I heard something.

It was utterly silent save for the sound of wind rushing and trees breaking. I didn't hear anything within Giant, no motor, no gears creaking, as it rushed toward us on all fours like a wild and dangerous beast. I looked back at Arwen and moved with instinct more than thought.

I felt the wind of Giant's motion upon me as I lifted the improvised stake over my head and slammed it down into the fleshy body.

The tenfish bucked and trembled. I dug deeper and twisted. Tentacles went flaccid and I heard Arwen groan in pain even as she struggled to right herself.

Giant barreled toward us. The machine's great momentum was going to crush us. I screamed.

Then it launched itself over us, over the pool. On the other side, it dug its back feet into the dirt as it fought to slow its body, turning itself, righting itself to face us.

Giant circled the pool, slowly, effortlessly transitioning to two legs. It stood, towering over me, focused on the tenfish. A gaping hole appeared in Giant's neck, and I screamed again. While the Deadlight Garde's body was a smooth layer of hard, flexible shell, the hole—the mouth—revealed a fleshlike wound. Sparse long hairs protruded from the gap, and Giant bent down close to Arwen. The hairs weren't such at all. They were thin feelers touching and caressing the tenfish's body, inhaling the animal's body into itself until it was completely devoured.

Then, Giant was gone. Silent once again, moving toward the trees.

I shook, recoiling at the brief alliance I had shared with the Deadlight Garde. I was wrong—it wasn't a demon, it was worse than a demon.

Arwen sputtered and coughed, and I turned to help her, dropping the stick. I couldn't lift Arwen, but she did something to unclasp her smashed helmet and tried to sit up. She lay heaving and coughed again. Her eyes were red, bloodshot. "Congratulations," she said.

I startled. "What?"

She cleared her throat. "You killed the first alien in this war." She held my gaze, face stern, then suddenly burst into rasping laughter. I started chuckling too and then abruptly broke into a sob.

"Yeah, it's pretty bad," she said.

"It's okay, it's over. Oh, are you hurt?"

"No, I mean…" Arwen paused, "it's bad. Our situation. Earth. The aliens." She shook her head. "When that thing rammed its tentacle up my nose, I thought I was dead until this huge pulse went straight up to my brain. I saw stuff."

"Like what?" I said apprehensively.

"When I was connected to the tenfish, I got, I guess, impressions. It was trying to project images in my head, that it was going to kill me, that it was going to compel the Deadlight Garde to kill you and hide our bodies, but I got snippets of things around the edges. Like I could read its mind, and it was trying not to think certain things. I don't know if that was Hetta's or James's experience." She said his name gently. "Or maybe the creature was more in control in those instances.

"But Hetta was right. They didn't come to Earth for us. They're vagabonds of a sort, collecting resources from planets across the galaxy. They'd been to Earth numerous times to collect oxygen to inject into the oceans on their ships. Humans weren't just collateral damage. They didn't need to go to such extremes to kill us if they could take what they wanted. We couldn't stop them."

"What do you mean?"

Arwen shook her head. "When they returned to Earth this time, they were surprised by our numbers and how our intelligence had progressed. They don't want competition. We're eons away from exploring the far reaches of space, but they know eventually it will happen. I felt the tenfish's hatred of me, and its panic at the thought that *we* could someday threaten *them*. So, they've annihilated us, crippling our numbers in the hopes that it pushes us back to living like animals. They've left small primitive groups of us because their, um, policy, for lack of a better word, is to not totally annihilate a species."

"Why not?" I found two pieces of flint and was working on building a fire.

"I don't know, but I can think of a few reasons, and I doubt it's for moral ones. It takes a long time for animals to evolve past the single cell organism stage. Maybe they let species evolve in case they can harvest or use us in some way later as we change. Maybe, even if they don't have a use for us now, it's easier to let us grow and change in case they eventually do."

Arwen peeled down her bodysuit. It made a weird suction noise as she pulled an arm out. I saw a deep red patch over one side of ribs. That was going to bruise terribly. I wondered if she had broken a rib and said as much.

"No, the suit protected me from the worst of it. Who knew a fish could do something like that?"

"Well, you've heard of sharks, right?"

Arwen barked a laugh and pulled her other arm out, that side less affected.

She continued, "Or maybe the aliens see us as part of an ecosystem and feared how the environment would destabilize if we kept growing the way we were. Even we knew that our huge numbers were damaging the Earth. Maybe they didn't want us to damage the garden they've grown here. But the real reason is probably one that we can't even understand. Their species has been traveling the universe for…an eternity. We're like insects to them— something to pare back. We're both a threat as we are and a potential future benefit."

A spark struck the kindling, but I shivered at Arwen's words.

She took a shaky breath. "The Deadlight Gardes are robots, like we thought, but we went wrong when we thought they were the product of a civilization that had grown so advanced they moved their consciousnesses from organic, carbon-based bodies to robotic ones. The robots are slaves. The tenfish are the true aliens. The robots protect them. That's why we've never seen the fish. They're utterly vulnerable. We've been fighting a war, and we never even got past the bodyguards." Arwen shook her head.

"But then why was that one here?"

I pulled my clothes off methodically while I listened. It was barely freezing, but if we stayed wet we'd be in trouble. I thought we could walk back to Lilium Springs and be okay, but I didn't know yet if Arwen could walk or what our reception would be when we got there.

"It was a criminal of sorts. It was going to be executed, um, but not executed. Frozen somehow, until later. I'm not sure. But the fish fled inside its Deadlight, taking its chances on Earth. The hot spring was a fine habitat for it. You were right, there's definitely some connection between the Deadlight and the tenfish, but I only got a fuzzy glimpse of it. The Deadlight was probably trying to get far away from us because it knew when we threatened the fish, it'd be compelled to come back and defend its master—the first Law of Robotics. You did good, Marah."

I didn't feel like I did good. Gooseflesh rose across my arms as I wrung out my clothes. I tried not to think of Arwen's gaze on me.

The flame took off, turning my haphazard fire into something powerful.

"They'll leave on their own?" I asked, glancing at the trees where Giant left.

Arwen gave me a hard look. "They'll leave of their own accord once they have all they need from our planet, now that they've slaughtered and possibly permanently set back our species."

Arwen moved to the fire and held her hands out to warm them before briskly rubbing her body, working her circulation. She was looking down when she said it.

"And they'll be back."

We stood drying ourselves until we heard low huffing and snorting coming from inside the tree line. Arwen raised a brow at me.

"Bear," I mouthed.

"Where's my Kronos?"

"I dropped it in the water."

Anger washed over Arwen's face. Then she nodded something to herself and cautiously made her way across the rock. I took a hefty branch from the fire to follow her, also naked. Whereas Arwen moved quietly, I purposefully made heavy stomps to scare the animal.

We went wide of the brush that concealed the bear. I heard the unmistakable sound of bones snapping. It wasn't a bear. We couldn't take our eyes off the scene, both startled and afraid. The strangled scream of a cougar greeted us, claiming its prize.

Arwen and I stood naked in the pine forests of the Rocky Mountains, like Eves in the Garden, the flame of knowledge in my hand. Lying on the ground in front of us was the limp, dead body of Elder Sister Hetta, reign ended at last.

23. Over Eden

My Titan Suit had had a hard winter too, but I hadn't taken it off in the forty-eight hours since Hetta died. It would need a nice cleaning once I got as far away from that little corner of the Rockies as I could. The reinforced canvas felt tight and rigid after months of jeans and button-down shirts, but I already felt like a different, stronger person than Sister Arwen.

I had spent much of the past two days in the church, explaining to Bethany, Jackie, and Candace what Marah and I had experienced and witnessed at the hot springs. When they first saw me in my Titan Suit, they understood that I was not there to be questioned or intimidated. I was there of my own free will to give them an explanation and a warning.

"All of this happened because of the blind faith you put in your leader." Jackie opened her mouth to interject, but I kept rolling. "Hetta has been letting an alien species stick its finger up her nose since last summer to fill her mind with images of the aliens' inner workings. She mistook those secrets for power when, in fact, she was abandoning her responsibility to her people. We all noticed she was getting sick. The experiences were too much for her body. But your unwillingness to question her authority put everyone around you in danger."

I spent hours outlining what Marah and I had discovered about the tenfish and their control of their robotic army, the Deadlight Garde. Then I spent an especially long time detailing the video monitors hidden in the back of Hetta's closet. I couldn't tell if the other Elders knew about their existence, but Bethany, the new Elder Sister, had sat quiet during my entire explanation, Hetta's usual seat hauntingly empty next to her.

She finally said, "I'll take all of this into consideration, soldier."

Bethany herself accompanied me to the storerooms as I selected food and supplies to take on my next journey. Everyone I met along the paths turned away, refusing to meet my face. It was as if I had turned into what Marah first feared I was—an angel of death.

To everyone except James, that is. He was at my cabin when I got back, his parents nowhere in sight, as was typical.

I nodded at him and stopped with Bethany a little way away. I wanted to say goodbye to him in private. Bethany spoke before I could.

"I'll destroy the technology you found Elder Sister Hetta using. Such things distract us from our true purpose and, though this might surprise you, I agree no leader should have that kind of power." She cleared her throat. "If it's true what the tenfish showed you, and the aliens do indeed leave Earth behind with some survivors, we'll have a new world before us. I hope wherever you settle, you consider connecting your new home with us as a trade partner and…" she paused. "I hope we will live up to the expectations of neighborly love. Godspeed, soldier." Bethany turned and left on the trail, heading to her new home.

James grinned as I approached. "Did you hear her? She called it the tenfish."

I smiled back broadly. "You are a true scientist—you made one of the biggest discoveries in human history."

We both looked awkwardly at the ground. Already, he looked different. His pinched face, always waiting for the criticism to come, was relaxed and more confident. I was sad I wasn't going to see him grow up.

"You remind me of my brother, Julian."

James flushed. "Oh? Did he—did he die?"

The wound was old. I could bear it. "Yeah. I never got to say goodbye. When I joined the army, I left home in the dark before he was awake. I think I was scared to see how much my leaving hurt him, the same way my dad and sister hurt me when they left."

"I don't want you to go either." It came out in a rush.

"And I don't want to leave you behind. This isn't my home though. At least this time I can accept that loving you is worth the pain of missing you." I half smiled.

He clumsily grasped at me and circled his arms around me. I felt a humid breath on my arm and a sob escaped. In a rush he pulled away, handed me a folded paper, and took off for the woods. I stood, watching the back of him recede as he wiped his nose. I opened the paper. It was a map. A map with a star in one place and an arrow pointing west with a question mark by it. I looked up quickly, but James was gone. I thought back to his bin of treasure. I'd seen a compass in there, but I hadn't realized he knew how to use it. Even I underestimated him. I folded the map carefully before adding it to the stack of papers in my belt, anticipating the day the atlas would help us find each other again.

I went inside my cabin for the last time. When I had arrived at the community, wearing the costume Marah all but forced me into, all I carried with me was the fake backpack stuffed with random supplies. I didn't need stuff then and I didn't need it now. I would only take my bodysuit and what I could carry on my belt—a water canister, wire for snares (I vowed to find a library book on the subject), a two-fist-size metal pot perfect for one, a tiny med kit, a menstrual cup I hoped would hold out, and a few bits of food. I planned to bring a big hunting knife too.

I put everything else in the cabin away. When I was done sorting and folding, I checked the cupboard and under the bed. The only thing resting in the dim shadows was the fervently transcribed book. For something that could control so much, it looked so plain, just a limp sheath of pages. I didn't want to touch it and hadn't since I finished it, trying to understand, trying to piece together the life Lilium Springs lived and the life I was expected to live.

I didn't want to linger, but I wanted to take away the hundreds of hours it took to write out the book laboriously line by line. I lit a fire quickly and shredded the pages, feeding the Bible to the hungry flames by the handful. It was a good enough pyre.

When I left the base, I was so eager to be alone. Then, when I was truly alone, I realized how vulnerable I was. That drove me into Marah's waiting arms, and once I was in, I was in deep. Sadness washed over me when I considered how quickly I had expected the only people I could find to fill the hole in my heart left behind by my family.

Nothing told me I'd be able to find other humans out there, but if I did, the next time I would choose wisely. I didn't just need other people; I needed people I could trust and love.

A specter appeared by the door, transparent and lithe in the noontime sun. Marah poked her head in. She looked slightly puffy, as if she had been crying.

"Are you sure about this, Arwen? Everything is clear. You could stay."

"No, I couldn't. And what we know about the Deadlight Gardes and the tenfish could maybe make a difference. I owe it to everyone that I try."

"You've always acted like you were above redemption. Like our desire for forgiveness was trivial. But you want it too. You just want it from the people you left behind instead of God." She didn't say her assessment bitingly, just as if she was taking one last moment to pull me apart and figure out what made me tick.

Marah circled the room and looked out the window. "Timothy's going to leave me too."

"He is?" He couldn't leave Marah for Rachel. Rachel was still married to Henry.

"He's going to take the kids on a hunting trip. Said they'd be out there for a few days as they hunted small game. Maybe set up some snares east of here, out of our normal range."

"Okay, well he's not *leaving* you, Marah." I should be used to the exaggerations by now. "They'll be back."

"He's going to take them to a town."

That *was* big. "A town. A deserted town? Like the kids will finally know how others lived?"

She nodded, nose wrinkling.

"Good," I said it with no qualms. James needed to see. The fairy-tale nightmare they were living needed to be over. "What is he going to tell them? About why they lived how they lived, where all the people went, and why you all live differently?"

"I don't know. Timothy didn't say."

I wondered if Marah ever had to sit with an ambiguity like that before. Probably not. That's why she was the way she was. Why all the women in Lilium Springs were.

"I'm sorry for what your family is going through, Marah. But I think you should take solace in the fact that you have family left."

I debated hard over the past two days if I should tell her about Rachel and Timothy's affair. I decided not to. It felt wrong keeping the information from Marah, but I wasn't going to sentence Timothy or Rachel to death or expulsion from the community. And, frankly, I thought a few secrets were the only way the Bennett family would stay together long enough for the kids to grow up.

"I don't want you to go." Marah literally, *literally* stepped in between me and the door.

I took a deep breath. As much as we were different, as much as she had obligations to other people, as much as she bugged me, I was sad to leave her too. "I can't live here. I never could."

Now a tear really did slip down her cheek. And she always said she wasn't a crier. "Don't you love me?"

I looked down, but I could almost see ourselves in an out-of-body experience. Her, a wife and mother of three, wearing a shirt and pants she made herself. Me, a disgraced former soldier in a Titan Suit on her way to dangerous territory once again, hopefully to find people who would shelter her not because God wanted them to, but because it was the right thing to do. I would never let someone make me feel like I was lucky just to tag along again.

"I'm pregnant," Marah blurted.

I opened my mouth and shut it. I didn't know if I should congratulate her or what.

"I haven't said it out loud yet," she said.

"This is what you wanted, right?" I asked, trying to remind her. She wanted a little girl so badly. Not for the right reasons, but I think on some level she wanted this more than anything in life.

"Yes. I just wish my life—my entire existence—wasn't falling apart." She sank to the floor. I sat next to her.

"It's called an existential crisis." I tried to smile. "The rest of us had it when we first learned about the aliens."

Marah whispered, "Maybe when I spotted you in the woods, I should have left you alone."

"If you had done that, I would probably be dead." I touched her shoulder lightly. "Thank you for caring." I put one hand on her shoulder, cupped her face with the other. "Goodbye, Marah."

I stood up and settled my belt once again. I stepped out before more could be said.

I was fully conscious of being only a step or two away from Marah, from a life I had tried to live. Another step, then another. I didn't take the path. I crashed right into the trees, muck clinging to my feet, the sun hanging over my head, ready to sink to my right.

I wondered where I could find a good dog on my journey back.

Acknowledgments

Let me first thank the professionals that helped in the creation of this book: copy editors Anne-Marie Rutella and Leah Brown, book designer Lance Buckley, blurb expert Staci Mitzman, book coach Nicole Van Den Eng, and photographer Graham Washatka.

I am also grateful to the many bloggers, experts, and book professionals that publish free content online to empower independent authors. Their collective expertise was invaluable, but I especially appreciated the guidance of Lindsay Buroker, Joseph R. Lallo, Meg LaTorre, Natalia Leigh, Kristen Martin, Andrea Pearson, and Joanna Penn.

Still, this book would not have been possible without the support I found in my personal life. My children Madeline and Pierce cheered me along the way, and Joe and Adriana McCleer, Beth and Paul Stevens, and Jane Zornow provided helpful childcare so I could work. I'm also glad for the support and keen editing skills of my aforementioned book coach, Nicole Van Den Eng, who is also my sister. Finally, my husband, Oliver Zornow, was endlessly enthusiastic, and problem-solved with me daily throughout this book's creation.

And thank you, Dear Reader, for breathing life into this project by reading it. Without your imagination and emotions, it is simple ink and paper.

About the Author

Rebecca M. Zornow is the author of *It's Over or It's Eden, Dangerous to Heal,* and *Negotiated Fate*. She is a Hal Prize winner, a full member of the Science Fiction and Fantasy Writers Association, and has written for numerous print and digital publications.

Rebecca is an alumna of Lawrence University. After graduation, she served in the Peace Corps where she started school libraries and an art club in rural eSwatini. Rebecca is also a board member of the Caneille Regional Development Fund that works in rural Haiti. She is a former magazine editor-in-chief and runs the book coaching business Conquer Books with writer and book coach Nicole Van Den Eng.

Learn more about Rebecca and sign up for her monthly newsletter at www.RebeccaMZornow.com.